THE VIGILANTE TE

By Joe Messerli

Table of Contents

Copyright Notice 4

Disclaimer 4

Chapter 1 5

Chapter 2 14

Chapter 3 21

Chapter 4 28

Chapter 5 45

Chapter 6 57

Chapter 7 61

Chapter 8 72

Chapter 9 76

Chapter 10 82

Chapter 11 87

Chapter 12 91

Chapter 13 108

Chapter 14 122

Chapter 15 128

Chapter 16 138

Chapter 17 145

Chapter 18 155

Chapter 19 159

Chapter 20 169

Chapter 21 177

Chapter 22 187

Chapter 23 197

Chapter 24 208

Chapter 25 223

Chapter 26	230
Chapter 27	236
Chapter 28	242
Chapter 29	249
Chapter 30	254
Chapter 31	261
Chapter 32	269
Chapter 33	276
Chapter 34	283
Acknowledgements	290
About the Author	290

Copyright Notice

Copyright © 2018 by Joe Messerli. All rights reserved. No part of this publication may be reproduced, distributed, or transmitted in any form or by any means, including photocopying, recording, or other electronic or mechanical methods, without the prior written permission of the author, except in the case of brief quotations embodied in critical reviews and certain other noncommercial uses permitted by copyright law. For permission requests, email jpmesserli@gmail.com.

Disclaimer

This book is a work of *fiction*. Some public figures and certain long-standing institutions, agencies, and public offices are mentioned, but *the story and characters involved are wholly imaginary*. Any resemblance to actual events, locales, or persons, living or dead, is entirely coincidental.

The author in no way endorses the terrorist actions taken within the book, and none of the fictional characters targeted by the terrorists correspond 1:1 to any real-life person. In other words, none of these characters correspond to a real-life person with simple name/detail changes. All actions of the characters and entities are *entirely fictional*.

Chapter 1

Most would call them "domestic terrorists." If they were terrorists though, they were unlike any typical terrorists that would come to mind. All were highly-educated and intelligent with a variety of ages and backgrounds. Although not atheists, none of them were particularly religious. None subscribed to any far-right or far-left political ideology. There were no convicted felons in their small, tight-knit group, and they certainly didn't consider themselves terrorists. The group was composed of a physician, two Navy SEALs, a police officer, a science teacher, two computer programmers, and their U.S. Marine leader. Despite their diverse backgrounds, they all had one thing in common—a passionate opposition to an unelected group of powerful people. A group who, for far too long, had dangerously manipulated the levers of American politics and destroyed countless lives without consequences. These terrorists considered themselves patriots gearing up to fight a war, a long overdue Revolution.

*****

"Ten goddamn points," said Media World leader Colin Bennett. "Martinez has gained ten points in the polls in one week."

The meeting took place off the coast of Cape Cod in a 100-foot luxury yacht owned by Facebook tycoon, Jack Zimmer. It included some of the most powerful financiers of both the Democratic and Republican parties, a few tech company executives, two high-ranking senators, and several behind-the-scenes coordinators of political action committees (PACs) & information-dissemination groups. They were there to discuss a rising star of American politics, third-party candidate, Brent Martinez.

Bennett cycled through the power point slides showing the breakdown of the poll. "Martinez is eating into both Republican & Democratic numbers equally and is gaining in all gender, age, and income groups." Bennett continued by playing clips of the previous week showing appearances from the Tonight Show, the Daily Show, and Hannity. "Martinez is wisely working both conservative and liberal audiences. His Tonight Show highlights included nonstop laughs and are the most shared videos on Facebook and Twitter so far this year. I'm telling you that every time this guy gets national airtime, his numbers go up. Every debate I've seen him in has been a one-sided thrashing. Not even stacking the debate audiences and appointing hostile moderators have been able to trip him up."

"No one votes for third party candidates in November. Every four years we seem to hear the same garbage about a third party run, but it always fades as election day approaches." said Zimmer.

"This is a whole new ballgame," said Google project manager, Craig Whitman. "People are disgusted with both Democrats and Republicans. Barack Obama and Donald Trump were largely elected because they were perceived as outsiders. However, neither could change the government as much as their supporters had hoped. A third party is seen as the only remaining option by many Americans. Last week the top Google searches were 'Brent Martinez' and 'Libertarian party'. And since Martinez doesn't have any obvious scandals in his background, the search results are so far returning only favorable stories and video clips at the top."

Bennett continued: "As most of you know, likely the only reason we've kept third parties out in the past is the widespread belief that the candidate can't possibly win, and voting for that person would only split votes and end up electing the other party, as happened with Ross Perot and Ralph Nader giving boosts to Bill Clinton and George W. Bush, respectively. But if a third-party candidate maintains poll numbers over the 15 percent threshold, he can participate in national debates based on current rules. Martinez is especially dangerous because he takes votes from both parties equally, and we're dead in the water if he debates the fossils running on our tickets."

"But all of you can relax," continued Bennett. "We haven't even started to hit this guy. While it's true that he doesn't have any surface-level weaknesses, we haven't dedicated any significant resources to researching his background. Can we all agree to temporarily halt Democrat vs. Republican attacks until we get this guy out of the picture? Possibly kick in about 25 million bucks each to start the offensive? We share everything equally on Martinez that we can dig up, and we each open up our media distribution networks to maximize the hit pieces?"

"Agreed," said Republican financier, David Backman.

"I'd spend half my fortune to assure Martinez doesn't get elected," said Democratic billionaire Henry Keller. "Republican slime are at least somewhat controllable. A third-party candidate could really fuck things up. Especially a damn naïve, idealist child like Martinez."

"Ditto for you Democrat scuzballs," winked Backman.

"We will do what we can to minimize any positive exposure for Martinez in Facebook news feeds," said Zimmer. "We can twist some algorithms to move positive Martinez comments and shared videos farther down 'Home' listings."

"I have a team that can tweak Google search results somewhat, but you have to give me *something* negative to filter to the top," said Whitman.

"Ok. Let's get started," said Bennett to one of his assistants. "Use all of our PAC's, think tanks, public relation firms, media fact checkers, and other front organizations. We'll start with the standard Phase One operation—comb every word of every speech, interview, campaign ad, and piece of writing Martinez has ever created. Set up interviews of all former employers, ex-girlfriends, college & high school acquaintances, and business associates. Get a hold of our IRS contacts to see if we can get his tax returns. Get his company's financial statements from our banking contacts. Run his donor lists through our databases. He had a libertarian website blog about ten years ago that has since been discontinued. Craig, please send us whatever you can pull from the archives. Jack, send us every Facebook post he's made as well as every 'like'. He hasn't been on Twitter long, but Henry has a friend who can get us a download of every click he's made in the app."

"What do you want to make the theme—racist, greedy, fascist, sexist?" said Keller.

"All of the above. Let's not limit our search to anything for now. It will be difficult to paint him as racist since he is half Hispanic, but it's not impossible. The media has orgasms whenever they can portray a conservative or libertarian as racist. 'Sexist' will also be difficult since he's a damn choir boy with a picture-perfect family, but he *is* divorced, so see where that leads. He's a businessman, so 'greedy' and 'heartless' are probably our best bets, but we'll see where the research takes us. Martinez is so fresh on the scene that I doubt anyone has had time to dig up any real dirt, but it will come. We will start the drip-drip of negative stories to our media contacts as soon as it comes in. Have no worries—we will destroy him ASAP, so we can resume hating and attacking each other," Bennett said with a smile. And with that, the political talk ended for the night. Although some of them disagreed politically, they laughed and socialized like the best of friends, basking in their power. Some attacked each other viciously in public, but there weren't any hard feelings. It was a game. The American people were their sheep. Everyone had their skeletons, misstatements, failed relationships, mental lapses, and mistakes in life. All you had to do was dig through and cherry pick the right phrases & facts, form them into some themes, then leave it to the mainstream media and Internet to do the rest. If that didn't do the trick, there were several more steps that could be taken with sufficient financing. Most candidates never made it past Phase One attacks, though. It was almost too easy.

*****

The buzzer blared, indicating it was time to switch from pull-ups to burpees. After that, a minute of push-ups, which would then earn the trainees a thirty-second rest. Ten sets of three-minute varied intervals total would need to be completely, immediately followed by a two-mile hike with sand-filled backpacks ranging in weight of 20-80 lbs, depending on the fitness level of the trainee. The workout would finish with a comparatively easy two-mile run. Training took place in a remote wooded area in Northern Wisconsin, where Dr. Abby Benton owned one hundred acres of fenced-in land.

"C'mon, dig deep," said Cole Foreman. "There's a saying in the SEALs, 'When you're under pressure, you don't rise to the occasion, you sink to the level of your training.'" And train they did. A Revolution was coming. Training, preparation, and group cohesion were vital to their mission. Despite the fact less than half of the group had a military background, everyone trained together. The ex-Marine and two former Navy SEALs easily had the highest fitness levels, while some of the others had spent most of their lives sitting at a desk. Each exercise set include modifications to make it easier or harder. The one female trainee, Abby, was more than holding her own, fresh off a year of half-marathon races and Insanity Program workouts on her own before the boot camp started.   She provided an extra kick of motivation to the men she was regularly exceeding in reps and speed.

Every hour of their custom-made boot camp was strictly regimented for both training and mission preparation. Today, the schedule was as follows:

  05:30-07:30: Physical training
  07:30-07:45: Shower
  07:45-08:30: Breakfast

08:45-10:00:   Firearms training
10:15-11:45:   Bombs/Demolitions training
12:00-12:45:   Lunch
13:00-14:00:   First Aid and Medical Weapons training
14:10-16:00:   Security and Military Technology training
16:15-17:00:   Dinner
17:00-18:00:   Counterintelligence techniques
18:15-20:30:   Mission research, planning, and rehearsal

    The running/calisthenics training alternated daily with martial arts/hand-to-hand combat in the morning, followed by the basics of mission-critical skills training throughout the day. On top of the base knowledge for everyone, each member perfected a primary expert skill and a secondary expert skill. For example, Cole Foreman was a demolitions expert in the Navy SEALS; therefore, he was the primary master of demolitions. Scott Koonce was a physics and chemistry expert from his years as a teacher, so he took the role of padawan learner in demolitions. Actual mission assignments would be performed only by the ones best trained for the particular duty, but the military vets had lost enough men in battle to know the rest of the team always had to be prepared to step up if things didn't go as planned.

    Monday-Saturday of the sixteen weeks in boot camp followed the same jam-packed routine. Sunday was a rest day divided into two parts for which every member participated. One part was fun, team-building activities such as sports, paintball, escape rooms, scavenger hunts, etc. The only requirements for activity choices were teamwork, competition, and an element of pressure. The second part of Sunday involved strategic and psychological planning. The selected actions they were about to take must efficiently achieve mission objectives with minimal risk. However, the planned actions were, to say the least, morally questionable.   Therefore, a strict code of ethics was being put together for their upcoming war, the main point of which was, "Every target in our Revolution must have a long and egregious history of abuse in the actions we're fighting, and each target must have *unanimous* consent from the team to make the list." To put it another way, everyone had to believe that each target thoroughly deserved the fate coming his or her way soon.

*****

"Republicans, Democrats, and the media have for decades been turning us against each other," thundered third-party Libertarian candidate, Brent Martinez, from the podium of the sold-out arena. "Democrats vs. Republicans, rich vs. poor, conservatives vs. liberals, black vs. white, immigrant vs. citizen. In every election, politicians must create 'boogeymen'—some enemy to re-direct your attention and anger away from their failures and corruption. Banks, insurance companies, Big Oil, Big Pharma, Big Tobacco, Big Labor unions. Politicians and their media lapdogs feed hate and divisiveness, speaking of 'our side' vs the evil other side. Instead of working together to develop mutually-beneficial solutions, all energy is devoted to maintaining power and destroying political enemies. Up until now, they've succeeded in maintaining this destructive process by convincing you there are only two options, Republican and Democrat. This is the election where we Americans stand up and say, 'None of the Above! Give us Option #3!'" The crowd of 15,000 roared their approval. Martinez was speaking for the fourth night in a row to sold out crowds in the state of Pennsylvania. Each one seemed to be more enthusiastic then the night before as his popularity and name recognition grew with each passing day.

Martinez was the classic American rags-to-riches success story. As the oldest of five siblings from a poor single mom, he put himself through college while working two jobs through most of his childhood. After finishing degrees in accounting and economics, he passed his CPA and worked ten years mastering the maze that is the U.S. tax code. Martinez then started up his own venture capital company that helped successfully launch hundreds of small businesses. His work ingrained in him an intense dislike for government, which he felt punished those who worked hard and risked everything, while enriching a power-hungry, corrupt, morally-bankrupt set of politicians. Martinez had dark, rugged, youthful good looks and natural charisma. Every time his quick-witted brilliance and encyclopedic knowledge were put on display, his popularity grew exponentially. His beautiful blonde wife, a registered nurse, and three college-bound kids only added to his allure.

His libertarian third party views were drawing voters equally from both the Democratic and Republican parties, and it represented one of the biggest threats in American history to the two-party stranglehold on power. He had even drawn the endorsement of three Republican congressmen and two Democratic senators, who themselves had ran for election on the hopes of making a difference but were fed up with the corruption and failures of their own parties.

"Excellent speech, sir!" said a campaign volunteer.

Martinez smiled. "Thanks for the complement, but 'Sir'? You better not start calling me 'Sir'. You can always call me Brent, even if by some miracle I win this election. I won't even let my cabinet or generals call me 'Sir' or 'Mr. President'. The office has become too king-like."

The smile on Martinez face turned into a frown as his pollster and acting campaign manager, Rick Morries, approached.

"You're killing it in the latest NBC/Wall Street Journal poll, Brent, especially after that story on Locklear's affair as a Democratic state senator came out."

"And it's pure coincidence that this story is leaked hours after we found out about it?"

"Sir, I know you don't like the personal attacks, but politics is a dirty business, and you have to use everything in your arsenal to win," said Morries. "Do you think the Republicans and Democrats are going to withhold any dirt on you or your family that comes out? There are plenty of ways to get this information to the media without any ties to you personally."

"Dammit, you know my policy. I'm not going to turn into one of these politicians without morals that will destroy anyone in their path to get elected. I don't even want to be president if the only way I can do it is turning into another dirt bag that lives off lies and personal attacks."

"But, Brent, this news would have come out anyway. Now that you're up in the polls, they'll be throwing out every attack in the book, true and untrue. I--"

"Rick, I appreciate all you've done for me, but I've warned you several times now. I'd like you to pack your things and leave the campaign. I've fired other staffers for this sort of thing. I can't make an exception."

Morries exited the room without saying another word. Several of the staffers appeared stunned, but they were learning quickly that Brent Martinez's words weren't just spoken for the camera.

*****

A smile crossed the pudgy face of Media World leader, Colin Bennett, as he watched the Martinez speech on MSNBC from his hotel room. Bennett had seen it all a thousand times. He cracked his knuckles and got to work. The squeaky-clean image would not last long.

Chapter 2

Aaron Newsome marveled at how much progress had been made in his team through the first twelve weeks of his custom-made training program. He was worried at first if it was going to be too rigorous for some of the group, but what they lacked in ability, they made up for in motivation and determination. It was testament to his uncompromising screening process in selecting the team.

Although Newsome insisted on making several decisions democratically, he was the founder and undisputed leader of the group that would come to be known as the RAPCAs. He had jet black hair, dark brown eyes, and a tall, Marine-chiseled physique that brought an air of authority. Newsome had three main screening tests for RAPCA team members. The first one was the only one he was flexible on, which was to have some kind of special skills or knowledge essential to the mission. Training could make up for a lot, but they didn't have unlimited time and budget to handle totally raw recruits. Newsome stubbornly enforced the last two requirements though, and they were the main reason the team stayed relatively small. Each team member had to have a strong personal connection to Newsome or some other member that earned unflinching loyalty and trust. Lastly, each person had to have a passionate motivation for the cause. In other words, they needed something in their background that would strongly drive them to fulfill the team mission.

Newsome started RAPCA with two other members—his childhood best friend, Cole Foreman, a former Navy SEAL, and Dr. Abby Benton, his friend & personal physician. All remaining members had a branched-out personal connection to one of the original three team members. Despite the loyal personal relationships, Newsome thoroughly background-checked everyone, researching everything from their childhoods to each of their jobs.

Nothing would be left to chance. Dr. Abby Benton was a beautiful brunette who had once been one of the top orthopedic surgeons in the country. She was constantly underestimated by her good looks and petite appearance. Cole Foreman was plain-looking but strong and fit from his years in the Navy SEALs. However, within the tough exterior was one of the brainiest scientists in the military, who could build virtually any kind of bomb given the right materials.

Dr. Benton and Foreman had worked with architects the previous year to construct the 4000-foot, seven-bedroom cabin buried in dense northern Wisconsin woods. The outside was equipped with several layers of brick, cement, and sound-proof glass. Laser sensors were set at checkpoints of the fenced-in land that fed to a custom-made security system which sent alerts to each team member's iPhone. Five smaller bedrooms housed team members. The largest bedroom was filled with PCs and laptops connected to a heavily-encrypted network that led to the living room, which was lined with ten big-screen TVs, several couches, and additional workstations. Handguns, sniper rifles, and ammunition filled the walls of the basement, while bomb-making materials and a laboratory of chemical and biological equipment occupied the rest of the basement. Newsome, Foreman, and Dr. Benton sat in the strategic planning room of the cabin, which contained maps of New York and Washington, D.C. with several pushpins in each city. A smaller map of Atlanta contained exactly one pushpin. Yellow stickies, drawings, and red markings surrounded each pushpin.

"I can handle Atlanta alone," said Foreman.

"I don't want you going without a wingman to handle some of the tech aspects of the assignment," said Newsome.

"We need the extra person for New York. Most of our Zero Day targets are there, and we don't know who we'll have to pull or re-direct at game time. We're not going to have the surprise element beyond a few hours at best," said Foreman.

"I agree," said Dr. Benton. "Cole is better than anyone at disappearing if things go south. We need the extra surveillance and I.T. expertise in New York. After day one, security will be so tight that we may not get another shot."

"I don't know," sighed Newsome. "Atlanta has only one set of targets, but it is a critical one. Cole, let's plan to have at least one of our I.T. guys go down with you for a couple weeks to help set up and do some extra surveillance, after which he can fly to New York. What time windows are we looking at?"

"Based on our early surveillance and research, we've identified three summer weeks where we have a shot at 70 percent of the primary targets," said Abby, "but I'm thinking the end of July during Congressional recesses is our best bet. Newsworthy events are usually at a low point, so we have peak predictability of schedules and locations."

"That's awfully close to the election. I'd hate to see the media turn this into an attempt to influence the outcome, but I think you're right, Abby. We will have to accelerate our follow-up timetable in Silicon Valley, so let's have the tickets purchased and ready to go as soon as we've wrapped up D.C., New York, and Atlanta. Make sure everyone flies to separate airports for their first destination. We don't want FBI data crunchers picking up the coincidence of all our team members flying to the Valley at once."

"I really hate this plan," said Foreman, "but as George Patton used to say, 'a good plan violently executed today is better than the perfect plan tomorrow.'"

*****

Dana, it won't be long until they pay, thought Aaron Newsome as he finished off an extra run, started at 10pm after a full day of training. He gritted his teeth and balled his hands into fists as he tried to suppress the rage that still burned freshly in his heart. Exactly four years ago, the course of his life had changed. It was on that fateful day he found the love of his life with a self-inflicted, blood-soaked head wound from his own Beretta M9 pistol.

Dana and Aaron were married only a few years after high school. Dana pursued a Communications degree at University of Wisconsin while Aaron was in training to be a police officer at a technical college. Then, 9/11 occurred. The sight of bodies jumping out of windows of the World Trade Center and New Yorkers holding the pictures of loved ones missing in the rubble aftermath was more than the very patriotic Aaron could take. He immediately enlisted in the Marines. Dana hated being away from her high school sweetheart, but she knew she couldn't stop Aaron once he set his mind to a cause he passionately believed in. It was part of the reason she loved him so much.

Aaron's patriotism, bravery, and natural leadership ability quickly moved him up the rankings to Captain, from which he had no desire to move further, as he cared far more about his country and his fellow soldiers than politics and personal achievement. He saved the lives of several Marines from a roadside bomb in Fallujah, but not before shrapnel to the leg & hip ended his service career prematurely.

Dana gave birth to a daughter while Aaron was overseas, and Dana became a popular local news anchor in Madison, WI. She was heavily involved in the community and helped develop a few veteran and survivor charities, making her one of the most well-known women in Wisconsin. Her popularity was so high that the Republican Party persuaded her to run for the U.S. Senate, with whispers of even a presidential run at some point down the road. That was the beginning of the end.

Dana closely followed current events and naively thought she could rise above the petty partisan politics to change the country for the better. She knew politics could get rough, but she had no idea just how vicious things could get. Wisconsin was an even-polling swing state in an election year where control of the U.S. Senate was likely going to come down to one or two seats. Tens of millions of dollars was poured into the race that drew constant national media attention, mostly spent to attack and ridicule.

    Dana expected to get attacked mostly on political inexperience. That was mentioned, but the focus of attacks went back twenty years. It started with an editorial she had written for a college newspaper in which she advocated for free speech. The issue came to the forefront that year of college when the KKK wanted to march on campus. Dana explained that true free speech had to apply even to despicable groups like the KKK, because the alternative is giving a governing body power to shut down *any* speech with which it disagrees. "Dana Newsome advocates for the KKK" was how the story was spun in the mainstream media. Context of the article was rarely given to readers & viewers. In the editorial, Dana had continued on to rip the KKK for everything it stood for, but that wasn't reported in stories as they were echoed thousands of times through the web. Despite the fact the article was written twenty years ago and despite the fact her best friend happened to be black, Dana was branded a racist for the rest of the campaign.

    Next, private detectives working for big-money donors tracked down a couple of jilted ex-boyfriends from Dana's past, both of who happened to now be firemen. One of them, who was still bitter from their breakup, described Dana as a wildly promiscuous woman who liked to play perverted sex games. The media went crazy with the story, with comedians regularly running sex jokes about Dana & firemen. *Saturday Night Live* ran skits about Dana for three consecutive weeks. *YouTube* comedy videos & naked photoshop images of Dana were viewed millions of time on the web, which crushed her every time she faced her 16-year-old daughter.

Opponent research groups poured through thousands of newscasts and speeches Dana had made through the years. It was easy to clip together a Top-20 list of misspeaks that made Dana look like a ditsy blonde. It was also discovered that she had played with a volleyball team ten years previously named "Light as a Feather, Stiff as a Board". The name was picked as a joke because one of the members was Wiccan. Dana was Christian and never judged anyone by their religious beliefs, but from that point on she was ridiculed as a "witch". The witch characterization seemed to fit the ditsy blonde profile that was carefully constructed for her by the media. That brought another two weeks of Saturday Night Live skits, several rounds of late night comedy jokes, and endless Internet memes.

Dana's poll numbers dropped considerably, but her opposition groups weren't taking any chances. They tracked down an abortion clinic Dana had visited while pregnant with her daughter. She was depressed and lonely with her husband fighting in Iraq, and she ultimately changed her mind, but that wasn't good enough for the media.

A private detective followed Dana's daughter and recorded her getting drunk at a party. That incident and the abortion clinic visit together destroyed what was left of her mother-of-the-year image she once had.

Those were just *some* of the highlights of dozens of negative attack stories on Dana. In two months, the media & Internet had turned Dana from an intelligent, caring, articulate woman to a racist, ditsy, slut who cared nothing about her family. Dana's poll numbers dropped so dramatically that she withdrew from the race. She was humiliated and disgraced, and when she tried to go back to her broadcasting career, she found that part of her life was also shattered. No networks wanted anyone with her reputation on their show. The destruction of her character was complete.

One day, Aaron went out to a rehab session for his shrapnel-shattered hip. When he came back he found Dana in the computer room with the Beretta in her hand, brains & blood splattered on the wall. On the computer screen was a *Time* news article describing the great rise and fall of Dana Newsome. Tears poured from the eyes of the battle-hardened Marine as he held her for hours until friends and paramedics dragged him away.

Aaron tried to shake the images from his head as he prepared for his daily mission research with his team. He had not shed a single tear since that day. The *Time* article Dana was reading that day was now blown up and plastered on a wall of the cabin, along with similar articles that reminded each of the team members why they trained and what they were fighting.

Chapter 3

In about a week of research, Media World head, Colin Bennett, had compiled over 25,000 pages of written material plus almost 1,000 audio & video recordings of candidate, Brent Martinez. Besides Bennett's quite substantial annual fees, the big-money donations mostly were used to hire staff to pour through the mountains of information. Recordings were fed into a voice transcription program, which together with the written material were loaded into the Media World databases.

Millions of dollars were spent annually on some of the best tech experts to optimize the searching and analysis database programs. The Internet, especially social media, had provided a treasure trove of information. The toughest part was sifting through all of it.

First level programs searched the material for racist words: *nigger, negro, Chink, Jap, spic, dago, gook, gringo, hymie, raghead, redskin,* and so on. Next, it searched for sexist words and phrases: *broad, chick, ballbuster, shrill, honey, catty, bitchy, shrew, ice queen, man-eater, cougar, slut, whore, hormonal, menstrual, PMS,* etc. Next, it checked for gay slurs: *fag, dike, homo,* etc. The easiest way to knock out a candidate was to find a recording of the candidate using politically-incorrect trigger words. It always would lead to several days of news coverage and replaying of the clip until it was burned into the minds of many voters. The coverage would go on until the candidate inevitably apologized. The apology itself would be another news story that extended the coverage another day. Multiple incidents of a slur on video was usually an instant death sentence of a candidacy, regardless if the recording was clipped out of context or if it happened thirty years ago. Bennett assigned two staffers to review the results. Not much was coming up on Martinez, but there were a few interesting tidbits.

Next came donor lists and past associations. Lists of Martinez's donors, business associates, relatives, and friends were cross-referenced with a separate database holding criminal and civil trial proceedings. The objective was to compile a collection of sinister, dishonest, and corrupt individuals that could be tied to the candidate. It didn't matter if it was a $100 donation, a third cousin, a friend from high school the candidate hadn't talked to in twenty years, or a minor vendor of a business subsidiary. If you could credibility make a connection, you could work with it. Brent Martinez had helped fund hundreds of startups and had done tax/accounting work for thousands of individuals. Computer programs were spitting out reams of material. Bennett assigned five staffers to go through the results. "Greedy, corrupt businessman" was looking like an easy attack strategy to have in the arsenal.

Next came voting records. Each policy position of the candidate was poll tested. Voting records were first cross-checked with each of the unpopular positions held by the candidate. Then, the records were checked with polarizing issues such as abortion and gay marriage, which would inevitably alienate a portion of the voters regardless of which side was taken. In some cases, other voting record strategies were applied, such as finding votes that contradicted a current position, which painted the candidate as a flip-flopper or wishy-washy. Examining past legislative experience should be the most honorable way to judge a candidate, but politicians in power had made even that questionable. Bills were often hundreds of pages of complex legalese, frequently with unrelated clauses to the main objective of the bill. For example, a bill to fund improved armor for soldiers in war zones is packaged with a completely unrelated item such as a change to immigration law. The candidate must choose to vote for or against the whole bill, so if the vote is a No because of the immigration change, the candidate is described as "voting against improved armor for soldiers." Brent Martinez had only held local office, so his voting record was limited. Bennett did however see some potential to add to other attack themes. Two staffers were assigned.

Next came social media. Thousands of posts, like's, share's, tweet's, re-tweet's, pin's on Facebook, Twitter, Pinterest, Snapchat, Instagram, LinkedIn, and other social media offered a mountain of attack material on a candidate. Bennett assigned five people to review Martinez's history since the search & analysis programs were not as advanced for the newer, constantly-changing technology.

Finally came the fun part—the juicy personal attacks and scandals. Secret recordings, off-mike jokes, drunken rants picked up on smart phones, voice mail messages, etc. provided a starting point for finding material. However, interviews of past acquaintances provided the best hit material. Jilted ex-lovers and fired employees especially were a gold mine. Bennett assigned some of his best private investigators to comb through the past of Brent Martinez. This phase of the smear operation usually took the most time but yielded the best results. Bennett laughed as he thought about the short, shallow attention span of the average American voter. Fifty intelligently framed news stories attacking a candidate on issues did only a fraction of the damage of one bad joke caught on tape that could be played endlessly on every news show and ridiculed by comedians & Internet memes.

This was so much fun. Colin Bennett knew he was the best at what he did. Although Bennett had worn dozens of fancy titles over the years such as media consultant, research analyst, content strategist, and new media coordinator, he was really nothing more than a smear merchant. And there was nothing wrong with that—both sides did it! Bennett himself was especially effective because he had worked as a Republican attack dog before he realized the money was better on the liberal Democrat side. Switching sides gave him the added advantage of being plugged in to both right-wing and left-wing media distribution networks. He knew both sides' playbooks inside and out, and he always would be one step ahead of the opposition. Bennett was well rewarded for his work—he currently earned annual "salaries" from 35 organizations in Washington, most of which were nonprofit and/or "nonpartisan".

Colin smiled as he pulled up on his iPad a recently opened Cayman bank account. A cool $300,000 was added to the balance this morning—a bonus for getting the Republican senator from New Hampshire to resign. As was his tradition whenever he claimed another victim, Bennett opened an expensive bottle of wine—this time an 1865 Chateau Lafite that cost $4500. Every bottle tasted better than the last one. He was the true kingmaker. Would it be an exaggeration to say he was the most powerful man in America? Bennett laughed—maybe an exaggeration, but not by much.

*****

"I can't follow this shit," said Nate Keeting, RAPCA security technology expert. "There must be a thousand organizations here. Some mega-rich donors appear to be involved in key areas, but the money seems to disappear into an endless web of unrelated nonprofits and PACs. I'm pretty sure drug money laundering structures aren't this complex. 'Follow the money' sounds like a great strategy if it actually leads somewhere. I'm getting a headache." Keeting pulled a few hairs of his balding head.

"Take it easy," said Jim Damon, RAPCA database/search guru and former MIT roommate of Keeting. "We just have to break down each funding source and cross-reference it with our other lists until we build the hierarchy. Clearly, we have foreign governments, politicians, and big-money donors funding these slime groups. Think of it like mob organizations. The Dons and Caporegimes can't be tied to the crimes of the button men. So, they introduce buffers of communication. They give orders to the middle-men, who then pass them to others, who finally pass the orders to the ones who do the dirty work. It works the same in politics. The big guys can act all innocent and uninvolved, when in reality, they're directing it."

Nate Keeting and Jim Damon were the core tech brains of RAPCA. They were roommates and best friends at Massachusetts Institute of Technology. Their competitive drives pushed each other to become some of the most talented experts in the country. Both had the distinction of working for one of the top tech firms in the country—Keeting at Facebook, Damon at Google. Both also had the distinction of being fired after going public about the practices at their companies.

Nate Keeting was a tall, skinny redhead who fit perfectly with most stereotypes of the nerdy computer geek. He started out a programmer at Facebook after graduation, and his hacking skills eventually brought him to a Security Director position. The information technology field is dominated by liberal-leaning Democrats, so Keeting didn't exactly fit the profile with his conservative/libertarian views. He mostly kept quiet about his strongly-held views until he observed systematic efforts by Facebook to suppress conservative & libertarian thought within news and timeline feeds, in some cases removing sources entirely. After a night of one-too-many rum & Cokes, he spilled his guts to a local newspaper reporter he met at a bar. The reporter used Keeting as the centerpiece of a Facebook-censorship editorial. The story was picked up by Fox News, which lead to national attention for days. Facebook immediately took away all security logins and duties from Keeting, then cut ties entirely a couple weeks later as part of a "corporate downsizing". Coincidentally, several other Facebook employees who held non-liberal views were pushed out the door. Afterwards, Keeting took odd jobs and spent his nights hacking into corporate systems until his cousin, Aaron Newsome, recruited him for a new mission.

Jim Damon was short but deceptively strong. Although in many ways he was an awkward computer nerd like Keeting, he held an inner confidence honed from a decade of martial arts training. In a few boot camp sessions, he had put the much larger Aaron Newsome and Cole Foreman on their asses. Damon had always been a live-and-let-live libertarian that didn't follow politics very closely while he worked 70-hour weeks as a database specialist at Google. That all changed as he observed increasingly morally-questionable behavior by his bosses. Search algorithms and Google news feeds were being regularly manipulated to help certain politicians & organizations while hurting others. The tweaking of the search programs was explained away by Google's seemingly noble desire to fight "hate groups" and "fake news", but those terms became subject to interpretation of the Google executives and programmers themselves. This interpretation flexibility turned into a sword that promoted leftist & socialist ideas while striking down conservative and libertarian ideas. Damon started tweeting about some of the more dubious Google practices, which ultimately led to his firing. After his dismissal, Damon started paying closer attention to politics and the media. He disliked Donald Trump, but he started to detect patterns of media propaganda and dishonesty seemingly coordinated to destroy him. What he witnessed at Google seemed to fit into that destroy-Trump character assassination, and it disgusted him. Nate Keeting followed his roommate's public discontent with Google and mainstream media. He recruited Jim Damon into an organization that was fighting back.

"Most of these groups don't have to disclose their donors, so I'm going to have to hack into several more systems and reverse-engineer the money trails," said Keeting. "Clearly, Republican financier, David Backman, and

Democrat billionaire, Henry Keller, are spending massive sums. And the DNC and RNC are of course directing quite a bit of funds to these groups," he said, referring to Democratic National Committee and Republican National Committee. "But money disappears into a maze of PACs, think tanks, lobbying groups, public relations firms, media communication centers, and on and on. This Media World guy, Colin Bennett, seems to keep popping up."

"How's the geek division doing?" said Newsome as he walked into the room.

"We've identified hundreds of millions of dollars flowing through Washington," said Damon. "The problem is that is most of these organizations are nonprofit or advertise as nonpartisan. Some of them may be completely legit, and most do at least some reputable work publicly. It's obvious though that many of these firms are receiving & spending a ton of cash that can't be traced to any discernable work."

"Keep at it. Your work is the key to our operation. Our first-level targets are simply the branches of the tree. If we don't get to the root of the problem—the big-money donors and smear puppet masters—then, we're never going to fulfill our mission."

"I think we have to start at the end of the chain," said Keeting. "Let's monitor and cross-check communications from all the media on our suspect list. If we monitor similar timing and wording of stories, we can work backwards to see who is directing these smear media distribution networks."

"Add on whatever research you can," said Newsome, "but let's build on work done by others. There are books and articles by some journalists that have traced quite a bit of these networks. I think we all know who the guiltiest parties are, but let's make sure we thoroughly confirm we have the correct people. You both know how we plan to deal with these people—we can't afford to be wrong, even once. By the way, we have six weeks. Zero Day is July 31st."

Chapter 4

MARTINEZ LEADS REPUBLICANS, DEMOCRATS IN PRESIDENTIAL RACE 40-30-29

Colin Bennett knew the funds would be pouring in as he read the very scary headline of the Washington Post. He took out a notebook as he observed the latest TV ad from Martinez that likely pushed him to his latest lead:

I'm Brent Martinez, and I approved this message. A lot of you are tired of the negativity and personal attacks in Washington. So much of today's politics is about making you hate the opposing candidates rather than solving problems. Let me first say that all my presidential opponents are good people. We all want the same things. We simply disagree on priorities and methods of accomplishing these goals. Here's what I stand for:

A balanced budget. I will veto any spending bill that has more expenses than revenue, even if I must shut down the government. We can't leave our children with over $25 trillion in debt that grows every year. Interest expense alone will soon exceed spending on defense and social security.

Term limits. We need new ideas and need to clean out the corrupt, divisive career politicians that currently dominate our government.

Less regulation and government intrusion in our lives. Citizens and businesses should have the freedom to do whatever they want, provided it doesn't hurt or infringe on the rights of others.

Strong defense, but non-interventionist foreign policy. We will keep our defenses strong but will stay out of other countries' business unless we're directly attacked.

Time limit on government benefits. Government can help you through brief struggles in life like unemployment, but it is not designed to support you forever. We will give you a hand up, not a handout. Only Social Security and Medicare, which you've paid for with payroll deductions, will be available long-term.

End of corporate welfare and special tax breaks. We will no longer allow politicians to pay off campaign contributors with bloated spending bills and tax loopholes.

Rollback of executive and legislative power. Every new law, regulation, and executive action erodes a little bit more of your freedom and increases power in Washington. We must reverse this trend.

New market-based healthcare system. We will implement a 20-point plan to cut healthcare costs in half, cover 100 percent of Americans, and get government out of the system for good.

If you go to my website, BrentMartinez.gov, you can read detailed plans on these and other positions. I pledge to you to focus my entire campaign on solutions and will not endorse a single negative or personal attack ad. I will work on bringing people together in compromise and stop the hate that is tearing this country apart. I look forward to serving you.

Bennett saw why his clients were so panicky. People like Martinez directly threatened the entire power structure of Washington. Luckily, there was a giant toolbox of methods to destroy such threats. Bennett mobilized several research and talking-point divisions of his network, which were designed to take down even the most common sense of issue positions, or at least plant enough doubts that his other attacks would take hold. His army of media personalities would be mobilized within the hour—*CNN*,

MSNBC, CBS, ABC, NY Times, Washington Post, Time, Politico, Huffington Post, Newsweek CNBC, and on and on. Martinez had no idea the power that he was up against.

*****

"Welcome to CNN, Mr. Martinez," said the interviewer, Jerome Jones. "We should be set up and ready to start in a few minutes. We're just going to ask you some basic easy questions on your issue positions, maybe a little about your family. Nothing controversial. Just a basic introduction to who you are for our viewers."

"Thank you, Mr. Jones," said Martinez. Brent Martinez was coming to an end of the most jam-packed campaign week of his life. He had done forty speeches and ten interviews in the past ten days while sleeping only a few hours per night. He was looking forward to finally getting five hours uninterrupted shuteye after the CNN interview.

"Call me Jerome. We're all friends here! Ok, here we go...5-4-3-2-1. Mr. Martinez, thank you for joining us today. Recently, Democratic Senator Locklear was subject to scrutiny about an affair she had fifteen years ago. You've mentioned many times how you don't believe in personal attacks in politics, but the leak of this affair was traced directly to your campaign manager, Rick Morries."

"Your information is correct, Jerome. The minute I found out about it, I dismissed him from my campaign. I can't always control what every one of my staffers say or do, but I can definitely send a message when they ignore my wishes."

"Yeah, well, critics say you had no choice when the news became public, but let's move on." The smile on the face of Jerome Jones and all friendliness had vanished. "The Libertarian Party is often criticized for its radical non-interventionist foreign policy, or even lack of foreign policy knowledge. For example, candidate Gary Johnson had his campaign torpedoed in 2016 when he didn't know Aleppo, the Syrian refugee area. Do you think it will be any different for you? For example, who is the prime minister of Britain?"

"Theresa May," answered Martinez. "Gary Johnson was-"

"Italy?"

"Paolo Gentiloni," said Martinez.

"How about Uzbekistan?"

"Sapar Isakov. Look Mr. Jones, I—"

Jones lips curled as he tried to suppress a smile. Martinez had made his first slip up—naming the leader of Kyrgyzstan instead of Uzbekistan. "How about Germany?"

"Mr. Jones, with all due respect, we can play a quiz game all night, but I think viewers probably have more important questions."

"Ok, let's move on. Mr. Martinez, you've mentioned many times how you want to crack down on companies that hire undocumented workers, but we've just received word that the Post will release a story tomorrow tracing over 300 of such workers directly to your companies. What do you say to that?

"I haven't seen the report, but if true, those companies definitely deserve to be fined. I don't own or manage any companies. I'm only a venture capitalist. I look at financial statements and business potential, then provide startup loans if a company is viable. I don't own more than five percent stock in any company, so I have no control over—"

"Our analysis shows that twenty of the companies you've invested in are now out of business or have gone through Chapter 11 bankruptcy. How can you be trusted to handle our nation's finances if you can't manage these small businesses?"

"Venture capital investing is the riskiest type you can do. Most businesses start out losing money and can't sustain the cash flow and revenue to continue going. We've helped launch over 400 successful businesses. As a venture capitalist, all I do is provide startup funds. We don't get involved in management and wouldn't want to. We—"

"Mr. Martinez, I have in my hands three tax returns you filed during your work as a tax accountant before switching to 'venture capitalist'," said Jones as he gestured air quotes. "Two of them are individuals who made over one million dollars but paid less than five percent in taxes. Another is a small business that earned five million but paid zero dollars in taxes. Is it your job to protect millionaires from paying their fair share of taxes?"

"I'm not sure the specifics of those returns you mention. I filed over 4,000 tax returns during my years as an accountant, most of which were for people with income under $100,000. I can assure you I've never broken a tax law. Less than 0.1 percent of those returns resulted in audit, and none of the audits resulted in any criminal accusations. I'm guessing the business you say made five million without paying taxes *lost* an amount equal to that in previous years. In other words, the net profit after adding previous year losses came to zero, meaning there were no net earnings to—"

"But doesn't your tax plan specifically do that—give more money to the rich?"

"First of all, the government isn't *giving* anything. Taxes represent money each person or business has earned which is being taken away by the government. So, a 'tax cut' is simply a way of lessening how much the government steals every year. I'd be happy to go through each point of my tax plan. We cut rates, but we eliminate loopholes and complexity. Most businesses and rich individuals will actually pay *more* because there is less incentive to park money overseas or invest in non-taxable investments such as municipal bonds. Plus, if you study the Laffer curve in economics, it shows how total revenues can actually *increase* due to the higher tax base. The—"

"The *Center for American Progress* released a study that showed your tax plan will blow up the deficit by up to a trillion per year. How does that fit into your balanced budget plan?"

"Mr. Jones, I'm trying to be respectful, but if you're not going to let me answer a question, why am I here? You've rudely interrupted me throughout this interview, and I'd appreciate if you let me finish an answer. Now, revenue estimations of tax plans are very much an inexact science. I've put together a team of the nation's best economists to draft this plan, and they project an *increase* in total tax revenue within two years. These economists are all unpaid and nonpartisan; thus, they have no incentive to fudge the numbers, unlike *Center for American Progress*, which was started by Clinton's Chief of Staff and is funded by communist George—"

"Mr. Martinez, let's talk about your family. A review of Facebook posts turned up these very revealing bikini posts of your wife and daughter. One appears to be a topless photo of your wife." Images flashed on the CNN screen. "Is this appropriate for a potential First Lady and First Family?"

"Thousands of pictures have been posted of our family over the years. For the one you have on screen of my wife, she has a brown top on which is hard to see with her dark complexion. Anyway, I think it is unprofessional and in poor taste to bring these up."

"Mr. Martinez, we've learned your wife has twenty traffic violations and parking tickets on her record. And according to her ex-husband, she is unstable and threatened violence during a custody battle for their daughter. What do you say to that?"

"This interview is officially over. My family is not part of this campaign. Thank you for your time. Good night." Martinez took his headset, tossed it on the chair, and walked off the set as he flashed a look of anger at Jerome Jones.

Colin Bennett was grinning ear to ear as he watched the interview live. It was a short interview but provided him several days of talking points and attack ads. Instructions were sent out to his media distribution network before the CNN telecast had finished.

*****

"We were dead-on accurate about Jerome Jones," said RAPCA leader, Aaron Newsome. "That was a hit piece on Martinez from beginning to end. Are you kidding me? Who the fuck knows the leader of Uzbekistan? And Jones had at least three or four items that weren't public knowledge. Let's pull all communications with him from the last couple days and run a back-trace."

"Look at the trending news on Facebook," said Nate Keeting.

Martinez can't name leaders of U.S. allies.

Martinez's wife and daughter pose for scantily-clad pictures.

Twenty businesses of Martinez bankrupt.

Potential First Lady received twenty traffic tickets, potentially unstable?

"The CNN interview finished less than ten minutes ago. There's no way the algorithm I worked on could have these stories on Martinez trending unless they were manipulated from the programming team," said Keeting.

"My guess is that all the usual suspects will be running the same stories and talking points," said Jim Damon. "I'm going to run some tests every five minutes to analyze Google search results. I saw this pattern all too often when I worked there. Let's see how long before these filters to the top of any searches on Martinez. We will back-trace the websites of the result links. I'm running our Twitter analytics for the next couple hours to see which hashtags magically appear at the top of rankings."

"Excellent," said Newsome. "The rest of the team is at your disposal. Tell us how we can help. Take a look at the media hierarchy Abby and I put together. I want to have this entire network mapped out in the next two weeks since we need at least three weeks to update our surveillance and preparation steps for Zero Day."

"Fox News, Townhall.com, and other conservative and Republican outlets are already running the same stuff," said Keeting. "Either response time and media analysis are dramatically improving, or we are seeing the beginning of a two-sided attack campaign even bigger than the one on Donald Trump."

*****

Colin Bennett started with the reporters he had on his payroll. None of them were paid directly by Media World. He always used one of the organizations indirectly under his umbrella of control, some of which opened for business only a month ago and would likely be discontinued at the end of the presidential race. It was expensive and risky to pay reporters directly to write hit pieces, which is why he concentrated on reporters from the most high-profile sources—the *New York Times*, *Washington Post*, *Fox News*, *CNN*, *MSNBC*, *CBS*, *Associated Press*, and *Huffington Post*. Bennett had paid about a hundred reporters and editors over the years, but less than twenty were on his regular payroll. Most journalists were happy enough just to get an exclusive and inside access. It was a sort of transactional journalism—Bennett gave a reporter first dibs on a story if the reporter wrote the story the way he wanted.

Once a story was put out by the so-called credible sources, it was easy for Facebook, Google, Twitter, local newspapers & TV newscasts, etc. to all echo the stories. He had over a thousand journalists on his mailing lists. Each of his subsidiaries sent suggestive stories to their assigned list of malleable reporters. Most journalists liked to think of themselves as independent and fair, but most frequented the same news/opinion websites and shared the same opinions that Bennett wanted to create, so it was an easy sell to get them to push Bennett's talking points, especially when they had the backing of the "credible-sourced" stories put out by journalists on his payroll. The 24-7 cable news stations were already following the script exactly as Bennett had crafted.

"Martinez can't name the leader of one of our most important allies," said the CNN commentator, *"then abruptly changes the subject when asked about the German leader? It is Gary Johnson all over again. Libertarians have no clue how to manage foreign policy."*

"We're not just electing a president, we're electing a First Family," said the Fox News commentator. *"I'm not sure the Martinez family is who we want to represent the United States."*

"Brent Martinez clearly doesn't have the temperament or experience to handle the job," stated the NY Times editorial. *"He couldn't handle the most basic of questions on national leaders and stormed off of an interview when given some tough questions."*

"Twenty businesses he bankrolled are now out of business," said the CNBC analyst. *"How can we trust him to manage a twenty-trillion-dollar economy if he can't handle these small startups?"*

"The Martinez family smells of corruption," said the MSNBC commentator. *"They clearly pick and choose which laws they want to obey."*

"Martinez flubs CNN interview questions," read the Associated Press headline, reprinted in hundreds of local newspapers.

Bennett had his comedy-writing division working on some jokes for the *Daily Show*, *Tonight Show*, and other nightly comedy shows. The bikini shots and parking tickets opened up plenty of *Saturday Night Live* skit ideas. Steady streams of Internet memes were being developed to show Martinez jokingly botching questions on other national leaders and basic foreign policy questions. Google, Apple, Twitter, MSN, and Yahoo news app feeds all linked to the other sources he dispatched to bombard Martinez.

Bennett's work depended on creating an image or caricature in the mind of voters. If you repeated almost any idea thousands of times, eventually it started to stick. Bennett thought of the quote on propaganda by Nazi Information Minister Joseph Goebbels, "*Those who are to be persuaded by it should be completely immersed in the ideas of the propaganda, without ever noticing that they are being immersed in it.*" The Nazi regime was terrible of course, thought Bennett, but it created some damn good techniques for gaining and holding power!

*****

After a few days of attacks on Martinez, Bennett switched to a talking-point strategy. Most of the public thought of themselves as above the petty attacks, even though they inevitably fell for many of the caricatures he created. People just needed some "intelligent" reasons they could use to justify their opposition to a candidate, so he sent well-trained commentators and writers to get the boring stuff out of the way. Libertarians generally are pro-choice, pro-gay marriage, pro-marijuana legalization, and for lower defense spending—all positions popular with Democrats but not Republicans, so Bennett sent reps to conservative new outlets like Fox News to repeatedly point out these facts but down played them on liberal outlets like CNN and MSNBC. On the flip side, Libertarians are in favor of tax cuts, limited government, lower spending, and less regulation—all positions popular with Republicans but not

Democrats, so his reps accentuated these points on liberal news outlets but downplayed them on conservative media sources. It was all a delicate balancing act designed to get as many people hating a candidate as much as possible.

Bennett always questioned whether the issues strategy really had a significant effect on votes, but his data models showed at least minimal work had to be done. Voters believed what they wanted to believe and would seek out information that confirmed their biases, while ignoring anything that went against their existing beliefs. As Bennett would explain it, most voters were sheep that would always fall in line, but they justified their votes with reasons that sounded good.

Bennett had already compiled hundreds of pieces of research that could be turned into negative stories. Some of the best stuff was preserved for closer to the election, should he not be able to knock Martinez out sooner. A couple of the stories were fed to his media distribution network each day to keep a steady stream of negativity going whenever the candidate's name was mentioned.

Martinez only thinks of himself, says ex-girlfriend.

Hundreds lost jobs immediately after Martinez business purchases.

Alyssa Martinez had restraining order put on her in 2005.

Martinez donor charged with embezzlement.

Martinez tax plan could raise deficit by one trillion according to one study.

It didn't matter that Martinez hadn't talked to his ex-girlfriend in thirty years, the wife's restraining order was only filed but not granted, the Martinez donor only gave $200 to the candidate, and the businesses described were already in Chapter 11 bankruptcy before the purchases. The facts and circumstances didn't matter, only the headlines. And one of the joys of Google was that you could find a study to "prove" virtually anything you wanted to prove. The anti-Libertarian mainstream media would run with any study that backed up the agenda they and Bennett wanted to push, even if Bennett's organizations themselves specifically *wrote* the study cited as "facts and evidence."

*****

WSJ/NBC Poll: Martinez Falls into Statistical Tie with Locklear and Miller: 34-33-33.

    Colin Bennett frowned as he stared at the latest headline. It was a start but definitely not good enough. His ultimate goal was to get him under the fifteen percent threshold, so Martinez couldn't take part in the presidential debates with the Democrat, Elizabeth Locklear, and Republican, Richard Miller. There was gold somewhere buried in the thousands of hours of video on Martinez, but his staff hadn't found much useful stuff yet. The voice transcription search programs had done most of the work so far. Bennett insisted his staff listen to all the material, and he was personally reviewing a couple dozen informal or secretly recorded videos.
    Bennett came across an iPhone video of Martinez a bit inebriated at a cousin's wedding. He and several groomsmen were singing and dancing to a drunken choreographed version of the Bruno Mars song *Uptown Funk*. Martinez was slurring and badly botching the lyrics.

    "This is that ice cold. Michelle fight for that white gold. This one for Ken's hood girls, them good girls, straight masterpieces. Dwalin, balling, living it up in the city."

Bennett chuckled to himself as he continued to listen to Martinez get virtually every lyric wrong. Bennett's eyes suddenly opened wide, and he jumped up to hit rewind. There it was—he had struck gold! Martinez was singing the lyric, "Stop, wait a minute, fill my cup, put some liquor in it," but instead, Martinez clearly sang the line, "Stop, wait a minute, fill my cup, put some *niggar* in it."

This opened a whole new line of attack against Martinez. Bennett immediately emailed the video to his favorite MSNBC commentator as a reward for his non-stop Martinez attacks over the past week. Bennett emailed his staff a new be-on-the-lookout order for anything that could be crafted into evidence of Martinez racism.

Cable news stations and comedians couldn't get enough of the Brent Martinez botched lyric. He estimated that CNN, Fox News, and MSNBC together played the video 500 times during a week of coverage. The *YouTube* video clip was played 35 million times and counting. Bennett put his ridicule division to work creating an endless stream of Internet memes of Martinez in mid-dance move singing different popular songs, each with a different racist slur. *Saturday Night Live* almost built half of a show of skits to make fun of the video.

Bennett pieced together several more daily attacks to hit the racist Martinez. One occurred when he was a guest in the commentator booth at a U.S. Open tennis match involving Venus Williams. Martinez casually remarked that she was fighting back in the match using *guerilla* tactics. Guerilla tactics was a term popularized by a Sampras-Agassi ad which came to describe an aggressive style of play. Bennett played tennis every Sunday and knew the term well, but luckily the public didn't. Martinez describes Venus's play as "gorilla tactics," clearly a racist comment.

Next, Bennett went through a series of Facebook like's and Twitter re-tweets from Martinez, who had a tendency to praise inspirational quotes. For example, Martinez had Facebook-liked the Mussolini quote, "*It is better to live one day as a lion than 100 years as a sheep."* Another example was a retweet from a former *KKK* member of Congress, Democrat Robert Byrd, *"There is no doubt that constitutional freedoms will never be abolished in one fell swoop, for the American people cherish their freedoms, and would not tolerate such a loss if they could perceive it. But the erosion of freedom rarely comes as an all-out frontal assault but rather as a gradual, noxious creeping, cloaked in secrecy, and glossed over by reassurances of greater security."* A third example came from one of Bennett's favorite white supremacists, Donald Trump, "*Criticism is easier to take when you realize that the only people who aren't criticized are those who don't take risks.*" Bennett cared little about the context of the quote, and he was confident his minions in the media wouldn't either. All that mattered is that there were three more days of headlines and cable news coverage of Martinez's love for fascists, white supremacists, and *KKK* members.

Lastly, Bennett clipped together an interview of a black employee Martinez had fired from his tax accounting firm fifteen years ago. The clearly bitter employee accused Martinez of mistreating him and firing him because of his race. Bennett didn't intend to use the interview since the employee had a checkered employment past, and fellow employees all confirmed he had been fired for chronic tardiness and making repeated mistakes on tax returns, costing clients hundreds of thousands of dollars. But now that ex-employee video would fit nicely in his racist hit piece collection.

Add it all up and Bennett received two weeks steady coverage of the new racist image he had created for Brent Martinez. That wasn't good enough though. He promised large donations to organizations for his favorite race-baiters Al Sharpton and Louis Holder if they start making speeches and organizing protests around every Martinez speaking event. Liberal billionaire Henry Keller was always helpful in providing funding for "spontaneous" protests. The important thing was, between now and election day, the racist ways of Brent Martinez could never leave the minds of voters.

*****

Each of the big screen TVs in the living room of RAPCA headquarters showed different pieces of analysis on the latest rounds of Martinez attacks—twitter hashtags rankings, Google search results, Internet memes, cable news shows, comedy show skits, and so on. Each member was charged with monitoring and summarizing a component of the research.

"A usual tactic is to use something called 'persona armies.'" said former Facebook employee, Nate Keeting, talking to the whole group. "These are programmed fake accounts that post, share, like, re-tweet, add comments to YouTube videos & other posts, etc. to manipulate rankings. It makes stories that most people don't care about seem like critical top story issues. On the flip side, the 'persona army' programs can manipulate links from low quality sites. For example, if a site is flagged as a Nazi group or conspiracy website known for posting fake stories, it is lowered in rankings, so the programs try to associate it with stories they want to drop in rankings or remove altogether."

"There are several other underhanded tactics that can be used, but Facebook, Twitter, Google, and others have started to wisen up to some of them," said former Google employee, Jim Damon. "The programming teams are large, and there are still plenty of good people in these places that try to program fairly and impartially, but unfortunately everything has a human component, and the I.T. field is notoriously leftist and liberal its politics. Algorithms can be manipulated, and insiders like our targets—Jack Zimmer at Facebook and Craig Whitman at Google—often feed formulas to the smear organizations. The popularization of the term 'fake news' has made things all too easy nowadays."

"Weeding out 'fake news' has given the search and social media groups the ability to assign rankings to groups they consider 'credible,'" said Keeting as he made air quotes. "They assign numerical values to what they call 'trust indicators.' In other words, they can weed out any alternative thought they don't agree with. This is why when you pull up the Google, Apple, Bing, and other news apps you rarely, if ever, see any links from *Fox News*, *Drudge Report*, Bill O'Reilly, Rush Limbaugh, Sean Hannity, *Townhall.com*, *Breitbart*, or other conservative & libertarian sources. Yet, you will regularly see posts from liberal sites like *Salon*, *Politico*, *CNN*, *New York Times*, *The Nation*, *Washington Post*, *Huffington Post*, Daily Beast, etc."

"Fox News is the most watched cable news network by far, and *DrudgeReport.com* is by far the most visited political & news website," said Damon, "So you would *think* that if these were really fair and impartial rankings, they'd appear almost daily on the news sites, but they don't."

"Great work, guys," said Aaron Newsome. "Look, this sums up exactly why our organization was founded. Almost all TV, newspaper, and magazine news sources are liberal or socialist. And the few remaining alternative viewpoints in TV and radio are relentlessly attacked. As media organizations buyout and combine, I see a day coming where 'fake news' and 'fairness' are used to completely silence or shutdown Fox News or radio shows like Rush Limbaugh. And as Jim and Nate have shown, the last savior of free speech—the Internet—is being manipulated to promote a one-sided viewpoint. Google, Apple, Facebook, and Microsoft are all gatekeepers of the web, the propaganda ministers of the 21st Century. Echoed stories from the clearly corrupted *Washington Post* and *New York Times* make their way into almost all national newspapers and daily news websites. Communist and anti-American thinking have taken over Hollywood and colleges around the country."

"In short, almost all the centers of influence of American thought have been taken over by leftists. The U.S. celebrated a supposed victory in the Cold War with the toppling of the Soviet Union in 1991. But if you look at the power influencers in this country now, we've clearly lost the propaganda war that can be traced back all the way to Soviet 'Active Measures,'" said Newsome, referring to a Soviet term for the actions of political warfare to influence the course of world events. "Polls show that people under 25 overwhelmingly support communist or socialist forms of government. As that generation grows up and is shaped by one-sided technology, movies, TV, education, etc., the U.S. and democracy as we know it will cease to exist. That's not going to change unless we do something about it.

"All of us have very personal reasons for fighting the war we're about to launch, but let's never lose sight of the big picture. We are attempting to save democracy. We're trying to bring accountability to the powerful people behind the scenes that have destroyed lives and weakened the long-term viability of America for their own selfish gain. We're the new Sons & Daughter of Liberty. The Revolution begins soon."

Chapter 5

"It's a Ponzi scheme": Wall Street Fears Martinez Deranged Tax Plan Could Kick Off Economic Euthanasia. – Vanity Fair

"Muslim Terrorists Want Brent Martinez as President," Says Defense Secretary. – Washington Post

Teenager Claims to Be Martinez Illegitimate Child. – Salon

Psychologists Wonder if Brent Martinez is a Sociopath. – Psychology Today

English Professor Claims Martinez Plagiarized Paper in 1992. – New York Daily News

Libertarian Party is the Biggest Threat to American Existence. – The Columbian

Rev. Louis Holder: "Brent Martinez Wants to Send Us Back to the 60s–the 1860s." – New York Times

Martinez Always Gets Two Pieces of Pie for Dessert, While Staffers Get One. – CNN

New Poll Shows Only Twenty Percent of Americans Have a Very Favorable Opinion of Brent Martinez. – NBC News

    Colin Bennett scanned his Google news app and marveled at how well his friend, Google programmer Craig Whitman, was helping tweak the daily headlines. All of the main links in the Headlines, World, U.S., and Business sections were coming back with stories his staff had helped craft or even write word for word. Bennett estimated that

95 percent of journalists were liberal-leaning. And journalists, like all humans, sought out information that confirmed their existing beliefs while avoiding alternative viewpoints. That lead them to the stories his staff had crafted into the daily media narratives. Therefore, Phase One attacks not only started to hit the politician's numbers, but more importantly, it brainwashed the mainstream media to dislike the candidate, after which they did much of the dirt digging and negative-story bombing for him.

Still, Martinez's popularity numbers weren't changing very much, despite the heavily-biased poll the Washington Post was trying to sell. Opinion polls nowadays were news themselves and were another tool in the media weapons arsenal. Polls would be worded to lead to a certain response, would oversample Democratic-leaning voters, and would be timed immediately after news or events that optimized the result Bennett wanted. The idea was to discourage supporters of Brent Martinez, to make them think they were in the minority and wrong in their support. The manipulation techniques partially explained why Donald Trump won his elections despite trailing in nearly every poll before Election Day.

"How are you, Colin?" said Democratic billionaire, Henry Keller. "You're doing an excellent job, judging by the daily headlines and poll numbers."

"It's a start," said Bennett, "but the polls aren't as good as they seem. All the hits on Donald Trump the past four years have destroyed the credibility of a lot of the sources in our network. I need more funding as I don't think a Phase One operation is going to take him out. Barring a miracle flub by Martinez, we're going to need at least a Phase Two operation and likely a Phase Three job."

"Which organizations do you want to receive the money?" said Keller.

"I'll send you the information through the usual channels."

"David is getting worried," said Keller, referring to Republican billionaire financier, David Backman. "We've agreed to raise your bonus to $500K each, which you'll receive only if Martinez either drops out of the race or falls below the fifteen-point threshold needed for presidential debates."

"You better queue up the cash transfers," said Bennett. "I never fail."

*****

"This is our last training session hitting the vulnerable spots on the body," said Dr. Abby Benton. We will do a timed session, starting from the bottom up, one minute each on instep, shin, knees, groin, solar plexus, trachea, chin, nose, eyes, and ear. After that, work with your partner to go through the sequence again, practicing the block and counter. Jim and I will be going around to check technique. At this point, everyone should have perfect form and anatomical strike location."

Abby Benton didn't look very imposing with her petite frame and girl-next-door good looks, but she possibly added more value to the RAPCAs than anyone else. Not only did she provide the training facility and most of the RAPCA start-up financing, but her wide range of knowledge added value in nearly every area of their preparation—first aid, research, bomb-making, fitness, biological weapons, and pretty much anything science-related. She even was above average in firearms, taught by her father who had fought in Iraq during Desert Storm and her police officer ex-husband. She was finishing up a training review of the weak & vulnerable locations on the human body—the pressure points, pain nerve centers, and easy ways to incapacitate almost any individual. As a former orthopedic surgeon, she also described some of the injuries that would be the toughest to rehab and recover from, which would become particularly important in the coming days.

She'd been having trouble sleeping lately, not so much from guilt or doubt in what they planned to do, but more from the stress and anticipation of the coming actions. She'd changed so much in the past three years—once one of the most respected surgeons in the country, now she was training to be a so-called "domestic terrorist."

She met Aaron Newsome when she performed three operations on him after his return from Fallujah. She became good friends with both Aaron and his wife, Dana, through the rehab as well as their work on various veterans' charities founded by Dana. Dr. Benton was the main reason Aaron was nearly fully recovered from his extensive war injuries.

However, it was Abby's work on another patient that changed the course of her life. A well-known NFL quarterback had come to her after suffering a particularly vicious hit that broke parts of both his collarbone and shoulder blade while tearing his rotator cuff, all in his throwing shoulder. The quarterback had become a very controversial one before his injury. NFL national anthem and flag protests had died down as an issue the previous year before they were revived by this QB. The $30-million-per-year QB had spit on the flag during a live broadcast and was regularly using interviews to rip on the United States and everything it stood for.

During a press conference after the QB's first surgery, Dr. Benton was answering questions on his recovery when a reporter asked her if she thought players should respect the flag and stand for the anthem? Being the daughter of a Persian Gulf war vet, Abby answered 'Yes, of course' without ever thinking about why the question was asked. The answer probably would never have become much of an issue, but the damage to the QB's shoulder was too extensive for him to continue his career. She repaired the damage enough so that he could resume normal activities, but he lost enough distance and velocity on throws that he never played another down again in the NFL.

The media, prodded by a well-known race-baiter named Reverend Louis Holder, accused Dr. Abby Benton of racism and charged her with intentionally botching the surgery to end his NFL career. He convinced the quarterback to sue her for malpractice, and both sports and news media viciously attacked her for weeks. During the peak of the coverage, a crazed fan attacked her leaving the hospital one day, breaking her arm, cracking three ribs, and nearly killing her in the process. Although Abby knew she did nothing wrong and had medical testimony on her side, she was eventually pressured to settle the malpractice suit for a substantial sum. This ended the legal proceedings and most of the media attention, but Reverend Louis Holder tried to keep the race issue going long after the suit was settled, trying to convince the QB to also sue the NFL, and most of the media obliged.

Eventually, the uproar died down, but the reputation of Dr. Abby Benton was destroyed. She was invited to leave by her partners in her medical practice. Afterwards, her friend Dana Newsome helped get her a job at a small clinic in Madison, Wisconsin.

Abby watched with rage the daily treatment of Dana Newsome as she ran for the Senate. After Dana's suicide, it didn't take more than a minute of persuasion for Aaron Newsome to recruit his first and most important RAPCA team member.

Abby brought with her two recruits to the RAPCA team. One was her ex-husband, Darren Williams. Darren was 6'3" and had blonde hair, blue eyes, and a powerful build. He had worked as a police officer in the Chicago P.D., at least he did until being let go the previous year after a shooting incident. Darren had fielded a robbery call around midnight when a fifteen-year-old black kid pointed a .22 pistol at him. Darren had won shooting contests with his Glock 17, so it wasn't an accident when he unloaded two non-lethal shots into the kid's right shoulder, unleashing the weapon from the boy's hands in the process. The .22 slid into a pothole and initially wasn't seen by witnesses. National media ran with the story of "yet another unarmed black kid shot by a white police officer." Coincidentally, the story was fed by Reverend Louis Holder, the same man who had stoked the hatred against Abby during her malpractice suit. The District Attorney didn't have any plans to charge Darren after the facts came out, but she had no choice with the possible riots egged on by Reverend Louis. Darren Williams spent his life savings in legal fees to defend the criminal case and follow-up civil case. Darren won both cases, but the Chicago P.D. couldn't keep him on without tearing the city apart.

The second person Abby recruited was science teacher and former classmate, Scott Koonce. Koonce was the only black member of the group. He was 5'10", slightly overweight, and wore glasses that made him look like the professor he was. He was once a top research scientist and professor for UCLA. Koonce made the mistake of writing some prominent articles questioning conclusions and research methods in some major climate change studies. His articles didn't draw any conclusions on the *existence* of climate change. He simply attacked the flawed measurements and the exaggeration of the predictions. It didn't matter, as politicians and the very environmentally-conscious California media attacked him as a "climate change denier." Colleagues were pressured to pile on the attacks. Koonce lost his job and was effectively blacklisted from any other university research positions. After many months out of work, he started over with a high school teaching position in Appleton, WI until being recruited to the RAPCAs by his former classmate, Abby Benton.

Abby gave Darren Williams and Scott Koonce a forearm bash as they exited class, sort of a martial arts high-five. She walked back into the empty classroom to unleash a few last kicks and punches. The final strike was saved for a wooden mannequin with a face picture of Reverend Louis Holder where the head was. She executed a perfect spinning back kick as she screamed a "KEEEEEEAA!" Covered in sweat, she exited the room as the decapitated wooden head rolled into the corner.

*****

Hi, my name is Brent Martinez, and I approved this message. Recently, you've heard many negative attacks on me calling me everything from a racist to a sociopath. What you're seeing is a very organized effort to destroy me by big-money interests and operatives of both the Democratic and Republican party. I refuse to respond in kind. All you are going to hear from me are solutions and positive ways we can bring people together.

I refuse to take any donations over $200, and the small donations I do receive will only be used to give my full-time campaign staff a living and pay for ads like you're hearing now. I will never be beholden to big-money powerful interests or any establishment parties. And I'm not going to fund any Super PAC's or other organizations who exist for no other reason than launching character attacks and digging up dirt, or in many cases, manufacturing it.

Please go to my website, BrentMartinez.gov and follow me on Twitter or Facebook if you want to hear my plans without the noise of the powerful people trying to destroy me in the same way they've done to political outsiders of the past.

I've made many mistakes in my life and learned lessons the hard way, and they have made me the person I am today. Please consider my policy positions—term limits, reducing the size of government, cutting spending, reversing rules that grant too much executive power of the president, and so on. I'm a major threat to the whole Washington power structure, and the relentless attacks of the past few weeks are an organized, coordinated attack to neutralize that threat.

I'm the only candidate who wants to return power to you, the American people. I want to restore freedom and get the government out of every aspect of our lives. I'm never going to be perfect, but I will always follow my principles to serve you the people, and only you. Please join me in taking back our country.

"I'm starting to really like this guy," said RAPCA tech expert, Jim Damon, as he watched the ad on Fox News. "He's the only politician I've ever seen who talks about issues, and I've never once, not one single time, seen him launch a personal attack on another candidate."

"Libertarians are a little too fruit-cakey on foreign policy for me," said the former Navy SEAL, Cole Foreman, "but he does seem like a respectable guy."

"And if you go through our media & political organization hierarchies we've mapped out," said Nate Keeting, "he's the *only* candidate that, so far, we've been unable to tie to a smear merchant, directly or indirectly. There are a few libertarian organizations formed without his authorization that are running some negative stuff, but from what we've seen, he's legitimately trying to do what he says."

*****

After being checked for weapons, recorders, and listening devices, Colin Bennett stepped into the steel encased room.

"I will need $100,000 wired to my numbered account in the Bahamas for this information," said National Security Agency agent, Tim Gordon. "You already have most of the publicly-available information, so I didn't include it here. This flash drive has every phone call, email, recording, and text we've ever made to date on Brent Martinez, his wife, and kids. Voice assistants like Alexa and Google Now are making our job even easier than it was before."

"Excellent. Don't worry, I'll invent some 'anonymous sources' for the good stuff. Nothing will trace back to you."

"Really, Bennett?! Do you want me to quote word-for-word your little conversation with Henry Keller yesterday? How do you plan to spend the $500,000 from both Keller and Backman?"

"Shit," said Bennett.

"Relax, I already removed the conversation from our archives, but don't be such a dipshit. Our listening devices are way more sophisticated than they used to be. I'm shipping you some modern noise-cancelling devices and jammers. Don't talk about anything remotely illegal over the phone or Internet, and try to use more intermediaries when you communicate with your slime network."

"Yes, sir, Agent Gordon, sir," said Bennett, giving a mocking salute. Phase Two of his destroy-Martinez was beginning. The candidate had moved back into a five-point lead in public polls, but it was more like 10-15 points in internal polls of likely voters. The stakes were getting serious.

*****

"All I can say is that if you don't pull your ads from Tucker Carlson's Fox News show, then you're every bit as racist as the candidate himself, and we will have no choice but to organize a boycott," said the Reverend Louis Holder. He was talking to his tenth advertiser today. Fox News had run ads purchased by Brent Martinez and had allowed him to be a guest on shows many times. Sometimes when you couldn't kill the message, it was best to go after the messenger. "The NAACP, Rainbow Push, National Urban League...you have no idea how many organizations I have at my disposal. Find some other way to sell your product or suffer the consequences. The boycotts start in 24 hours unless I see a press release saying you've stopped your advertising. Good day, sir."

Louis Holder had learned his extortion techniques from the greats, Al Sharpton and Jesse Jackson. It's amazing after all these years this bullshit still worked, thought

Holder. The billionaire Henry Keller funded dozens of organizations whose only purpose was to organize protests and boycotts of anyone that didn't fall in line with his big government, socialist, politically-correct ideals. Louis Holder and others like him were the front men, the ones who called for the "resistance."

The support for the political platform of Brent Martinez was spreading like wildfire. Any reporter or news organization perpetuating that support had to be attacked every bit as ruthlessly as the candidate himself.

*****

"Bad news," said Cole Foreman. "We can't get to Bennett. His place is protected like Fort Knox. He's not stupid. He's made *a lot* of enemies over the years, and he's paid for the best security money can buy. He has dogs, motion sensors, electric fencing, and what I suspect are one or two ex-special forces protecting his mansion." Foreman and fellow Navy SEAL, Kyle Topper, had just returned from a scouting mission.

"Fuck," said Aaron Newsome. "What if we put the whole team on him before Zero Day?"

"It won't work. With the element of surprise, we *may* be able to take him out, but the likelihood of killing innocents and losing team members is way too high."

"Alright, we'll deal with him at a later time. Let's do your final class."

Cole Foreman was Aaron Newsome's best friend growing up. He obtained degrees in physics and electrical engineering before joining the Navy. He completed his BUD/S training to become a SEAL two years before 9/11. With his science background, it was an easy transition for him to become a demolitions expert. Serving tours in both Afghanistan and Iraq, he spent most of his time dealing with Improvised Explosive Devices (IEDs), the most prevalent weapon used by the terrorists they were fighting.

Foreman became friends with Dana Newsome through his friendship with Aaron, and he was almost as deeply angered as Aaron by the media's treatment of her. It didn't take much persuasion for Aaron to recruit Foreman for his new mission. Though even before Dana's death, it would have been easy to convince Foreman to join. A near-universal feeling among U.S. special forces was a hatred of politicians and the media, who they felt diminished their sacrifices and acted like judge & jury on things they knew nothing about.

Foreman recruited his fellow SEAL, Kyle Topper, who he had served with ever since BUD/S training. Topper was one of the deadliest snipers in special forces. The two of them deserved as much credit as anyone in taking down Saddam Hussein and freeing Baghdad. Half of their SEAL team was killed during the course of their missions, so they were especially infuriated by the constant media attacks on the Iraqi war effort, which pressured politicians to pull troops too soon and opened the door for ISIS terrorists to walk right in and undo all their accomplishments.

The U.S. government normally keeps track of ex-special forces with the skill levels of Topper and Foreman, and they would definitely be flagged after the upcoming actions, so the two of them officially became residents of another country and had re-entered the U.S. through Mexico using fake passports. Cole Foreman had a place in Panama, while Kyle Topper was living in Dominican Republic.

"Your final exam will be to build your own IED inside a burn phone, which we will test by remotely detonating using your own iPhone," said Foreman. "Remember our safety guidelines and simply run through the basic steps we've discussed—power supply, trigger, detonator, explosive material, and container. Use exactly the amount of C-4 we plan to use on Zero Day and not a speck more. We won't always know how close some bystanders may be to the targets."

Most of the explosive material was synthesized in their basement makeshift lab. Foreman and the chemistry teacher, Scott Koonce, did most of the work in putting together the lab. Aaron Newsome and Abby Benton had procured the raw materials over a year prior to construction of the lab using some of their many fake ID sets. Abby's ex-husband, the police officer Darren Williams, showed them all the tricks needed to get around detection from law enforcement.

Each of them built their own burn-phone IED and tested it inside a six-foot steel-encased cube from a hundred yards away. All operated flawlessly. Cole Foreman and Scott Koonce would do all the actual bomb construction in the first wave of attacks, but as with other training, everyone learned the basics. They had no idea how long the war would last nor who would be lost from their team.

*****

The last wave of RAPCA training exams involved pistol and sniper shooting. Former Navy SEAL, Kyle Topper, led the sniper training using his M64 semi-automatic rifle. He could hit the center of a quarter reliably from under 2000 yards but had hit many targets 3000 yards away over his years of service. Aaron Newsome and Cole Foreman weren't in the same league as Topper, but both were respectable shots.

Former police officer, Darren Williams, led the pistol review. The entire RAPCA team had grown efficient with each one's preferred Glock or Beretta model. All members hit 95 percent or more of targets from 50 yards away except the I.T. guys, Jim Damon and Nate Keeting, who each only missed by a couple of points.

Boot camp was finished. Despite their wildly varied backgrounds, ages, and training, they were now an elite cohesive team. Experience, education, and motivation made them as lethal as any special forces unit in the world. It was time for their war to begin.

Chapter 6

"I need you to work your magic, buddy," said Colin Bennett, referring to NBC editor, Mike Mathers.

"Let me hear the original again," said Mathers.

> "So, I met my sister's new boyfriend, …{garbled}" said Brent Martinez.
>
> "Is he white or black?" said an unknown voice. "Uh, he's black," said Martinez.
>
> "He's also a socialist who voted for both Obama and Hillary," said a second unknown voice.
>
> "See, I told you my sister sucks at picking boyfriends," said Martinez.
>
> {Laughter}

"So, I just want you to silence the unknown background voices," said Bennett.

Mathers made some tweaks at his computer. "How's this?"

> "So, I met my sister's new boyfriend…Uh, he's black. See, I told you my sister sucks at picking boyfriends," said Martinez

"Perfect! Now let's playback sound clip three."

> "Are you sure you want to run a fire sale on this company?" said an unknown voice. "Thousands of people will be put out of work."

> "Kill it. It's already gone through Chapter 11 bankruptcy and won't last long with its massive negative cash flow. We'll provide re-training and a nice severance package to all the employees who lose their jobs," said Martinez.
>
> "Ok, consider it done."

"Take out everything after 'Kill it' in Martinez's reply, then go directly to the response," said Bennett.

> "Are you sure you want to run a fire sale on this company?" said an unknown voice. "Thousands of people will be put out of work."
>
> "Kill it," said Martinez.
>
> "Ok, consider it done."

"Good," said Bennett, patting the NBC journalist on the back. "Please play the next one."

> "I like being able to fire people who don't do their jobs, steal money from the company, or sexually harass their employees. The great thing about the private sector is that you're held accountable for your actions. In government, programs can fail year after year, then instead of losing funding they get increases in their budgets, and employees in government keep their jobs and get regularly scheduled raises regardless of performance."

"I just want to hear 'I like being able to fire people' from that quote. The rest of that response can disappear."
"Ok. How many more of these do you have? I don't want to ask where you got all these recordings."
"Seven," said Bennett. "Don't worry, you're going to have a nice Christmas bonus this year, Mike."

Bennett had about fifteen new sound and video clips he could form into stories. Some of them could be released unedited since he knew he could count on like-minded friends in the media to leave out context and make them sound shadier they really were. The authenticity and editing were sure to be questioned, so he'd have to dispatch his own paid experts to provide cover. His favorite clips would be mixed in with a larger dump of recordings that contained nothing of interest. He knew reporters would sift through and find exactly what he wanted, then breathlessly turn them into "breaking news" stories. Bennett laughed—American voters were generally easy to manipulate, but it was even more of a cake walk to manipulate the average mainstream media journalist.

*****

Anonymous Hacker Group Leaks Hundreds of Martinez Videos, Phone Calls, and Recordings. — Politico

Martinez Claims Recordings are Taken Out of Context and Edited, Experts Disagree. — Los Angeles Times

Yet Another Racist Statement from Martinez Found in Recording Dump. – Washington Post

"'Plantation owner' Brent Martinez should resign immediately," says Rev. Louis Holder. – BET

Martinez is the Epitome of the Heartless CEO. – CNN Business

Martinez Shows Shades of Mitt Romney and Gordon Gekko. – New York Times

One-Percenter Brent Martinez Puts Profits Ahead of the American People. – MSNBC

Three More Companies Pull Ads from Tucker Carlson Show after Martinez Interview. — Daily Beast

Poll: Martinez Maintains Lead, but "Strongly Disapprove" Numbers Increase to Highest Ever. – ABC

Colin Bennett closed the Apple News app and flipped to his wine shopping app. He had plenty of $5000 wines in his cellar, but he might have to crack open something *really* special when he received his bonus for taking Martinez out of the presidential race.

*****

The Reverend Louis Holder used to have a weight problem, but he was much thinner nowadays thanks to a better diet and his daily run/walk, which he did every day at 5:00am sharp. He avoided the more scenic trails since he enjoyed his solitude, except for his loyal bodyguard, Marshawn, who always dutifully did the same daily run/walk, generally staying about ten yards behind him.

It was cloudy and darker than usual as Holder turned the corner around an old building, when he was startled by what appeared to be a homeless person stumbling into a trash can across the street. Turning his head distracted him from the female runner coming the other direction, who collided hard with him.

"Oh, I'm sorry. I didn't see you coming," she said.

Holder picked himself up off the ground and scanned the gorgeous woman covered in sweat, with cleavage peaking from the top of her sports bra. "No problem at all, pretty lady. I wasn't watching where I was going. I don't see many other runners out this way. Do you know who I am?"

"Of course, I know who you are, Reverend Holder. Do you remember who I am?" The smile on the woman's face curled into an expression of anger.

"I don't think--," Holder initial face of confusion turned in wide-eyed surprise. "Dr. Benton?" Holder turned around to locate Marshawn, only to see him unconscious, being dragged away by a man. "What the--?"

Abby delivered a stabbing knuckle punch to the throat of Holder, followed by a front kick to the groin. Holder staggered forward and grabbed his throat as he tried to get out the word "help", but to no avail. "I'm going to enjoy this." Abby extended two quick kicks to each shin. The only thing stopping Holder from howling in pain was his heavily damaged voice box. His pain was ended temporarily, though, when Aaron Newsome put Holder in a sleeper hold until he was unconscious.

"What in the hell are you thinking, Abby?" said Newsome.

"Sorry, I couldn't resist. The fear and pain in his eyes was too priceless to end so quickly. Let's get out of here." Kyle Topper finished dragging the bodyguard, Marshawn, to an empty alley. He was injected with an opioid called Etorphine and would wake up in a few hours. The Reverend Louis Holder wouldn't be so lucky, but first they needed to find out some information from him. The disguised homeless man, Nate Keeting, crossed the street to help the others throw Holder into a van that just pulled up, driven by Scott Koonce.

Their Revolution had begun. There was no turning back now.

Chapter 7

"I've never in my life been accused of being racist until I became a threat to the establishment power in Washington," said Brent Martinez from the podium of a sold-out 10,000 seat arena in Green Bay, WI. *"All of you know by now that this racist attack strategy is a standard operating procedure of politicians and the media to destroy candidates. They cherry-pick phrases from hundreds of thousands of pages of material taken out of context to turn people into evil caricatures. It has been so common for the media to use this strategy that when* real *racism occurs in society, it's belittled and ignored.*

"Political correctness is the most dangerous threat to free speech in existence nowadays. It is not only a control on free speech. It controls free thought. You're not *allowed to have certain thoughts, regardless if they're true or not. You're not allowed to point out obvious facts like most NBA players and the fastest world runners are black. You're not allowed to point out obvious differences between men & women, like men are more likely to want to pursue math & computer professions, while women are more likely to want to pursue nursing and care-giving professions. Political correctness says throw out science, logic, and all common sense; instead, follow the thoughts and speech of what some unknown authority says is OK, which seems to change every year, by the way.*

"Screw it. If you want someone who follows the standard politician-speak script, pick someone else as president. If you want to follow the same formula for picking politicians that lead to our current 535 people in Congress and recent presidents, have at it. I'm a flawed human being, just like everyone else. I've made many mistakes and learned many lessons. I'm not perfect, but I'm not going to apologize for who I am.

"I'm the only candidate who wants to give up presidential power, place term limits on Congress, and reduce the size of government and its intrusion into your lives. I'm the only one not beholden to lobbyists and big-money donors. In our nearly 250 years as a nation, we've never had a president that wasn't Democrat or Republican or some earlier version of one of those parties. I ask you, are you happy with what we have in power now? Maybe it's time to finally try a third option."

Colin Bennett listened to the crowd roar its approval on the TV as he formulated his next attack story.

*****

"In this Donald Trumpian speech, Martinez is basically admitting he is racist and doesn't care," said the CNN commentator.

"Martinez said in this Trumpian speech that only men should work math and tech jobs, while women should only be in nursing and caregiving roles," said the MSNBC anchor.

"How many more Trumpian statements from Martinez do we need to hear before we realize he may be the most racist presidential candidate we've ever had?" said the Washington Post editorial.

"Martinez's reference to NBA players being black is reminiscent of Donald Trump's racist attack on NFL players," said the ESPN commentator.

Colin Bennett listened and read almost twenty stories that used basically the same language. He loved that most of mainstream media personalities were lemmings, but could they at least think enough for themselves to change the wording of their statements? This last round of attacks might easily backfire as Rush Limbaugh and other right-wing commentators could easily highlight all the common phrases to make it look like a coordinated attack, which it sort of was, but success depended on the American people not knowing of the propaganda effort. It was possibly the biggest reason Donald Trump overcame all the coordinated attacks on him to win an election.

"You have to give up on this whole 'racist' thing, Colin," said Google executive Craig Whitman, as he walked into the room. "My analytics show the only positive is you're strengthening the strong disapproval numbers in the people that would vote against him no matter what anyway. You're equally strengthening his strongly-approve numbers and you're pushing independents in his direction."

"Noted," said Bennett. "So, what have you got for me, Craig?"

"This wasn't easy to get with all the privacy bullshit being put in at Google, but here is the search history from Martinez for the last ten years."

"Did you slip in the searches I sent you?"

"Yeah. I'm not exactly feeling right about it, though. It's a pretty sleazy thing to do," said Whitman.

"Politics *is* a sleazy business. Martinez knew the risks when he got into this election. What's going to bother your conscious more, Craig. Releasing this altered search history or letting Martinez get elected and screwing up the whole course of American and world history?"

"Yeah yeah, I know. Ends justifies the means, but it doesn't mean I have to like it. This can't get traced back to me. Right-wing nuts are going to question the authenticity and go after the source. If I'm caught, not only will I lose my job and stock options, I could be facing civil and maybe even criminal liability."

"Relax, Craig. Anyone who goes through the history is going to see 99.9 percent of the searches completely fit the profile of Brent Martinez because it *is*, in fact, authentic. I'm going to give this to David," said Bennett, referring to Republican billionaire, David Backman. "He will take care of leaking it through his media and PAC network. The

Republicans are scared shitless by the fact that not only is Martinez widening his lead, but he's starting to pull more votes from their side than the Democrat side. Republican voters are *far* more anti-media than Democratic voters, so this little media jihad against Martinez is garnering him sympathy. This has been part of our strategy from the beginning. If we can't get him out of the race, at least siphon off enough Republican votes so maybe we can have another situation like 1992 where Bill Clinton won the election with only 43 percent of the popular vote. And if there's a right-wing investigation into the source, it'll be traced back to Backman, after which they'll be the usual Republican circular firing squad routine."

"This may destroy Martinez, not just politically, but personally. You're awfully cold, Bennett."

"I think the word you're looking for is 'brilliant.'"

*****

New York Times reporter, Patrick Adams, was fuming as he walked into the office of his editor, Marilyn Kahn. "Why are killing my story?"

"It just doesn't seem believable to me, and it may hurt the reputation of a charity that is helping a lot of people," said Kahn.

"This is potentially the next president we're talking about here. It doesn't take a genius to see Elizabeth Locklear has been using her charity as a slush fund for Democratic political donations. Did you even look at my research? I have a detailed paper trail and three different on-the-record sources, including a CPA with an impeccable reputation who terminated his business with the company once he found out what was going on. Less than five percent of the so-called donations are making it to the stated beneficiaries."

"Yes, I read your research, and I didn't find it very convincing. Your 'impeccable' CPA is a registered Republican, so what he says means nothing to me. And most public charities have a low percentage of donations that reach beneficiaries. It's normal to have a high overhead rate for such a diverse group of donees. Let's also keep in mind how many people this charity employs."

"I cannot believe I'm hearing this."

"Why are you even working on this story, anyway? I told you we're focusing our resources right now on Martinez. I emailed you at least ten different story directions you can pursue. Locklear has been in the public eye for decades. Anything on her is old news. Martinez is the new kid on the block, and it's our job to fully vet him."

"So, you're telling me we're going to spend our time digging for stupid, meaningless stories like racist language in cell phone videos rather than pursuing obvious evidence of corruption?"

"I don't know how things ran in that piss-ant newspaper you worked for in Wisconsin, but here at the *Times*, you do as you're told if you want to keep your job. Why don't you take a mini-vacation and fly down to Virginia to meet with Martinez's ex-wife and a couple of his ex-girlfriends. A handsome young man like you could probably get them talking."

Adams exited the office without saying another word, slamming the door on the way out. Patrick Adams had never really fit in with the staff at the *New York Times*. He was born and raised in a small town in Wisconsin, and unlike most of his fellow reporters who had graduated from Ivy League universities, he had attended a small state school in Whitewater, WI. While most *Times* columnists were unapologetically liberal in almost all their political views, Adams was all over the map in his views—Republican, Democratic, Libertarian, Reform Party—it all depended on the issue. But he believed it was the job of reporters to bury all biases as much as possible and just report facts on all sides of every issue.

Adams had gained notoriety with an investigative piece for the *Wisconsin State Journal* in which he broke a corruption ring of mostly Republican legislators in the State Senate. His series of articles on the topic was the only reason he was granted an interview with the *Times*. Being an investigative reporter for the *New York Times* or *Washington Post* was always his dream, but lately he was starting to become jaded on what had become the state of American journalism. Truth, justice, balance, facts, and unbiased investigation no longer seemed to matter. Now, it was all about finding ways to destroy any undesirable candidates and maintain the status quo of power in Washington.

Adams sat as his desk staring at his own picture with Bob Woodward, the *Washington Post* journalist who had helped break Watergate. This *New York Times* gig wasn't fulfilling his life's mission. If only he didn't have nine months left of the lease on that $4500/month New York apartment, he seriously would consider giving his notice that very moment. Regardless, it was time to start planning his life after the *Times*.

*****

The 75-year-old ex-ABC anchor, Dan Irvin, desperately missed the limelight of his former job. Very few of his loyal viewers would recognize him nowadays due to the effects of age and plastic surgeries. Luckily, his name still carried considerable value in the journalism community, which allowed him to write regular guest editorials for the *New York Times*, *Washington Post*, *Politico*, and *Newsweek*.

He was universally hated and mocked by the Rush Limbaugh's and Sean Hannity's of the world for his liberally-slanted decades of reporting, which he regarded as more centrist. But they were just right-wing crazies who were jealous of the amount of damage his "October surprises" did to so many of their conservative candidates. More than any reporter, Irvin was famous for withholding bombshell stories, often based on shoddy evidence, until a few weeks before the election when they could do the most damage.

Almost none of the stories were the result of his own investigative work but instead just fell into his lap from one of his friends or political insider contacts. Irvin was still convinced Donald Trump would never have been elected had he still been at his old anchor job to bring more credibility to all the huge scandals that came out before the election.

Irvin was in the middle of typing an editorial on why Brent Martinez should resign from the presidential race when he heard pounding on the door. Strange. It was rare for him to have visitors in his cabin for which he stayed one day per week to write. He looked through the peephole to see a pretty woman in a bike helmet crying with blood on her face and arm. He cracked the door.

"Hello miss. Can I help you?"

"Please sir. I had a bit of a wipeout on my bike. My iPhone busted when I hit the pavement. Do you mind if I use your phone? And do you happen to have a first-aid kit?"

As a celebrity, Irvin knew to be extra cautious around strangers, but few people recognized him nowadays, and this girl seemed harmless and legitimately injured. "I suppose. Come on in. You can use my cell. I think I might have some bandages and rubbing alcohol." He opened the door and turned as she followed him in.

"Thank you so much, Mr. Irvin."

Irvin felt a chill down his spine as he heard his name called. He turned around towards the girl. He couldn't get a word out, though, before Aaron Newsome stepped up behind him and put him in a tight headlock until he fell into unconsciousness.

*****

Irvin was startled awake four hours later from the smelling salt waved in front of his nose. He looked around to see what appeared to be the inside of a barn containing only a table, a few laptops & papers, and six other people.

Irvin was shirtless, bound by duct tape to a chair. He recognized one other man in the same situation sitting ten feet across from him—the Reverend Louis Holder.

"Feel free to scream if you want," said Aaron Newsome, "but we're in the middle of nowhere, so it won't accomplish anything other than to annoy me, which is not something you want to do in your situation right now." Newsome walked up and ripped off the duct tape on each of their faces. Irvin was too petrified to speak.

"What the hell is this," said Holder, "Do you have any idea who you're fucking with? I'm Louis Holder! If you dumb-ass crackers don't release me now, you're going to have fifty million pissed-off niggers ready to hunt you down and rip you limb from limb."

"Save the rap, Holder. There are no media cameras here. We've all heard your race-baiting and hate-mongering bullshit, and believe me, you're going to pay for it very soon. We have your phone, and thanks to your logged-in Dropbox account, we now have all your personal documents and account information. Interesting group of contacts you have—bankers, lobbyists, hundreds of journalists, corporate CEOs. What the hell kind of 'reverend' carries $3000 in cash with him, while exercising, no less?"

"Fuck you! If you really have all that information, you should know the kind of power I have at my disposal. The best thing you can do is let me go and disappear to some tropical location where you'll never be found."

"Why exactly are we here?" said Irvin. "We haven't done anything to you?"

"Oh, I'm sure you know my history with the great Reverend Louis," said Abby Benton. "And you, don't act so innocent. You've spent decades destroying lives and turning the nation against each other. People like you and Holder have done more harm to this country than any politician could ever hope to do in a lifetime."

"That's not true, I've always been fair--AH!" Cole Foreman stepped behind Dan Irvin and administered a pinch in the neck that silenced him.

"You'll have plenty of time to talk in a few minutes," said Newsome. "We have blueprints of several media locations in New York, Washington, Atlanta, Chicago, and Los Angeles. Both of you have spent considerable time in these locations during your visits with your other media contacts. Irvin, I know you worked for years at both the *Washington Post* and *New York Times*. We want to know more about the layout. We want to know security routines and other intel we can't gather from surveillance."

"I'm not telling you a goddamn thing!" said Holder.

"Reverend Holder. Mr. Irvin. I'm only going to ask nicely once. We're not monsters and don't want to torture, but we have little time and even less patience."

"Fuck off, snow white," said Holder.

"Sir, I'm not sure what you want to do with this information, but I don't want to see my friends harmed. I have to agree with the reverend," said Irvin.

"I'm sure you both have seen torture in movies, but have you ever thought about what it would be like to have pain administered by a trained physician like Dr. Benton, here? Especially one who was nearly killed and had her career wrecked by your bullshit antics?"

"Yes," said Dr. Benton, "for example, I know from my expertise in anatomy that there is a bundle of nerves near your shoulder underneath the clavicle right about here, and if you take a knife like this and plunge it like so."

"AAAAHHH!" screamed Holder as Abby stuck the knife in and twisted.

"I'm betting you don't want to me to demonstrate the most painful locations in other male anatomy locations," said Abby as she lowered the knife to his groin. "My friends Cole and Aaron here have sacrificed in the military for decades and have withstood unspeakable amounts of pain. I'm guessing you two haven't learned much about enduring pain in your cushy media bubbles back home." Abby moved the knife over to the other prisoner's groin and pinched a pressure point on his inner thigh with her fingers.

"No. What do you want? I'll tell you what you want. Please anything! Stop, anything," said Irvin in an increasingly panicky voice.

Newsome tapped on Abby's shoulder and walked her back, gently maneuvering the knife out of her hand unseen by Holder or Irvin. "Look," he said, "if we wanted to kill a ton of people, we would blow up their buildings or set up sniper rifles and start shooting. Our I.T. guys Jim and Nate are going to go over the blueprints with you. Darren is going to go over security measures. We've already done extensive research, and if we catch you in a lie, we'll have Dr. Benton start slicing off body parts and administer drugs to keep you conscious and alert, so you can thoroughly enjoy the pain as long as possible."

The last bit of defiance was fading from Reverend Louis as he nodded his head. Irvin looked near catatonic but also nodded. "The only thing I want to hear from either of you from this point on are answers to our questions. Let's get to work."

Chapter 8

Two things annoyed Colin Bennett about the sudden disappearance of Reverend Louis Holder. One, Holder was instrumental in whipping up protests and media attention to his various attack strategies. Few were better at inciting hatred and keeping voters divided enough to get his lousy candidates elected. Second and more importantly, his disappearance was dominating TV and newspaper top stories, which meant the media campaigns against Martinez were taking a backseat.

The FBI was being pressured to investigate the KKK, Aryan Nation, and other racist hate groups, but it seemed obvious to Bennett, this was something different. The kidnapping was too professional and low-profile for those groups, and didn't these idiot politicians realize if it was a race-based crime, they would have kidnapped or killed the bodyguard of Holder instead of just drugging him?

"Ugh." Bennett rolled his eyes as he grabbed for the remote. How many of these damn FBI press conferences were they going to have? Why even *have* a press conference if 99 percent of your answers are "no comment" or "we have no information on that?" Politicians and bureaucrats were such gutless weasels. All of them had to pretend Holder was some great loss at the risk of being labeled *racially insensitive*. Bennett didn't give a shit about Holder personally, but he needed him the next few weeks. Right now, more importantly, he needed him *out of the news*.

He wanted to wait until September to launch his Google search history strategy. Summer vacations would be over, and it would be closer to the election, so people would be paying closer attention to the news. However, the latest developments had forced his hand. He picked up the phone. "Connect me with David Backman."

*****

Iconic News Anchor Dan Irvin Found Dead in Cabin of Apparent Heart Attack. – CNN

Still No Leads on Disappearance of Reverend Louis Holder. – Washington Post

Wikileaks Releases Stolen Google Search History of Brent Martinez. – New York Times

Democratic and Republican Parties Trying to Change Presidential Debate Rules to Force Higher Poll Vote Percentage Threshold to Participate in Debates. – Fox News

"Fuck!" said Colin Bennett as he skimmed through the latest news summaries put together by his assistants. Another cog in his propaganda machine was now out of the picture. The old bastard couldn't stay alive for another month? Oh well, it was a minor setback, but it was yet another story pushing down the headlines he wanted. And fucking *Fox News*, how the hell did they get wind of the debate rule change attempt? It was the one story he *wanted* to keep buried. Both Republican and Democratic big-money donors wanted to put in a contingency plan to raise the debate participation threshold to twenty percent in case they couldn't get Martinez down in the polls under fifteen. Voters definitely wouldn't like it, so this was supposed to stay buried in the avalanche of other news. He'd have to ramp up the *Fox News* credibility attacks.

He was confident the Google search history would eventually lead to weeks of negative stories on Martinez, but there were almost 50,000 searches in the released history. It would take some time for media departments to go through it all. He didn't want his Media World network to point out any searches for them since he didn't want to be tied to the *Wikileaks* release in any way. It was time to goose them in the right direction and start building a new attack narrative. He picked up the phone.

"Henry," he said, referring to Democratic billionaire Henry Keller, "we have five million bucks set aside in the Martinez budget for TV/radio ads and robocalls, but you know my opinion on the uselessness of these. I'm thinking we should carve out most of that money for a Phase Three strategy."

"We've reached that point already?"

"Unfortunately, yes. Martinez is still leading the polls, and we're coming up dry in our searches of his texts, emails, phone calls, and social media history. The guy's a damn Boy Scout—no evidence of any infidelities, no cash kickbacks or the usual political payoffs. I've never seen anyone so squeaky clean get this far up the power structure. There are a few things we can tweak to sound a little nefarious, but I doubt much of it will stick."

"You're sure, Colin? We can't keep going to the same well. The strategy is going to lose effectiveness each time if we keep using it."

"Trust me. We will be extra careful in selecting the women, and I have some other ammunition that will feed right into the narrative. I'm also going to ask Dutch Marcello to help us out," said Bennett.

Keller sighed. "That Mafia union thug of yours scares the hell out of me."

"Yeah, he scares me too. But he always comes through for us. He doesn't ask too many questions, and for the right price he'll do whatever we ask. Nowadays, he's been hiring professional mercs instead of his unpredictable fellow dago goombah wops."

"Alright, you have my authorization, but don't use any of the usual budgets. I'll send you some Swiss account numbers. Bounce the money around to several banks in the Caribbean before you direct any of the cash to these women or Marcello, and make sure the payments are given in installments since I'm sure the white trash you'll be paying are too stupid to keep the money off the IRS radar."

"Sounds good. Martinez will get hit so hard and so fast he may jump off a building rather than just withdraw from the race." Bennett ended the call with Keller and dialed an internal number. "Bill, it's a go," said Bennett, referring to one of his assistants, Bill Reines. "As we talked about, I want you to compile a list of ten women who've had some kind of interaction with Martinez in their lives—acquaintances, ex-girlfriends, employees, relatives, former classmates, whatever. All of them should be low on the food chain in the income/savings department, and it's an absolute *must* that all of them have at least one child. I'd prefer they were anti-libertarian in their political leanings, and it would definitely be golden if on top of everything, they have an axe to grind with Martinez. Oh, and I need it done by Monday."

*****

WSJ/NBC Poll: - Martinez Back in Lead over Locklear, Miller 36-32-31

Brent Martinez was hitting his stride. He had shaken off a couple bad TV interviews brought on by fatigue and was now smoothly dominating every speech and appearance. All the negative stories were starting to backfire as it increased his name recognition and viability as a candidate. As in the Donald Trump campaign, voters who hated the mainstream media were flocking to Martinez. Every negative story seemed to push a few more people from that segment of the population into his column. Upon reading the Wall Street Journal poll headline, for the first time in the race, Martinez himself was starting to believe he really could be the next President of the United States.

Chapter 9

"Do you have references?" asked the *New York Times* cleaning staff supervisor, not that it really mattered. He knew he was going to hire the gorgeous red head in the low-cut blouse the minute she walked into his office. Almost all the cleaning ladies were black or Latino, which helped to nicely fill the *Times* diversity quotas, but he supposed adding one white woman would be ok, especially one this hot!

"Yes, here ya go," said Dr. Abby Benton. She was wearing a full redheaded wig and had dyed her eyebrows to match. She wore blue contacts over her brown eyes and used some light makeup to give herself a slightly pale complexion. A temporary tattoo was used to give her what appeared to be a small scar on her left cheek. If the FBI later came looking for her, the scar would be put in the profile as a distinguishing feature. She dressed provocatively for the interview, but from that point on she would be as non-descript as possible—baggy clothes, hair in a ponytail, no cleavage or any sexiness showing whatsoever.

"Great. I'll call your references today. Assuming everything checks out, you can start on Monday."

"Sounds great! Thank you."

"The receptionist will show you where you can pick up your uniform and security card. Don't lose your card. Security is always tight here since that asshole Trump fired up all the anti-media nutballs out there."

"Understandable. See ya Monday." Abby slowly walked out of the office and intentionally went the wrong direction at first. She was wearing several hidden recording devices pointed in different directions, all being fed back to Nate Keeting's laptop as he worked in the visitor waiting area. She already had located two journalists from their target list.

"You lost, miss?" said the reporter, Patrick Adams.

"Sorry, yes, this is such a maze. I'm looking for the reception desk. I came here for an interview for a cleaning staff position."

"No problem. Go down that aisle, turn right at the cube with all the Obama, Hillary, and Locklear posters. Straight ahead from there."

"Thank you so much," said Abby. Abby swore under her breath, put her face down, and quickly followed the way out. Adams sensed something vaguely familiar as he returned to his desk. Maybe she was some former model or actress. He definitely recognized the voice. Anyway, it was time to get back to his Martinez research.

*****

"Dammit," said Abby. "I almost got made."

"What are you talking about?" said Nate Keeting.

"One of the reporters was a patient of mine back in Madison who I went on a date with after my divorce. It was an alright date, but I couldn't stomach going on a second one after I found out he was a reporter. His name was Patrick something."

"Patrick Adams. Yeah, I remember reading about him when we were doing all our first-level screenings. He's one of the few *Times* reporters that actually practices journalism now and then."

"He was a nice guy. Anyway, don't tell Captain Newsome. He'll probably want to pull me out. I'll be working nights, so I doubt I'll see him again."

"Based on the video feeds I picked up, it looks like all the information from Irvin and Holder checks out. I hit a few snags getting into their internal network, but we should be able to do everything we need using their guest Wi-Fi. I've programmed the burners to all use it. As we talked about, put the cameras anywhere concealed within Bluetooth range of the phone. If you can find a location to plug in a charger while keeping the phone hidden, go with it. Otherwise, use the backup battery packs."

"Thanks, Nate. I got it. Tomorrow, you can move on to the next target. I'll buzz you if I need you."

*****

After reviewing the profile of over 100 *Washington Post* employees, they finally found their man. Leroy Evans was 32 years old, black, single, and almost a spitting image of RAPCA member, Scott Koonce. He worked on the janitorial staff at the *Post*, although that's not the job title he described when he flashed his *Post* security badge while trying to pick up college girls every Thursday night. He didn't have any relatives or close friends in Washington, so it looked doubtful any red flags would be raised if he disappeared for a few days.

Aaron Newsome thought about flying Abby down to use as bait in luring him somewhere secluded, but she was too critical to the *New York Times* operation right now. He decided to take the chance of hiring a local call girl to do the job. She went by the name of Cherry, which wasn't very original, but in her tight Georgetown sweater, she perfectly looked the part of the all-American girl.

Newsome sat at the bar within earshot as she perfectly played the part of the gullible journalism student celebrating the success of a summer session exam, who was in awe of the cute "assistant editor" of the great *Washington Post*. He followed them out of the bar and back to the hotel room she was told to go. If Evans was a little more sober, he might have questioned why Cherry had a hotel room reserved, but he wouldn't be conscious much longer to think about it. About a minute after Cherry and Evans walked out of the bar, the look-a-like Scott Koonce walked in and sat in the same seat Evans had vacated.

"Struck out, eh?" said the bartender. "I thought you had her. It's rare a college girl that hot would fall for the editor pickup routine."

"It was worth a shot," shrugged Koonce. Koonce turned in the other direction, so the bartender wouldn't see his face too closely. He sipped his drink as he tried a couple purposely lame attempts at picking up other college girls before he finally walked out. Witnesses would later say the janitor hit on a few girls before finally leaving alone.

Newsome waited outside the hotel room. It was a cheap, rundown highway motel that still used old-fashioned keys in which you entered your room directly from outside the building. He waited for about fifteen minutes before knocking twice, pausing, then knocking four times more. Cherry opened the door to let him in. "I put the whole container in his drink just like you said. He's out cold."

"Great job. Here's your money. We may have more easy jobs for you in the future, but that depends on if you can keep your mouth shut. You never met us, and if anyone asks, your john tonight was a 60-year-old Asian." Cherry pecked him on the cheek and left the room. Koonce arrived five minutes later.

"Coast is clear," said Koonce. The two of them wrapped Evans in a sheet and quickly carried him the short walk to the trunk of the car from the first-floor hotel room. Leroy Evans would have to spend an unpleasant week chained up in the company of Reverend Louis Holder, but unlike Holder, Evans had a hope of being released unharmed.

*****

Cole Foreman pedaled at a swift pace during a morning bike ride, following about a half mile behind a 50-year-old man, trying not to be seen. His MapMyRun app was saving the exact route taken by the biker ahead. Foreman had sometimes watched the man while on foot, sometimes by car, each time with a different disguise. His surveillance was supplemented by scattered traffic cams hacked by RAPCA tech guru, Jim Damon. The person who interested them so much was CNN Executive Vice President of Programming, Mohammed Malik. They established that he did a 20-mile bike ride five mornings per week, mostly sticking to the same route, but sometimes varying it slightly. Malik was a creature of routine, his bike workout starting each time at precisely 5:15 am. It would be his downfall.

The RAPCAs had identified ten potential targets at CNN, five of which were very high value. With the element of surprise, they could probably get to any single one of them, but once one went down, the others would go on alert, so coordination and timing were paramount. Foreman and Damon had set up cameras outside the homes of half the targets and had driven the neighborhood of the others. The two of them had toured CNN several times over the past year to supplement the mountain of publicly-available information on the layout of the studio surrounding area. After a year of study and preparation, Cole Foreman had a mental map of every target's home address, their exact route to work, where they parked, and where they spent most of their workdays.

"Any signs he saw me?" said Foreman.

"Not that I could tell. Malik is in another world with his Beats headphones and tunnel vision," said Damon.

"Have you come up with any other ways to get to the secondary targets?"

"Not without blowing your cover on the primaries. As we talked about, concentrate on Jones, Malik, and Lewis. You can plant some car bombs on a couple of the others, but as soon as one goes off, you can bet none of the others will be stupid enough to start their ignitions."

"Did we get a time frame from Captain Newsome, yet?" said Foreman.

"Most likely between 9 am and 11 am."

"That should work. I'll take out Malik in the morning on his bike ride. Jones leaves for CNN around 10-10:30ish, so I'll have him in his car. Candy Lewis will meet her untimely demise when she arrives home later that afternoon. I'll plant a few goodies for the others, but I doubt much will come of them. Excellent work, Jim. I don't think you can do much more here. I'm sure Captain Newsome and Scott can use you in D.C."

Aaron Newsome had been planning this operation for four years. He estimated his team together had spent over 10,000 hours of preparation and training for what would likely take place over an 8-hour window on July 31st. The brainpower and skill sets were divided evenly over the three cities. Former Navy SEAL Cole Foreman was handling Atlanta. Dr. Abby Benton, ex-Facebook employee Nate Keeting, ex-SEAL Kyle Topper, and police officer Darren Williams were working the New York operations. Newsome and the science teacher, Scott Koonce, were working Washington ops. Ex-Google employee, Jim Damon was helping in both D.C. and Atlanta.

Google and Facebook together could tell you almost everything you wanted to know about a person—what were their interests & hobbies, where they lived, where they worked, where they shopped, who they were related to, what were their political leanings, what were their strengths & weaknesses—the list was endless. Having ex-employees of both companies allowed the RAPCAs to compile a thorough profile on every target before they even set foot in the cities.

Major operations were set for the *New York Times*, *CNN*, and *Washington Post*. However, the RAPCAs had many smaller, specific targets in mind for Zero Day from the surrounding area—*Fox News*, *MSNBC*, *CBS*, *ABC*, *Time*, *Newsweek*, *Politico*, *Salon*, *Daily Beast*, and more. With limited resources, they had to be selective on targets— security, risk, opportunity, and value of each target were all taken into consideration.

Mission training and preparation were complete. Everyone had their assignments. With ten days left until Zero Day, there were no more drills, it was time for battle.

Chapter 10

"You can spend up to $250,000 on each woman," said Colin Bennett, "or if you think you can get by with less, go with it, we just need to make absolute sure these women stick to their stories no matter what heat gets put on them. So, if you could supplement the payments with some of your Sicilian charm to frighten them against retraction, it'd be greatly appreciated."

"Wow, 250k, eh? The price of October surprise whoring has really gone up these days," said Dutch Marcello. "With my cut, you guys will be out over $5,000,000. Must be getting pretty desperate?!"

"It's a sound investment when you think about it. In past elections endless millions have been wasted on TV ads, radio ads, robocalls, print ads, and other useless crap. Why not take that money and spend it on something that actually works?"

"Heh, you're a cold-hearted bastard, Bennett. It's why I love working with you."

"We've done most of the legwork for you," said Bennett, handing a binder to Marcello. "We selected ten women most susceptible to the payoffs based on income, political leanings, history with Martinez, and psych profile. Can you believe we have an ex-FBI criminal profiler on staff now? She's the best. It's spooky sometimes how she can predict behavior."

"Wow, she can predict that poor people will take $250K for a few lies with a threat of major bodily harm if they don't? Sounds like a genius to me!" said Marcello sarcastically.

"Point taken. Still, with these kind of stakes and the heat that will rain down on them, at least one or two of the women may develop a *conscience*. It makes me sick."

"You don't have to worry about that."

"By the way, all these women have at least one kid if you need to give them some extra motivation."

"I'll have it taken care of in the next couple days. I'll put my top people on it. And I want more than just money. I want your assurances you'll get the union rules I mentioned pushed through in the next term. Our unions don't bring in the cash of drugs and gambling, of course, but they're still a significant source of our income. You guys haven't gotten much done the past few years. Though it's been entertaining. I still love calling a law that gets rid of secret ballots the 'Employee *Free Choice* Act'. That's cute."

"No worries. Anti-Trump hysteria has fired up our base. With Martinez out of the picture, we'll ride a major wave to power to take the presidency and both houses. We could almost have you write the union laws for us after that."

Marcello laughed. "Ok, will do. What about timing?"

"I put some dates in the profiles and the order I'd like them to go public. This will be earlier than usual since we want Martinez out before the debates. I'll make sure the first woman gets national attention for a couple days. After that, each of the rest will *courageously* come forward to tell their story on a staggered basis each day or two. Give it a few weeks and Brent Martinez will soon be known as one of the sickest perverts in American political history."

*****

Woman Says Brent Martinez Raped Her When She Was 17. – CNN

Intern Claims Martinez Made Sexual Advances on Her and Her 15-Year-Old Daughter While He Was a State Senator. – Washington Post

Boys and Girls Club Volunteer Says Martinez Regularly Patted Children on the Butt While Volunteering – Mother Jones

Martinez Google Searches Discovered: -- New York Times
- *Lesbian Teen Seduction Nude*
- *Grade School Girls Underwear*
- *High School Girl Locker Room Hidden Camera Nude*
- *How to Seduce Teen Girls*
- *What State Has Lowest Age of Consent*
- *What Countries Have Youngest Prostitutes*
- *Young Girl Tinder for Married Men*
- *How to Seduce Middle School Virgin Girls*
- *Twin Sister Teen Three-Way*

Two More Women Come Forward with Accusations Against Martinez. – ABC

"Your Daughter Should Grow Up to Be a Real Heartbreaker." Ten Voice Recordings and Emails Uncovered of Martinez Complimenting Underage Girls. – MSNBC

Echoes of Hillary: Martinez Claims Vast Conspiracy to Take Him Down. – Fox News

Ninth Woman Comes Forward with Sexual Deviancy Claims Against Martinez. – Politico

Martinez Claims "All" of His Sexual Accusers are Lying. – CNN

Martinez Plummeting in Polls. – Rasmussen

Latest Poll: Locklear 40, Miller 36, Martinez 23. -- Gallup

    Bennett marveled how fast Marcello worked. He maybe should arrange a little bonus to stay on his good side. As usual, Bennett knew he just needed to start the ball rolling and then let the rabidly Martinez-hating media take over. A couple of likely attention-seeking women had piled on the accusations. CNN and MSNBC both kept running scorecards on their screens near 24-7 that showed the number of Martinez accusers. Of course, the definition of "Martinez sexual accuser" continued to expand each day. Any woman that claimed Martinez *flirted* or *complimented them* was added to the scorecard. Pat on back of the shoulder? Hug? High-five initiation? Add them all to the total. MSNBC anchors were regularly throwing around "25" as the number of women that had made accusations.

How the hell was Martinez still at 23 points in polls? Bennett was running out of techniques in the toolkit to throw at him. Maybe Keller was right in that they had gone to this well too often. For future candidates he may have to refine the timing of attacks. In the new media world, character destruction was constantly a learning process. Momentum was on his side though.

Bennett hit his interoffice line. "Bill, let's pull a couple people from the Miller opposition research team. Martinez supporters are clearly moving towards our candidate. We need the extra people to help come up with some good jokes, skits, memes, etc. for *SNL*, the *Daily Show*, Jimmy Kimmel, Samantha B, and so on. I don't want anyone in America with an electronic device to go an hour without hearing something about how perverted Brent Martinez is."

Bennett hung up the phone and took out a secure satellite phone given to him by his NSA buddy. Dutch Marcello picked up his matching model phone. "Dutch, great job! I've arranged a nice bonus for you. Have you talked to Marie Martinez yet?"

"She's been tough to get alone. She's working two jobs and spends almost every second of the rest of her time with her kids. Her second husband is a real slimeball. He keeps all his money in his girlfriend's name and hasn't paid a cent more than what's kept him out of jail. Marie still has a nice shiner from the last time she took him to court for child support. I may have to pay the guy a visit to set him straight."

"You're always the humanitarian, Dutch. We really need Marie to go on record against her ex-husband. The other accusations are starting to stick, but there's a large chunk of voters who seem like they'll never be convinced. We need someone super-close to Martinez to get us into the end zone. Their marriage seemed to end amicably, and they've exchanged Christmas cards every year since the divorce and the occasional how-you-doing email. So, we may need some of your extra special persuasion. You can use the rest of the allocated funds if you have to."

"Do you want to wait a few weeks? October surprise?" said Marcello.

"No, I want him out of the race well before then. Libertarian organizations are already pushing him to resign from the race, and the other candidates are so bad they'll be lucky to get into the five percent range."

"I will take care of it personally."

Chapter 11

"How do I look?" said Abby Benton.

"Minus the pony tail, like a teenage boy," said Abby's ex-husband, Darren Williams.

"Perfect. That cleaning supervisor gave me the creeps. He's probably staying late just to hang around to leer. Good luck at MSNBC. See ya in a day or two."

Abby had her hair bundled tightly and tucked into a baseball cap, wore a tight sports bra to compress her chest, and had put on the two-sizes-too-big cleaning uniform. Indeed, the supervisor was staying an hour late hoping to run into her. He couldn't hide his disappointment as he waved to her on the way out. He may have to fire whoever was in charge of handing out uniforms.

The first couple days on the job would be learning the lay of the land, locating all offices & cubicles of targets, and spotting security cameras & guard checkpoints. Hopefully, she wouldn't get fired from getting lost around the building too many times. Several reporters worked late, so getting to certain locations unnoticed would be a challenge. The front of her ballcap and the hairclip holding her pony tail both contained recording devices that captured almost everything around her for later study.

Cafeterias and break rooms were not popular with the cleaning staff, so they were happy to see the new girl volunteer to take on that duty. Abby made note of empty donut boxes and popular snacks for each floor in question. It would become important later.

Abby quickly crossed off half the targets on her list as off limits. There was just no way to get to them without blowing her cover. At least five of the top-level targets seemed accessible though. She'd have to work fast as Zero Day was less than a week away.

*****

"Why are you doing this to me?" whimpered Washington Post janitor, Leroy Evans.

"I'm really sorry, Leroy," said Aaron Newsome, "You don't deserve this, but your face and security badge make you particularly valuable. The last thing we need are your finger prints. Relax, if we wanted to kill you, we would have done so. If you cooperate, you'll be released by the end of the week unharmed."

"Why? They're not going to help you get around the *Post* offices?"

"Let us worry about that. Our 3D printer will do the job. Alternatively, we can cut off your fingers."

Evans reluctantly stuck out his hands. Reverend Louis Williams squawked behind his duct-taped mouth. Newsome walked over and put on another piece of tape, then yanked him by the ear until he returned to a seated position.

Scott Koonce had fastened a temporary wart to his face and shaved his head to match his appearance even closer to the tied-up Evans. He added some padding to his gut and bought matching clothes. The heat patterns they'd picked up in the building indicated Evans worked alone almost the whole night, so he just needed to get past a few security guards. Unlike Abby, he didn't have free rein to show his face around the building. Beyond a few days, the risk grew too high of being spotted by someone who knew Evans. Day one would be reconnaissance. Day two would be installing the devices and reviewing functionality with Jim Damon. Day three would be tweaking and fixing technical glitches, plus paying a visit to a few break rooms and snack areas. Day four would be execution on July 31st, Zero Day.

Aaron Newsome periodically questioned the morality of what he had set in motion. Seeing Evans whimper like his world was ending triggered one of those bouts of conscience. He had taken every precaution he could possibly think of to protect the innocent, but it was inevitable that at some point some bystander would be in the wrong place at the wrong time. He rationalized that what he was doing was righting a wrong that hurt billions of people every year.

Yet all he had to do to really steel his nerves was turn on the news and see the usual politics of personal destruction. Watching the carnage of the Brent Martinez campaign brought back fresh memories of Dana. This had to stop, so Newsome must proceed to fight back in the only way he knew how.

*****

"Can you filter out some of the noise," said RAPCA sniper, Kyle Topper. "This directional mic is the most powerful I've ever heard, but it's picking up everything."

"I'll see what I can do," said Nate Keeting.

"Wait, go back. I heard a Russian accent. I think Keller is talking to his SVR contact again," referring to the Russian foreign intelligence service.

"There's no need to make any donations to my charity foundation groups," said Henry Keller. *"There are too many people exploring money trails nowadays. Just continue to feed me the information on the Ruble and Euro moves."*

"...{garbled voice on phone}...."

"Yes, we have an all-out blitz going on Martinez. Even David Backman and the Republicans are helping. Personally, I'd spend every cent I have to make the U.S. a socialist/communist nation. The Martinez brand of Libertarianism is against everything I stand for. If you keep on getting me the currency information I need, you'll never have to worry about funding."

"....{garbled voice on phone}..."

"What? No, get that thought out of your head. I don't want to make Martinez a martyr. Our strategies are working. He'll be out of the race in a few weeks. I'm meeting Dem PAC coordinator, Bill Reines, here for brunch on Wednesday to exchange some more opposition research. I would say by mid-August we can turn our attention back to the Republicans."

"I hope you're recording this," said Topper. "Looks like we finally caught a break. I didn't think we'd have any shot at any of the big-money guys on Zero Day. Let's get a room booked in one of the hotel floors we talked about that have a clear line to Keller's penthouse suite.

Henry Keller had grown his fortune to over $25 billion, making his money almost entirely on stock option & real estate trading based on politician-provided insider information, a highly unethical but legal practice. Born in Ukraine, he had dual citizenship there and in the United States. He had over 100 organizations through his charitable foundations that publicly advocated for various philanthropic goals, but in actuality, they were nothing more than communist/anti-capitalist organizations designed to sow unrest in the U.S. and sway public thought away from that of its founders.

"Get a message to Captain Newsome that I'll be changing my Zero Day location from MSNBC to here," said Topper. "One of our Big Five targets is about to be crossed off."

Chapter 12

The marriage of Marie and Brent Martinez was doomed from the start, as they were polar opposites on almost everything. He was active, socially-outgoing, and ambitious. She was an introverted home body who didn't want much more in life than to have a couple kids and be a stay-at-home mom. He wanted kids also but wanted to wait until they were a little more financially secure before starting, which was a constant source of contention. Marie never really was in love with Brent but married him because he was the textbox description of the ideal guy—handsome, soon-to-be-rich, intelligent, and romantic. He always treated her like a queen, but she could never shake her attraction to the "bad boys". Marie eventually ended the marriage to resume a relationship with her on-again, off-again boyfriend from high school, who soon became her second husband.

After the divorce, Brent's career, family, and social life rocketed to the top in every area of the American dream. Marie's life, on the other hand, went into a downward spiral. She and her new husband blew the large savings Brent left her on drugs and travel before Marie got pregnant with the first of her two kids. Her new husband made decent money as a truck driver until getting fired after a DWI on the job when he rear-ended another vehicle. He became abusive after bouncing around odd jobs before Marie filed for her second divorce.

The government tried to collect as much child support from Marie's deadbeat ex as it could, but he worked mostly cash-paying jobs and kept the money in his new girlfriend's accounts whenever possible. Marie had been working two jobs for over five years now and lived in a constant state of exhaustion and depression. She had gained over 100 pounds since her second divorce and spent all her time doing nothing but working, sleeping, or attending to the needs of her kids. She hadn't spoken to Brent in almost ten years, but she still sent a Christmas card every year and an email once a year or so, too proud to confess to him how terrible her life had been since she left him. Despite the fact Brent would definitely have offered to help her out if he knew her state of affairs, she had become somewhat resentful of his seemingly perfect life.

"Rough day?" a man said to Marie, shaking her awake on the park bench.

"What? Shit, what time is it?" said Marie.

"It's about 1 pm," said Dutch Marcello.

"Oh, ok thanks," said Marie. The two of them sat alone on a bench in a park where dozens of kids screamed and played.

"It's Sunday. You sound like you have a time deadline of some kind."

"Yeah, I have to drop the munchkins at the babysitter at 2 pm before heading to my shift."

"Wow, your boss must be a slave driver making you work on such a beautiful Sunday," said Dutch.

"Yeah, the manager is a little shit barely out of high school. At least I get to take home a free Big Mac supersize meal on Sunday."

"Oh, sorry. Are those two on the swings your wonderful bundles of joy?"

"Why do you ask so many questions?" said Marie.

"Just trying to be friendly. You look like you've had a rough day. I see you have quite the bruise on your eye. Were you in an accident of some kind?"

"No, that was a gift from the kid's piece-of-shit father. I filed a court motion to get more money after I found out he was hiding money in his girlfriend's account. Look, you seem like a nice guy. I don't want to be rude, but I really don't feel like talking to anyone."

"What an ass! Seems like this guy needs someone to knock some sense into him," said Dutch. "Would you like me to have it taken care of for you, Marie?"

"How did you know my name? Who are you?" she said, backing away.

"Relax, I mean you no harm. You can call me Dutch. I'm sort of an acquaintance of your first husband, Brent."

"You mean, Mr. Perfect? At least he seemed like Mr. Perfect until the past month. We were only together for a few years, but the guy described in the media is a complete stranger from the man I knew."

"Don't you resent his success a tad? He has a wonderful wife and kids, plus he's worth almost $20 million dollars while you work two jobs to make ends meet. This after you filed bankruptcy two years ago. His presidential campaign is nose-diving, but you know he still has a near-perfect life," said Marcello.

"Are you stalking me?! Who are you really?"

"I'm your white knight, Marie. I represent some powerful interests that can totally turn your life around. If you'll go to the press and say a few things about your marriage to Brent, we can definitely make it worth your while."

"Is that the reason all these women are making accusations—they're being paid to do so?"

"No, from what I know, they're all legit. Brent really is that much of a sleazebag, but a significant portion of the population just refuses to believe it. My employers want to make sure that such a monster never becomes president," said Marcello.

"I've never seen even a trace of what they're describing about Brent. I can't lie."

"Two hundred thousand bucks."

Marie's jaw dropped. With that kind of money, she could move out of the crappy one-bedroom apartment and drop down to one job. She could pay off the rest of her student loan and the new credit card debt she'd run up since her bankruptcy. "No, this is wrong. I can't do that to Brent. He's always treated me good."

"Don't think about the money, think about what it'd be like to have a racist, greedy, child molester as the most powerful man in the world. Do you really think *all* these women are lying? I tell you what, I'll make it $250,000. And as a bonus, I will guarantee your second husband never lays a hand on you again, nor will he ever miss another child support payment."

Could it really be true about Brent? A lot can change about a person in 18 years. A part of her knew this was wrong, but could she really pass up her one chance to turn her life around? Brent would recover from this. He was highly unlikely to be president at this point anyway. It would be nothing but a blip in his perfect life. Her kids didn't deserve to live in squalor. Yes, she'd be doing it for them. Reluctantly, she said, "When do I get the money?"

Marcello flipped her a large yellow envelop. "There's $100,000. You'll get another $50,000 immediately after you give an interview to the media. The rest will be paid in $5,000 installments per week. I cannot stress enough that you cannot deposit this money in the bank. The IRS and political allies of Brent will likely wonder where that amount of cash came from. You can spend some, but you'll have to stash the rest for a while. I can set you up with someone that can help you wash the cash if you like. Everything you have to say is written on the paper in the envelop. You'll receive a call from one of our media contacts tonight after your shift. Do we have a deal?"

Marie had never seen this much cash in her life. Maybe she could give her kids their first real Christmas. "I guess."

"Excellent. We are in business. If you stick to the script and do what you're told, you'll have a very happy year. I must say though, that there is no going back now. There will be no retractions or changes of story. I am *not* the type of person you want to disappoint. Do we understand each other?"

For the first time, Dutch Marcello's grinning face turned into a cold, stern, dead-eyed expression. Marie's body temperature seemed to instantly drop fifty degrees. The thoughts of the cash vanished as she suddenly was thinking about the safety of her and her children.

*****

Marie Martinez received a call the same night from MSNBC's Ryan Mathews, a close friend of Colin Bennett. Mathews had never received a cent in payment from Bennett for a story. He was a true believer communist who absolutely hated conservatives, Libertarians, and Republicans. In truth, his show should have been limited to opinion/editorial content only, but he usually worked a 5 pm news slot at the network, sometimes deviating if the story was big enough. He didn't need the slightest bit of prodding to run a Bennett hit piece as "breaking news".

MSNBC had a camera crew arrive at Marie's house at 8am the next morning. Mathews was chomping at the bits to personally put the nail in the coffin of the Brent Martinez campaign.

"Sexual allegations have rocked the already-shaky Martinez campaign over the last two weeks," said Mathews on the air. "The candidate has claimed *all* his accusers are lying and are part of an orchestrated campaign to destroy him, despite up to 25 women making various charges. Today, we will be talking to the person who probably knows him better than anyone in the world outside his immediate family, and she has some pretty shocking things to say. Let's go to Marie Martinez, ex-wife of the presidential candidate. Ms. Martinez, thank you for joining us. Can you tell us a little about your marriage?"

"Well, we were young and dumb, never really a match. I fell for his good looks, sense of humor, and charisma. In the beginning, things were ok," said Marie. "We both had good jobs. He did well financially, and we thought about starting a family."

"But you never did have any kids with him, and your marriage ended rather quickly, correct?" said Mathews.

"Yes, I filed for divorce about a year after we got married. It took about nine months before it was finalized."

"Why did it end so quickly?" said Mathews.

"Well, in the beginning, it was a lot of little things. Brent was never home much and was a bit obsessed with making money. He wasn't very affectionate or romantic. He never helped out around the house. That sort of thing. As time went by though, he became a bit controlling and verbally-abusive. One time during an argument he threw me out of the car, causing me to hit my head on the cement."

"Sounds terrible! Why didn't you call the police or report him?"

"He said it was an accident, and we were married. We made a promise to be together forever, so I wanted to work everything out. But what really bothered me though was, um, his sexual needs."

"Would you care to elaborate?"

"Well, he had to, you know, have it *all* the time. Every day without fail. It didn't matter if I was tired, sick, or said no, he would throw me on the bed and force himself on me."

"He raped you?!"

"I don't know if you can call a husband forcing his wife to have sex 'rape', but yes. Sometimes he would get very rough, and I ended up with bruises and would have trouble walking."

"How awful! Why stay with him as long as you did? Why not file charges?"

"I was young and naïve. I didn't think a husband could be charged for a sex crime against his wife. Anyway, each time we had relations, he wanted more outrageous things. Sick fantasies. He wanted to do slave & master things, act out porn films, bring other women into our bedroom. It disgusted me. But the final straw was when I saw him watching kiddie porn films. I think he got them in Thailand or something. And he wanted me to pretend to be a grade school girl in his sex fantasies. We had been trying to have a baby at the time. I couldn't imagine exposing a child of mine to him. I immediately went back on birth control and called a lawyer to start divorce proceedings."

"Sounds like an absolute nightmare! How come you're just going public with this now?"

"I didn't think anyone would believe me. On the surface he seems so innocent and nice. Behind closed doors though, he's a different person. Seeing all these other women come forward finally gave me the courage."

"So, you believe all the allegations that have come out against him the past couple weeks?" said Mathews.

"Yes. I—," Marie couldn't finish her sentence as she started bawling uncontrollably. "I don't want to talk about this anymore. You have what you need." She put her hand in front of the camera and left the room.

"There you have it. The ex-wife of Brent Martinez making some shocking allegations. I'll be back with more after this." After the commercial started, Mathew said to his editing staff, "I think we can run it almost unedited, except for that 'You have what you need' statement. Chop that off and run it."

Nate Keeting and Aaron Newsome halted their surveillance camera reviews long enough to watch the breaking news interview from MSNBC.

"Those fuckers!" said Newsome. "Did you see what I saw in that interview?"

"Yeah, it was almost like she was coached. Who says the type of things she did in a monotone voice? At the end it seemed like she was sobbing more from guilt or remorse," said Keeting.

"There's just no doubt in my mind anymore. Martinez is telling the truth that this is an orchestrated campaign. I want you to stop what you're doing and spend the next couple days researching every single woman that has made an allegation against him the past few weeks. Hack whatever email, texts, or calls that you can. Check their bank accounts and credit cards. Find out if any of them have bills suddenly being paid off or if any have suddenly gone on shopping spree. This has Media World written all over it. I want to expose these shitbags to the public for who they are...or as of a few days from now, who they *were*."

*****

Ten Women's Groups Calling for Martinez to Drop Out of Race. – Mother Jones

Brent Martinez Falls to Single Digits in Polls After Explosive Ex-wife Interview. – MSNBC

Martinez Continues to Deny All Accusations, Including Those of His Ex-wife. – Yahoo News

Attorney Generals Exploring Statute of Limitations for Martinez Sex Crimes. – New York Times

Potential First Lady, Alyssa Martinez, Reportedly Has Hysterical Crying Fit After Campaign Event. – CNN

Psychologists Say Sociopath Brent Martinez Has At least Five Major Disorders. – Salon

Libertarian Groups and Candidates Calling for Martinez to Drop Out of Race. – Los Angeles Times

Martinez Non-committal on Staying in Race Despite Continuing to Deny Accusations. – NBC News

"Bill, I think we can start shifting our focus to the Republicans now," said Colin Bennett as he browsed on his iPad through some of the most expensive wines in the world. "David Backman and his conservative media contacts are starting to shift towards attacks on Locklear. Even he believes that Martinez is as good as dead in this race."

*****

"Leroy, it's about time for us to part ways," said Aaron Newsome to the tied-up *Washington Post* janitor. "In about 24 hours someone will come to release you. I'll send an anonymous tip on your location. Sorry again for all the unpleasantness. Here take these." Newsome ripped the duct tape from his mouth and handed him two pills. Leroy Evans hesitated, looking back and forth between Newsome and the pills.

"As I said, if we wanted you dead, you'd be dead. It's just a sedative to relax you. You'll sleep most of the next half day." Reluctantly, Evans did as he was told.

"Before your nap, we want you to watch one thing. Go ahead, Scott."

"Reverend Holder, I can't say it's been a pleasure. I hope you've enjoyed your last few hours. You destroyed the lives of two people I now consider family, and you hurt more people than we can count over the past decade. People like you have divided this nation and created unnecessary hate and division for far too long. It's time for you to leave this world. You're lucky it's me punching your ticket and not Dr. Benton. She would have inflicted more pain than you can possibly imagine."

Holder starting shrieking and struggling with the duct tape as Scott Koonce took out a large hypodermic needle and proceeded to give Holder two injections from a small bottle. Holder formed a smile, then his eyes went wide as he let out a deep breath and fell unconscious.

"What...what did you give him?" said Evans.

"Such a large dose of opium that he's not going to wake up, Leroy," said Newsome. "Look, we've treated you humanely and don't have a beef with you personally. In a couple days you will see the reach and power we have. We can get to anyone, anywhere. I suggest you give the FBI and Homeland Security exactly zero information on us and our time together, or you'll be praying for a death as easy as Holder just received."

"FBI? Homeland Security? Who the hell are you people? What are you going to do?!"

Newsome and Koonce exited without saying another word as Evans dosed off.

*****

Abby Benton carried with her a bigger purse than the previous few days on her job at the *New York Times*. Her too-big uniform was also tighter than usual as she had several devices taped to her body.

"Wow, five boxes of donuts and snacks, Ms. Benton," said the security guard. "What's the occasion?"

"It's my birthday, and everyone here has been so nice to me. I have a friend who works at a bakery that gave me a nice discount and prepared them for me fresh," said Abby.

"Sweet. Mind if I snag one of them?"

"You don't want one of these sugar bombs. You look so fit, I don't want to ruin it for you," said Abby as she walked on without stopping to give the guard a donut.

That was kind of rude, thought the guard. She's probably right, though. He didn't need the sugar, and it was nice she noticed his physique. She looked very different from the knockout that had come for an interview the week before. Must be a work thing. He might have to ask her out when he saw her tomorrow.

Abby proceeded to specific breakrooms frequented by reporters and editors. The boxes contained not only donuts but also cheese spread & low-carb crackers, gluten-free bagels, and other assorted organic and healthy snacks. She wanted snacks that would appeal to everyone on each floor.

She pulled off all the devices attached to her body and tossed them into a bag stashed with her purse in the bottom of her cleaning cart. She had about six hours before the early birds started trickling in, and she wanted to be long gone before then. Yesterday, she had installed a few devices to verify reception, power, and Internet connectivity with Nate Keeting. Now it was time to install the rest.

Abby walked to her first office and took out a burn phone coated with stickum. She reached under the desk out of sight of the person who'd be sitting there tomorrow. After scanning the room, she found a plant at the window that conveniently disguised the recording device she pointed towards the desk and switched it on.

"P7 is activated," Abby texted to Nate Keeting. "P" was used to signify a primary target, "S" was used to signify a secondary target. The numbers corresponded to a person on their list. After Keeting responded with a thumbs-up text, she moved to a nearby cube outside the office. Abby stuck the same kind of C-4-packed burn phone underneath the desk. She located an out-of-sight outlet for which she attached a charging cord. Abby had backup battery packs she would attach if a convenient, out-of-sight outlet wasn't available, but with Bluetooth connectivity to the camera and the regular transmission over the Internet, the power would drain quickly. The recording device for this cube would have to be attached with stickum next to the phone as the cube didn't have any plants or obvious hiding locations. "S14 is up," she texted.

"Got it. Only seeing a chair for now but it should do the job," came the text reply from Keeting.

Abby proceeded to install the same burn phone & recording devices in ten more cube and office locations. With each device installation, she emptied the trash or performed some other cleaning type of duty in case the *Times* security staff were watching a little too closely.

"Camera on S17 isn't coming through," texted Keeting.

"Power is on. Bluetooth is connected. Not sure what problem is," replied Abby.

"Enough with the damn texting, Abby," said a co-worker. "You're going to get fired after a week on the job."

"Sorry, my mom is in the hospital, so my sister has been texting me updates."

"Oh, I'm sorry to hear that. I'm sure they'd let you leave if you need to."

"No, it sounds like the surgery came out alright. I can finish my shift."

Secondary target 17 would just have to be skipped. There was too much risk in trying to fix it now. It was likely that at least half the explosives wouldn't be used anyway. Nothing was going to be set off unless the target was nearby and there were no innocent bystanders in the immediate area.

Abby still had three burn phones packed with the most C-4 explosive material at her disposal. These were to be planted at her discretion for shock value, not directed at any human targets. She placed two of them in empty offices located towards stairwell exits. They would scare people from running in that direction tomorrow when all hell broke loose. The last explosive device she had set aside for a room full of computer servers. As with most server rooms, the door was locked and rarely visited by I.T. staff unless an installation was scheduled. Abby didn't have a key, but she noticed a gap in the bottom of the floor wide enough to slide a phone. She reached down and slid it with a strong flick of the wrist, enough that it ended up underneath a rack, not visible to a passerby.

"Done. Any tech issues?" texted Abby.

"No, looks good. You can get out of there," replied Keeting. Abby let out a nervous exhale, retrieved her purse, and headed for the exit.

"Headed out already?" said the security guard that she had talked to earlier.

"Yeah, my mom just got out of surgery. She's alright, nothing serious, but I want to be there when she wakes up."

"Oh, sorry. Hope everything works out." The guard noticed the cute new cleaning lady was sweating quite a bit and had frazzled hair. She must be more worried about her mom than she was letting on. He thought about asking her out, but this wasn't the right time. There was always tomorrow.

*****

Since Cole Foreman was now the only RAPCA member in Atlanta, he had to concentrate on fewer targets, but high-quality ones. He'd been stalking the early morning biker, CNN VP of programming, Mohammed Malik. All prep work was done for him. Also, all his shock-value explosive targets at CNN were taken care of and ready to go off whenever he hit the arming signals. Two targets remained.

The first belonged to CNN news anchor, Candy Lewis. Lewis was to put it lightly, an angry, man-hating feminist, an attitude she unapologetically let shine through every day of her journalistic work. She considered white men the cause of almost all misery in the world. Over the past two weeks, she had dedicated nearly 80 percent of her daily hour shows pursuing attack stories against candidate Brent Martinez. Foreman choose tonight to visit her house after he learned she was out on a date with someone she had met on a lesbian online dating service.

Foreman easily got around her security system using a few tricks from his team member, Jim Damon. Getting into the house was not the problem, re-wiring the security system into a weapon would be the greater challenge. Since Lewis lived alone, she was likely to be the only one to know the code; thus, it was the perfect arming device. Foreman packed a healthy amount of explosives into a nearby grandfather clock, then went through a series of steps given to him by Damon. After running some arming & verification tests, he exited the back door. Only 45 minutes had passed. Not bad. It was plenty of time to get to the house of Jerome Jones, the CNN interviewer who had kicked off the attack campaign against Brent Martinez.

It was starting to seem like all their targets were enemies of the third-party candidate, but most of them were selected long before Martinez became nationally known. The slimy techniques the RAPCAs had tracked over the past couple months made it easy to see Martinez had become their enemy number one.

Jerome Jones had a wife and kid, so getting him at his house was out of the question. Foreman just needed access to the car in his garage for a short time. All the lights were out, and judging by the heat patterns in the house, everyone was in bed. Nothing was showing up on the cameras Foreman had installed on the front and garage windows. It was time to move. Foreman picked the garage door lock and entered with his tool belt and explosives. Newer cars used far more electronics than the old days, so his device would be much more sophisticated than the crude car bombs used in the past by the mob. For an expert like Foreman, it was an easy job. Rather than wire it to the car's starter, Foreman's bomb would be detonated with a remote trigger. Timing would be tricky, but it was likely Jones only had one or two car rides left in his life.

*****

Scott Koonce, wearing the uniform tag of Leroy Evans, entered the *Washington Post* for what would become his final day on the job. Koonce had set up most of his camera/burn phone devices the previous night. He was there only to tweak a few malfunctioning devices and install two more explosive sets for primary and secondary targets he was unable to get to yesterday without blowing his cover.

Koonce also generously brought a few boxes of donuts to be set up in some breakrooms visited occasionally by *Post* journalists. Things had gone rather smoothly with the operation. He concluded that Evans must not have had many close friends there since he'd only receive one passerby wave in the hall by a security guard. Intelligence gathered from the capture & interrogation of Dan Irvin had been invaluable in skirting around building security and locating his targets.

Koonce walked directly to the breakrooms and set up the donuts and assorted healthy snacks, displayed with the sign "Free donuts and snacks for all your journalistic work." Hopefully, no one would overindulge on the free food.

Koonce didn't waste any time with his normal janitorial duties. He wanted to get in and get out.

"Receiving video on S24 yet?" he texted to Jim Damon after re-booting the recording device.

"Nothing. Reboot the phone also," replied Damon. Koonce did as he was instructed. Two minutes later came the reply, "It's up."

Damon walked up a floor to the office of primary target 13, a Washington Post editor who had cleared hundreds of articles over the past year backed only by unconfirmed anonymous sources, a great number of which turned out to be wildly inaccurate. "P13 is online."

"Got it," replied Damon.

Damon took the elevator down to the basement and proceeded to one of the server rooms. Using Leroy Evans's security card and a few hacks, Jim Damon was able to program another security card that would open the room of computers. He stuck an explosive device with a healthy amount of C-4 explosives to the back of a server rack and quickly closed the door.

"Hey Leroy? How's it going, bud?" came a voice down the hall. "I didn't know they assigned you to this floor." Koonce tried to turn and quickly walk the other direction, but it was too late. "Uh sorry, I thought you were someone else. You look almost exactly like my co-worker, Leroy. Oh, I apologize, I suppose that is a racist thing to say."

"No worries. Have a good day," said Koonce as he continued to walk on down the hall.

"Wait a minute. Stop. Why does your name tag say 'Leroy Evans'?" The two of them made eye contact for a long second. "Security!"

Koonce hit him with a quick punch to the solar plexus, knocking the wind out of him, then followed it up with an uppercut punch to the jaw. As the man stood dazed, Koonce reached into his jacket and pulled out a syringe which he injected into the man's neck. Koonce's heart was racing as the man fell unconscious. Koonce stood for a full two minutes as he debated what steps to take next.

Finally, he grabbed the man's legs and dragged him to the elevator. He re-loaded the syringe on the trip to the third floor in case he came across someone else. When the elevator came to a stop, he dragged the man to a janitorial closet and swiped his card to open. After retrieving some duct tape from a supply closet, he wrapped up the legs, arms, and mouth.

"Dammit," said Koonce as he noticed for the first time, sporadic drops of a blood trail leading from the elevator to the closet. He must have dislodged a tooth with the uppercut. He quickly grabbed a mop and retraced his steps to the elevator and back to the basement server room. This was taking too long. "Shit." An I.T. guy exited a room down the hall and was headed straight for him. Koonce reached into his jacket for the syringe, but the guy turned and went into the restroom.

That was enough excitement for today. Koonce found the closest exit and left the building. The last couple malfunctioning devices would just have to be left as is.

*****

Kyle Topper finished up some of his assigned tasks the previous week at CBS, Fox News and MSNBC, but his main operation would be taking place from a hotel window approximately 1500 yards from the penthouse room of Democrat billionaire, Henry Keller.

His room was two floors beneath the level of Keller's penthouse, but the line of sight was clear enough that it would be a fairly easy shot if Keller poked his head out, especially if he and Bill Reines ate brunch on the deck.

Topper unpacked his gear, dragged a hotel table to the window, and put together his M-64 rifle.

It was time to catch a few hours of shuteye before setting up in the morning. After that, it was just a waiting game.

*****

Aaron Newsome looked at his watch as he walked into his Four Seasons hotel room in Washington D.C.—3 am, July 31st. There was no way he was going to be able to sleep a wink before morning. He couldn't stop going over preparations and rechecking every detail. He'd be regularly sending text messages and entering codes on the apps connected to all his team members as he made decisions over the next 12 hours.

Newsome booked his room at Four Seasons due to the reliable wi-fi, but more importantly, because two primary targets were staying in the hotel.

"Everyone check in at exactly 5:00:00 am," he texted. "Cole, Darren, and Kyle, execute at your discretion. Everyone else, wait for my go-ahead. This is what we trained for. It's time to wake up the world."

Chapter 13

July 31st, 5:00 am

All eight RAPCA team members clicked on a sync-time app installed on all their phones at precisely 5:00:00 am. Everyone now had the time synchronized to the exact second. Dr. Abby Benton and ex-Facebook employee, Nate Keeting, sat in an Extended Stay hotel apartment near LaGuardia airport in New York. Eight large computer monitors were set up, four controlled from Dr. Benton's laptop, four controlled from Keetings's laptop. Each monitor displayed eight video recording feed squares that were turned on an off at their command. In the middle of each of the recording squares a short code displayed indicating whose cube or office was being recorded and where they were located. For example, a Benton laptop box displayed "P7 NYT", indicating primary target 7, located at the *New York Times*. A Keeting laptop box displayed "S34 CBS", indicating secondary target 34 at CBS. Beyond hourly tests, the recording devices were powered down to save the battery lives for office hours.

Much the same scene played out at an Extended Stay hotel apartment near Dulles airport in Washington. Tech guru Jim Damon and the former science teacher, Scott Koonce, each tracked four computer monitors full of video recording boxes. Since the cameras were feeding over the Internet, they also were monitoring video feeds from New York in addition to the D.C. locations.

The ex-police officer, Darren Williams, was getting set to check out of a dinky Manhattan hotel in a few hours. He was on call to go to any locations in New York should they experience a glitch that required on-site detonation. Until then, he'd be hanging around the ABC/Disney headquarters, monitoring high-value targets for opportunities.

Sniper Kyle Topper grabbed eggs, a muffin, and coffee as he headed back to his hotel room. He flipped the do-not-disturb sign and put a chair against the door in case it was ignored by housekeeping. As he ate, the sniper set up his M-64 rifle on the hotel table. Billionaire Henry Keller had appeared briefly in range last night, but Topper was waiting for Democratic PAC leader, Bill Reines, to arrive for brunch.

Aaron Newsome had only one laptop at his Four Seasons room in Washington split into two displays. On the left showed text message feeds from all team members. On the right was a listing of all media locations and a number which indicated the number of recording devices picking up movement. Almost all of them had a zero at this early hour, but a few locations were starting to tick up to 1 or 2.

Ex-Navy SEAL, Cole Foreman sat on a rented Harley in an Atlanta park, waiting a few miles away from bike trails that would soon be visited by CNN programming executive, Mohammed Malik.

5:15 am

New York Times reporter, Patrick Adams, stepped off the elevator and walked towards the employee break room to put away his brown-bag lunch. He was usually the first one in each morning on his floor, so he was surprised to see a box of donuts and snacks on the table. Someone must be way behind on a story deadline. Adams usually avoided sugar, but the protein bar he grabbed for breakfast wasn't quieting hunger pangs. One jelly donut and a cheese cracker should be Ok after his long workout last night.

5:45 am

CNN VP, Mohammed Malik, hit the 10-mile mark on his morning bike ride. He was riding a bit faster than usual as he strived to reach his 400-mile goal for the month. His peripheral vision picked up a Harley heading in the opposite direction as he sang an Eminem song, *"Started whoopin' her ass worse than before, they first get divorced, throwing her over furniture..."*

Malik steered towards a bike trail along the water. He didn't notice the Harley pull up behind him until he had hit a curve in the trail. Cole Foreman pulled a Glock pistol from his belt and fired a shot into the middle of Malik's ear right below his helmet. Malik was thrown violently from the bike and went flying into a rock along the water. Foreman stopped the motorcycle and walked over to Malik. He fired one more bullet into Malik's heart, then submerged Malik's body into the water. He lifted a couple large rocks he specifically had set aside and stacked them on top of the body to keep it weighted down. Foreman splashed some water to rinse trails of blood, then hurled the bike into the river. Foreman stepped back on the trail and checked from several angles to make sure Malik and has bike weren't visible. "P8 is down," he texted to the team.

7:00 am

Keeting, Benton, Damon, and Koonce ran through hourly system checks. Newsome watched as most locations registered camera-movement numbers above zero, indicating journalists were trickling in for work on this Wednesday morning. The organic and gluten-free snacks were proving popular at the *Washington Post* and *New York Times*, but there were still a couple getting their sugar fixes with the donuts.

Darren Williams walked around the ABC headquarters parking area. The reserved spots of his targets were still open.

Patrick Adams made his second trip to the bathroom in the past half-hour. He was starting to feel a tad nauseous and dizzy. Hopefully, it wasn't the flu. He was behind on too many stories.

8:00 am

Systems checks were looking good. Aaron Newsome counted 20 targets with some kind of movement. Of course, he couldn't see what kind of movement. Each camera was there not only to verify the target was in the correct location but also that there were no bystanders in the surrounding area.

8:15 am

Darren Williams watched behind a pillar of the parking structure as the ABC/Disney program director arrived for work. Williams was a huge sports fan and looked on in disgust at the man who had purged the ESPN he once loved of all but politically-charged liberal voices. He never watched ABC much but knew the director had also packed it with shows that no longer entertained but instead preached his own brand of politically-correct propaganda. The news division had lost all sense of real journalism long before he arrived, but this programming director did everything he could to make sure it stayed that way. The program director had just returned from a two-week trip to Europe, courtesy of the billionaire, Henry Keller.

"Freeze!" said Williams as pulled out his Glock pistol with an attached silencer.

"Ok, relax. I'm putting my hands up. Just please take my wallet. I have a family."

"I don't want your damn wallet. Open the trunk." Williams scanned in both directions. They were alone, but for how much longer?

"Ok, I'm going, but it's empty. I think you have the wrong person."

"Get in the trunk."

"What? I--."

Williams clubbed him on the top of the head. "Now! I'm not going to ask again."

"Ok, ok. I'm going. Please, there isn't much air in here."

"Get tucked in there. Put your head against the back of the trunk." Williams leaned in and fired two quick shots into the side of the director's head. He looked around once more in all directions before slamming the trunk and walking on. "Cross off P14. Stealth takedown," he texted.

8:20 am

Patrick Adams stepped into the men's room stall and vomited violently for 30 seconds straight. Maybe it was something he ate, or maybe he was indeed coming down with the flu or something. He felt a little better after puking but was feeling sharp abdominal pain. Should he go home? No, he'd hadn't had a sick day since he started at the *Times* and he wasn't about to start. He staggered back to his cube and went to sit down, but he missed the chair and fell to the floor.

"Geez Patrick, have you been mixing some Jack Daniel's with your coffee?" said a co-worker.

"No, just a little under the weather. "

"You look like death."

"Thanks, you're too kind. How's your Martinez piece coming?" said Adams

"Good. I have an inside source that tells me the piece of shit is going to drop out of the race within the week."

"If he's guilty of all he's been accused of, that's definitely a good thing."

"*If*? *If* he's guilty? You sound like a Fox News anchor."

"I don't know. It just seems suspicious to me that someone with not even a hint of sex issues in his history suddenly gets hit repeatedly after he takes a big lead in polls. It all seems a little coordinated and convenient and…" Adams started coughing and grabbed his trash can to spit out a bit more puke.

"Man, I think you need to head home, Patrick. You know, I heard Tom yacking in the restroom earlier. I wonder if you two are coming down with the same bug."

"Thanks for your concern. I better get back to work. Marilyn wants my story done by noon."

9:00 am

There were no more tests or systems checks. All cameras were online and would stay that way. Most of the donuts and snacks in the break rooms of the *New York Times* and *Washington Post* were gone. Damon, Keeting, Benton, and Koonce monitored each of their assigned cameras, occasionally zooming in and zooming out of specific devices, entering status codes on each that were fed to Aaron Newsome in Washington."

"We're at 30 targets right now. I want at least 3 primary targets both at *Post* and *Times* before launch," texted Newsome.

"We have at best a couple hours before symptoms of our special ingredients hit majority," texted Dr. Benton.

"Reines arrives for brunch 9:30ish. Let's try to hold off until then unless numbers reach 40+," replied Newsome.

"Seen a couple pukers at *Post*. No one has gone home yet," texted Koonce.

"Same at *Times*," texted Keeting.

"*Post* employee meeting set for 10-11," texted Koonce.

"Hold tight," said Newsome. "We have maybe 15-30-minute window after initial launch to hit rest of targets."

9:20 am

Bill Reines arrived for brunch with Henry Keller in the hotel penthouse. It was a little too close to the 9:30 am scheduled time, as Keller was not a man who tolerated tardiness, not even from the second most powerful man in the Media World network. Reines managed several political action committees, public relations groups, and opposition research organizations. However, his most important duty was to act as a go-between from Colin Bennett to Henry Keller and other big-money donors as well as the Democratic National Committee and various politicians.

"Welcome, Bill. Good to see you again," said Keller. "Hope you're hungry. My chef is the best and has prepared all your favorites."

"Thanks, Henry. You're too kind. Things are looking good on the Martinez campaign. I'm guessing you're ready to shift to Miller."

"Yes and no. I want to keep up the pressure on Martinez. Let's continue to push at least one story on him per day until the debates. Not only will it assure he's gone, it also will push women's issues to the forefront again, which should be a jolt to Elizabeth's campaign numbers." Keller was among only a handful of people on a first-name basis with the Democratic nominee, Elizabeth Locklear.

"Consider it done. What are your preferences for re-launching the Miller attack strategy?" said Reines.

"Come, let's sit at our table. It's out on the deck. The weather's perfect today. How's your wife? I hear she's under consideration for a role at the State Department if, sorry *when*, Elizabeth is elected," said Keller.

Kyle Topper lined up his sights. "I'm going to have a clear shot of P6 and P1 as soon as chef and waiters clear," texted Topper.

"Hold off," said Newsome. "Nate, Jim, how's it look? I show movements on 35 total targets."

"Negative," responded Nate Keeting. "A bunch of co-workers talking in circles near two of the targets."

"Two of primaries away from desk at *Post*," responded Jim Damon. "Looks like secretaries triggering motion."

"They just started breakfast. I can wait a few minutes," texted Topper.

Ten tension-filled minutes passed. "Numbers have ticked up to 42," typed Newsome. "We're not going to get a better time."

"One secretary gone. One primary back at desk," texted Damon.

"Still have a crowd at *Times*, but it's thinning," responded Keeting.

"Kyle, fire at will. Jim, as soon as last secretary clears, light 'em up at *Post*. Abby and Nate, wait for Jim's first launch, then start with *Times*. Hit within 15 minutes max. After that, everyone hit rest of targets at your discretion."

Kyle Topper took aim through the removed window pane at the laughing, celebratory billionaire 1500 yards away. With almost no wind today, it would be an easy shot. The bullet from the rifle sounded like a light gust of wind as it hit directly between the eyes of Henry Keller and exited the back of his head, spraying blood and brains against the hotel deck wall.

One of Keller's two bodyguards recognized what was happening immediately and yelled, "Gun!" Bill Reines struggled to process what was going on. Was this a joke? Was this real? He didn't hear a gun shot? "Everyone GET DOWN!" It was too late as a bullet entered the right temple of the stunned Reines. One of Keller's assistants ran for the hotel room sliding door. Topper recognized the assistant who came one vote short of making the list of RAPCA targets. He couldn't kill the slimeball, but he couldn't let him off with nothing. He lowered his aim and fired twice into his hip. Keller's right-hand man would spend the next year in pain and rehab, but he'd live, which was more than he deserved.

"P1 and P6 are out of the picture," texted Topper. "A few bodyguards and assistants there, so word will spread fast. Do you need me anywhere?"

"No," replied Newsome. "Pack up and head to JFK. See ya in a few days."

9:35 am

"Come on, come on, get the hell out of there," said Jim Damon as he watched the *Post* secretary linger in the office of one of their top targets.

"We've dropped to 40 targets, skip P13 and blow the rest if secretary doesn't leave soon," texted Newsome.

"She's wrapping it up," replied Damon. Damon typed in the sequence *P13 P17 S24 S25 S26 S40* and paused as he watched the secretary leave the office. "About damn time," he said out loud. Damon looked at the *Detonate* button on his screen for a long five seconds. He closed his eyes, took a deep breath, then opened them and clicked on the button.

Damon's laptop sent signals over the web to apps running on the first six burn phones, which initiated the explosion sequence of the C-4 packed in each device. All six devices exploded within a half second of each other, producing high-pressure shock waves of energy and shrapnel, devouring everything in its short path. The phones were packed with only a small amount of explosive so collateral damage would be limited, but it was enough to kill five of the first six targets almost instantaneously. The sixth would lay bleeding for another ten minutes before finally closing his eyes.

"Six down at *Post*," texted Damon.

"Abby, how does it look at *Times*?" texted Newsome.

"Two targets just walked away from desk. Restroom I think. One primary having conversation with two others. Give us ten minutes."

"Everyone copy?" replied Newsome. After receiving affirmative responses, Newsome texted. "Abby, let us know ASAP. I'm heading down to hit my targets."

9:40 am

Newsome took the stairs down a floor and found the hotel room of the *Infowars* right-wing conspiracy theorist famous for spreading fake news stories on the web. Based on Jim Damon's hack of the check-in records, the man was alone. Newsome heard the TV blaring as he stepped to the room. Newsome took out an IED that looked like a hockey puck and slid it under the door. He counted to five as he quickly walked on. Newsome reached the stairwell before hearing the concussion of the blast. Primary target 15 was out of the picture.

The noise and flames quickly created chaos in the hotel, which provided perfect cover as Newsome walked up two flights of stairs, then flipped down the fire alarm switch on the wall. He pulled up his collar to hide his face and tightened his ballcap as people started exiting rooms. Mike Mathers, the NBC editor who regularly altered videos for Colin Bennett, was one of the last to exit. He walked up behind Mathers and fired two quick shots from his silenced Beretta. He stepped over Mathers and walked on to the stairwell. As far as he could tell, no one had witnessed the shooting. He was down a full floor before he heard a scream.

"Cross off P9 and P15."

9:43 am

"Setting off shock and awe devices at *Post* now," said Scott Koonce. Seconds later two computer rooms and two empty offices were engulfed with noise and flames. Screams and cries for help came in all directions. Most were trying to flee the building, but with explosions coming in all directions with seemingly no rhyme or reason, many just ducked for cover.

9:45 am

After vomiting into his trash can, Patrick Adams said to his co-worker, "This is ridiculous. I think I'm going to head home before I pass out."

"Did you guys hear?" said another co-worker. "There have been a bunch of explosions over at *Washington Post* headquarters. I got a text from a friend there saying at least five killed. Dozens wounded."

As the co-worker read off some of the deceased, the names started to click in the head of Adams. Two of them were editors, one of which was a close friend of his boss. A sinking feeling hit his stomach as he got up and ran towards her office, "Marilyn!" As Adams arrived at the door, the desk of Marilyn Kahn exploded out. The concussive power of the blast slammed him backwards far enough that his head hit the wall and knocked him unconscious.

Ten more explosions followed in quick succession from other areas of the building. Three floors were filled with flames and flying metal & wood. Scattered blood and body parts added to the war-zone type feeling.

"11 targets down at *Times*," texted Abby Benton.

"Light up the rest," replied Newsome.

Scattered explosions rocked throughout the headquarters of the media world over the next half hour—Fox News, CBS, ABC, NBC, *Time*, *Politico*, *Salon*, *Newsweek*, MSNBC, *Slate*, *The Nation*, *Huffington Post*, CNBC, Associated Press, and *Newsmax*. About a quarter of the explosions occurred near a journalist target; the rest were set off in unoccupied areas.

10:15 am

CNN anchor, Jerome Jones, navigated the interstate as he watched a *Samantha Bee* show recording on his dashboard-set iPad. He laughed hysterically as the comedian started in on her third joke about Brent Martinez. About a half-mile back behind him, Cole Foreman maneuvered in his Harley, trying to stay out of sight. Jones was most likely heading to work, but as word spread of the media attacks, there was no telling when he may divert.

Jones remained happily clueless about the war that had been launched as he pulled into his reserved parking space. Oddly, dozens of people were starting to walk out of the buildings in view. Foreman did a quick scan of the cars around Jones before entering a code into his phone. Five seconds later the Cadillac driven by Jones exploded into a fireball.

People streamed out of each building as full evacuation orders had been given. Foreman entered two more codes, setting off harmless but noisy firecrackers around the buildings. Panicked screams filled the area as CNN employees sprinted for their cars. Few wanted to hang around long enough to find out what was going on and started their vehicles up without hesitation, despite the sight of the smoldering Cadillac in one of the lots. It was just what Foreman was counting on as primary target 16 dove into his Mercedes. Foreman entered one final code into his phone, erasing P16 from the world.

"Done at CNN. X off P10 and P16. Heading to HJ Airport."

10:30 am

A full evacuation order had come through at ABC headquarters. Darren Williams had walked the parking ramp for about the tenth time when his last target finally came into view. The news anchor sprinted towards his car, anxious to get out of the area as soon as possible. Several witnesses were in view, so getting close up was out of the question. Williams stepped behind a pillar and fired his pistol from 50 yards away, hitting the anchor in the jugular area of the neck. He couldn't get a second shot off as the man fell to the ground, but judging by the amount of blood spreading by his car, it wouldn't be necessary. Williams didn't pause to text a status update as he double-timed it to his vehicle a mile away.

11:00 am

Jim Damon and Scott Koonce dropped off their packed-up equipment at the UPS office and headed to Dulles Airport. They would both be taking separate flights on three different airlines over the next two days. Kyle Topper was onboard his plane at JFK airport in New York. Abby Benton, Darren Williams, and Nate Keeting would soon board separate planes at LaGuardia. The only RAPCA team member that wouldn't be flying that day was Aaron Newsome, who was now speeding north on Interstate 80.

11:15 am

Time-based charges set off thousands of firecrackers throughout the filming studios of *Saturday Night Live*, the *Daily Show*, *Jimmy Kimmel*, and *Full Frontal with Samantha Bee*. No deaths or injuries occurred at the locations from the fireworks, although a few were hurt in the panicked stampedes that followed.

12:00 pm

Chaos raged throughout newsrooms across the country. Although attacks were concentrated in New York, Washington, and Atlanta, most media offices weren't taking chances, operating with skeleton crews if broadcasting at all. Most reports of the attacks were being handled by local news affiliates, as it was clear the national media were the targets. A handful of defiant national journalists continued to broadcast through the crisis.

The lesser-covered story was the rampant sickness hitting employees of the *New York Times* and *Washington Post*. A total of 80 employees at the locations suffered from severe abdominal pain, nausea, headaches, and dizziness. Several were having seizures, and a couple were already in the hospital in critical condition.

1:00 pm

"I'm not sure how many died, mom," said CNN anchor Candy Lewis. "I just wanted to get the hell out of there. Yes, yes, I'll be there soon. I just want to stop at my place to pack a bag and grab a couple more clips for my gun. See you soon. Love you too."

Lewis stepped out of her car and walked into her place. The comforting buzz of her security system eased her mind as she entered her code. As she finished typing, an unfamiliar beep echoed through the house and Lewis instantly knew something was horribly wrong. The grandfather clock beside her exploded out, engulfing half the house into flames. Candy Lewis became the final casualty of what would come to be known as the "Media 9/11".

Chapter 14

WAR! TERRORISTS LAUNCH COORDINATED ATTACKS ON MEDIA! – Los Angeles Times

Terrorists Launch Jihad Against Mainstream Media: 38 Dead, 295 Injured or Sick. – Fox News

Traces of Salmonella, Antifreeze, Emetic Tartar, and Other Substances Detected in Break Room Snacks at NYT and Washington Post. – Chicago Tribune

Billionaire Henry Keller and Democratic PAC Head Bill Reines Assassinated at Hotel. – Daily Beast

Connection to 7/31 Attacks? Police Re-Opening Investigation into Death of Dan Irvin. – MSNBC

FBI Investigating Dozens of Domestic Hate Groups in Terror Attacks. – ABC

No Claims of Responsibility in Deadliest Terror Attacks Since 9/11. – CBS

"Terrorists Were Professionals Who Had Specific Targets in Mind," Says FBI Director. – Boston Globe

Did the CIA Coordinate 7/31 Media Attacks? – Daily Kos

Aaron Newsome scanned the Google News headlines as he ate breakfast at a Cracker Barrel restaurant near Lake Hopatcong in New York. He'd never seen the media use the word "terrorist" so quickly. Maybe if they had painted "Allah Akbar" at the explosion locations, the media would wonder more about a motive or call it "workplace violence?"

Newsome scanned the list of casualties for the tenth time. There were far more injured than he had hoped, but so far no one except those on their target lists had died, although it sounded like a couple were hanging by a thread in the hospital. Were they really doing the right thing? He would not lose a single hour of sleep over the targets they *intended* to hit, and Newsome had undoubtedly killed some innocents unintentionally in Iraq and Afghanistan, but it was very different when you were giving the orders.

His team was dispersing to airports around the country before all re-connecting in California. There would be no email, text, phone, or any other kinds of communication for at least the next three days. He would likely be joining them before the weekend was over, but he had one more thing to take care of.

*****

"FUUUUUCK!" shouted Colin Bennett as he hurled his iPad into a brick wall, shattering it into several pieces. Almost half of his most trusted media connections were dead. It would take years to replace and rebuild his network, and he didn't want to think about how much money. More importantly, with Henry Keller dead, $500,000 of his Martinez bonus was in jeopardy as well as the long-term financing of Media World. The loss of Bill Reines was no big deal—he could pay another subordinate less money to do the same job. Hopefully those dipshits at the FBI would track down the bastards who had done this quickly. If not, he may have to take matters into his own hands. Bennett looked down at his iPhone, which was receiving a call from the phone of Henry Keller.

"Who is this?"

"Mr. Bennett, this is Henry Keller, *Jr.* calling you. I found your number in my dad's phone. He has talked to me a lot about you and your history together."

Bennett hesitated. "I'm so sorry about your loss."

"Save it. I know you didn't really care about my dad personally, and I'm guessing you're freaking out about the massive funding source that was just killed."

"No, I liked your father a lot. We had more than just a working friendship. We--."

"I don't really care. All I want is retribution and to continue my father's work. It's clear these terrorists were going after my father and his media network. I want to rebuild it twice as strong as a big 'fuck you' to the bastards. You can rest assured that the Media World funding will be continued, as well as your $500,000 bonus, assuming Martinez stays where he is in polls. And if something happens to David Backman or he backs out of paying his matching $500K, I will cover it."

"Ok, sir. Thank you. And I wholeheartedly agree, your father would want exactly what you're doing." Bennett managed a smile for the first time in the last 24 hours.

"I also want to track down these terrorists and deal with them my own way. You knew quite a few of the people killed yesterday, so you must have some insight into who perpetrated these attacks, and I know you have contacts in the NSA and FBI. I will pay you an extra half million per terrorist that you help me track down. From what I hear so far, they don't know shit about who did this."

"That's what it sounds like from the press conferences. What about the media campaign against the Republican candidate, Richard Miller?"

"Nothing changes. Keep lobbing daily hit pieces at Martinez, but start shifting the hit pieces to Miller. He's going to get a nice bump in the polls for his tough-on-terror reputation, so we have to go after that. Tracking down the terrorists will be a side project for you, but I still want to focus on bringing my dad's dream of Communism in America to fruition."

"Any stories we release are going to be low-priority with all the terrorist investigation news."

"I know it will be further down in headlines, but keep the distributions going. Libertarians are perceived as weak on terror, so that will be another nail in the coffin of Martinez, but we have to hit Miller hard."

"I'll do what I can."

"I'll be in touch." Keller, Jr. ended the call. Bennett laughed at how quickly fortunes could change. These terrorist attacks may turn out to be a blessing in disguise and make him richer and more powerful than he ever dreamed."

*****

Steve Myers had not stopped shaking since the first set of firecrackers was set off at the studios of Comedy Central. No one working in comedy-related media had died on 7/31, but the terrorists were clearly trying to send a message. *You're next?*

Myers had written *Saturday Night Live* skits for five years while doing guest comedy appearances on the *Daily Show*. Nowadays, he had his own regular political comedy/news show on Comedy Central. Consequently, he knew he likely was on the media radar of these terrorists.

He had no intention of going back to work for a long while, and he wasn't going home after he heard about CNN's Candy Lewis blowing up in her own home. It was time to lay low at his dad's cabin on the lake. He unpacked three weeks of groceries, a Ruger revolver, and a 12-gauge shotgun from his Chevy Volt and carried them to the isolated vacation home. His boyfriend, Martin, was planning to join him tomorrow, so that would ease the tension.

Myers flipped on the TV as he walked around the cabin to verify all doors and windows were tightly secured. Every damn channel had something on about the attacks. Maybe a Netflix binge would get his mind off the attacks.

As Myers browsed through his watchlist, music started blaring from outside the house. Did Martin surprise him a day early? He grabbed his shotgun and stepped outside. The music was coming from his own Chevy. Myers must be losing his mind. He couldn't even keep it together to turn off his car radio before he walked in? As he took a step towards his car, he heard someone step behind him and shove a pistol in his back.

"Drop the shotgun if you don't want to live the rest of your life in a wheel chair."

"Look, I'm just a comedian. I'm not a journalist. No one takes what I say seriously."

"Not a journalist? An entire new generation is getting their news from shows like yours. I like a joke as much as the next person, but you don't do jokes. Shows like yours stopped doing jokes years ago. All you do now is spread propaganda, take quotes out of context to humiliate & deceive, perpetuate lies and character assassination, and hurt anyone who disagrees with you politically."

"Look, I never meant to hurt anyone. It was all in good fun."

"Do you remember the name, Dana Newsome? Seven. Seven *Saturday Night Live* skits you wrote making fun of her, and *all* of them were based on lies and bullshit that happened decades ago. And through your comedy show appearances, you referenced Dana in 65 joke segments—*45,* in less than two months!"

"I don't..."

"You've told thousands of jokes on your show over the years. Can you name five of them that reference someone who disagrees with you politically?"

"I can't help it if one side sets themselves up so well for jokes while one side honorably serves the nation. Politicians know they're going to be mocked when they make the decision to run for office."

"You're a tool. It's sad how gullible, brainwashed assholes like yourself unknowingly do the bidding of rich powerful people, destroying everyone that gets in their way. Dana was one of the sweetest persons you could ever meet, and she wanted nothing more than to help people and improve the world. You, as much as anyone, turned her into a caricature. You humiliated her, destroyed her reputation, and ruined her career, all because she didn't have the political opinions you wanted her to have."

"I'm not responsible for what happened to her. I--."

"A little over four years ago, she used this Beretta I'm holding to end her life. It hasn't been fired since."

Newsome unloaded four shots into the chest of Myers. As Myers lay awake struggling for breath, Newsome looked him in the eye and fired one more bullet into his forehead.

"That one was for you, Dana, but I'm not done making them pay. Not by a long shot."

Chapter 15

"Water?" Patrick Adams struggled to say as he glanced around the blurry hospital room.

"Well, hello. I was wondering if you were ever going to wake up," said a nurse. "You've been out for quite a while."

"My head is killing me."

"Yeah, you sustained quite a concussion. You've been in and out of consciousness a few times over the last few days. There were some poisons in the breakroom snacks at your office, so we pumped your stomach, just to be safe. A piece of metal also cut a nice big gash in your leg during the explosion."

Explosion, poison, it was all coming back to him. "Marilyn? Marilyn Kahn? Is she alright?"

"I'm very sorry, but she didn't make it," said the nurse.

His heart sank. He never got along professionally with Marilyn, but he liked her personally. "How many are dead?"

"Why don't you just concentrate on getting better, Mr. Adams. I'm sure you'll—."

"How many?"

"I'm not sure how many died where you work. The news says 40 have died, 42 if you count Dan Irvin and Louis Holder, plus hundreds more injured or sick," said the nurse.

"Irvin and Holder? They're connected to this? Who all was hit?"

"The *Times*, the *Post*, and CNN were hit the hardest, but the psychos hit just about everyone in media—Fox, NBC, CBS, ABC, you name it. Some billionaire also got killed along with a political bigwig that he was eating with."

"Henry Keller, by chance?"

"Yeah, that's him. I guess maybe you had some awareness after all when you were seemingly out of it."

"No, it was just a hunch." Connections were starting to swirl in his head. "Do they know who did this?"

"They're fucking clueless. Pardon my French. All kinds of theories out there—CIA, right-wing hate groups, the mob, foreign intelligence organizations."

"I need to get the hell out of here." As Adams sat up, wooziness and blackness knocked him back into the bed.

"It's out of the question. Maybe in a day or two."

"Can you at least have someone bring me my laptop and some notebooks. I have to find these people. I owe that to Marilyn, and everyone else who lost their lives to those bastards."

*****

Google, and its parent company Alphabet, hired some of the most gifted individuals in the world as its employees. It was perhaps the most sought-after career choice by graduates in the technology field. And why not? In addition to receiving great pay and developing cutting-edge technology, Google was famous for its employee perks— free gourmet cafeterias, massage rooms, game rooms, nap pods, onsite health care, fitness facilities, and more.

Abby Benton, now a blonde, applied for a job in one of the employee organic restaurants at Google headquarters in Mountain View, CA. She was a skilled baker, although she wasn't going to brag about her last recipe prepared for *New York Times* reporters. Abby had changed her hairstyle and eye color, added some freckles, and tweaked her makeup enough that if you put a picture of her now side-by-side with one taken at the *Times* a week ago, you'd never guess it was the same person.

There was nothing 9-to-5 about Google employee hours, so it was relatively easy for Abby to get hired on for a mix of second and third shifts. It didn't hurt to be an attractive blonde when you applied for a company that overwhelmingly employed men. She didn't expect to be there for long. Thanks to former Google employee, Jim Damon, she knew the layout and security measures inside and out. It was time to start preparations for opening the next front in their Revolution.

*****

In three days, mostly from his hospital bed, Patrick Adams had compiled a research folder on every person killed in the 7/31 attacks, in addition to Dan Irvin and Louis Holder. Each folder included a small personal biography, a job history, the ten most notable writings or speeches, groups & media organizations that had criticized the person, and their top ten most-likely enemies.

The attacks were highly-focused with just enough explosives to kill the target while minimizing collateral damage. The poisons in the break-room snacks were not high enough in concentration to cause death, so they were obviously there to send a message. Fireworks and explosions of non-populated areas did the same. However, there was no mistaking the fact that the terrorist wanted specific people dead. There had to be a connection or similarity among the deceased.

So far, Adams had found one very common similarity. Almost all had been flagged repeatedly by various fact-check sites such as *Media Research Center*, *Snopes*, *Politifact*, and *Open Secrets* for spreading fake news, reporting uncorroborated claims, or telling outright lies. Louis Holder was one of the worst offenders. Most targets were reporters, and the ones that did verify sources usually only reported one side of stories and acted as hired attack dogs.

The FBI seemed to be focusing its investigation on foreign intelligence services and right-wing domestic groups that hated the media. Press conferences made it sound almost like the attacks were random, but they clearly were not. What made the investigation so confusing was the diversity of the attacks. Most were liberal-leaning journalists, but there were plenty of Republican-leaning ones killed. So why were the targets chosen?

The TV coverage of the past few days had been filled with heart-wrenching memorials and puffy pieces about the great journalistic careers of the people killed. It is custom in our society not to trample on a person's grave, but was that blinding everyone to the fact that these people had one thing in common—they were shoddy journalists! How did you even bring up that fact with authorities? How could Adams even suggest to his mourning co-workers that their friends were killed because they had thrown away their journalistic integrity?

The more research Adams compiled, the more he disliked the victims. Adams didn't believe in violence—they definitely did *not* deserve to die, but you couldn't ignore the evidence that may help find the terrorists and their motives. Adams had heard many conspiracy theories about Henry Keller that were regularly lampooned by his co-workers as right-wing drivel. Maybe it was time to give those theories a look.

*****

"You said on the phone you interned at Google," said the Facebook interviewer. "How come you didn't take a full-time position?"

"I'm still considering one, but Google is ranked as the *second*-best place to work in America. I want the best," said Jim Damon, using a co-opted identity of a recent MIT graduate. "I also am considering an offer at Microsoft in its LinkedIn division. As you can tell by my posts, I'm kind of a social media nut, so Facebook is where it's at."

"Yes, you sure are passionate about your Socialist politics, which is good, we have *a lot* of Bernie lovers around here," said the interviewer, referring to the former presidential candidate, Bernie Sanders. "Your Trump and Martinez posts are hilarious. You'll fit right in."

"Thanks. Yes, I get worked up a bit. It's all in fun," said Damon.

"You look much better in person than your pictures if you don't mind my saying so. You must have lost a lot of weight," said the interviewer.

"Yes, about fifty pounds. Organic and paleo eating combined with a ton of running."

"Nice. So, this is a six-month contracting position, which will likely lead to a full-time offer if you do well. You plan to move to Menlo Park?"

"Definitely. I don't miss the Cambridge winters."

"By your resume, it's sounds like you have all the web programming experience we need, as well Oracle and SQL Server experience. I'm sure you've read about our little programming tech exam we use to verify your skills are up to snuff. Don't worry, we won't make you drink shots every few minutes like the *Social Network* movie."

"I wouldn't mind if you did. Creative stimulation."

"Sorry for all the interviews. We're a pretty tight group at Facebook, and we want to make sure everyone fits into our culture."

RAPCA member, Nate Keeting, knew from his years of working at Facebook the inside information on getting hired, which he passed on to Jim Damon. Damon had all the technical skills to satisfy the interviewers. It was just a matter of getting through the lengthy interview process in a timely manner.

*****

Kyle Topper and Cole Foreman never did too much golfing when serving as Navy SEALs, but today it was part of their mission prep. They were golfing 18 holes in California at one of the most exclusive golf courses in the country, trying not to stand out by how bad they swung a club. This golf course was the only weakness they could find in the security around David Backman, the Republican billionaire. Now that Henry Keller was out of the picture, Backman had become their number one target.

Virtually every attack story on Martinez from the conservative media could be traced directly or indirectly to Backman. Usually Backman and Keller funded opposite sides of the political spectrum, but it was clear from the money trails and email chains the RAPCAs had put together that the two were united in wanting to destroy Martinez.

"Based on course diagrams, holes 6, 8, and 12 give me the best line of sight," said Topper.

"Backman is scheduled for 9 am tomorrow," said Foreman, "and there's no way we can get a tee time on the weekend, so we'll have to find a location for a spotter."

"I'm guessing I have maybe ten minutes before someone spots me on the ridge, so we have to set up and take down quickly."

"According to Darren's intel, he usually has two guards on the course when he golfs. He may raise that after the takedown of Keller."

"I'm thinking I can set up in the left woods by the green around hole 6. So, I can give you around a T-15 minutes warning if set up for a shot at the green on 8."

"Where do you want me?" said Darren Williams.

"Find a location around holes 5-7 to stage a distraction, then get the hell back to the clubhouse parking lot. We won't get another shot at this anytime soon, so be ready for anything."

*****

Aaron Newsome had driven from New York to Wisconsin and was now back at the training headquarters facility. He had spent most of the last 24 hours reviewing transcripts and videos of press conferences and news sources.

"We have an APB out on two persons of interest in the investigation, an African-American man and a red-headed woman," said the FBI investigator.

"Attacking the press means attacking free speech and America itself," said the President.

"Make no mistake, this is an attack on democracy," said the CNN anchor.

"There is no justification for violence, and these attacks should be universally condemned," said Brent Martinez.

"KKK, Aryan Brotherhood, and other right-wing groups should be under investigation," said the Democratic Senator.

"All Islamic terror groups have been ruled out as suspects," said the Fox News anchor.

"Donald Trump and Brent Martinez are directly responsible for these attacks with their media hate rhetoric," said the CNN commentator.

"These attacks were a hit to the nation greater than 9/11 and the attack on Pearl Harbor," said the MSNBC commentator.

Newsome rolled his eyes more times than he could count. It was all predictable. He had not come across one single story in the mainstream media that said anything negative about any of the victims or honestly explained why they might have been chosen as targets. Everyone killed was described as a great contributor to humanity, as unbiased and fair journalists. By the glowing reports, you would think the attacks were a purge of saints in the media.

That was about to change. Newsome was putting together twenty USB flash drives, each containing a packet of charts, spreadsheets, documents, videos, and recordings. It started with a hierarchy of organizations related to the Democrat National Committee, Republican National Committee, billionaires David Backman & Henry Keller, and other big donors including some foreign governments. Payments were traced from the donors to networks such as Keller's charitable foundations and Media World, which included subcomponents of public relation firms, political action committees, nonprofits, think tanks, lobbyists, websites, opposition research organizations, media fact checkers, and other miscellaneous political organizations.

Newsome detailed financial transactions and money trail information going in and out of the media/political hierarchy. Cash payments from the network had been directly connected to 28 of the 40 people killed on 7/31, with several more connected to relatives. If it wasn't cash, then other kinds of transactional relationships between the donor network and media personnel were detailed in the packet.

Newsome copied 100 subfolders on each USB flash drive. Most of the subfolders had the name of a person that was killed, injured, or listed as a RAPCA target they were unable to hit. Each subfolder showed a history of dubious journalism and shady activities of the person mentioned— false or misleading stories, one-sided attack pieces, overuse of anonymous and unconfirmed sources, and so on. Newsome added whatever hacked email and text correspondence could be collected between the money/political network and the journalist.

To put it another way, the information on the flash drives made it crystal clear that the people targeted were no angels and were hit for very specific reasons. Newsome added four file folders that contained the names of women who had made sexual accusations against Brent Martinez. They included email communications with organizations in the Media World hierarchy as well as financial transactions and deposits made by the women or a close relative. It was clear from the spreadsheets that they had large cash windfalls right around the time they went public with their accusations.

Newsome packed each USB flash drive in separate envelops. He added a one-page summary of the drive contents. No signature or claims of responsibility for the attacks were included.

*****

"I don't like this one bit," said David Backman into his Samsung Galaxy as walked the golf course to the green on the 4th hole. "Sooner or later it's going to become obvious why the terrorists picked them, and the trail is going to lead to us. Start a purge of every correspondence we've ever had with anyone connected to these people. Delete every email and shred anything printed. Don't forget to wipe backup servers. Close any bank accounts that have been used for funneling any cash directly or indirectly to them." Backman paused. "Yes, I agree. I'm starting to get some really bad vibes, like these terrorists aren't done. If they went after Keller, they may be coming after me. I have four of my best security guys with me now, but I think I'm flying back to my island after this round. I shouldn't even be out here, but this is the first stress-free hour I've had since I heard of the attacks. I'll call you later tonight. Stay safe."

"He's headed to hole five now," said Darren Williams into his wired mic, which fed into the earpieces of Kyle Topper and Cole Foreman. "I see four security guys, corner formation around Backman and one other bigwig. No holes worse than bogey so far, so expect them soon."

"See if you can take down the back-right guard mid-hole if you can get him out of sight of the others. He'll be in best position to spot our sniper."

"Copy that." Williams headed for the 10th hole driving a golf cart that carried two coolers of drinks and a sign with prices.

Fifteen minutes later, Foreman glanced through binoculars from a wooded position on the 6th hole as Backman set up for a birdie putt. "They're finishing up on the 6th. Be advised, security all appear to have vests on. Backman is open though."

"Copy. Setting up in ten minutes," said Topper.

Williams took a curving route past hole 10, then 9, selling drinks to a couple of golfers before heading towards hole 8.

"Any of you want a cold one?" he said the security guy stationed to the front right of the two golfers. The guard looked back towards Backman, who shook his head as he grabbed his wedge for the 3rd shot of the par 4 hole.

"Nothing for any of us, thanks," said the guard.

Williams drove in the direction of the 7th hole, then slowed up by the trailing guard on the right as he heard Topper say, "Got 'em in sight now."

"David, get down!" yelled the front right guard, "Sniper at 3 o'clock on the ridge!"

David Backman turned his head slightly, causing the bullet to hit the side of his head instead of between the eyes, where Topper had lined his sights. Before the trailing right guard could react, Williams reached into a cooler and took out a gun and shot tranquilizer darts into both his legs. The other three security men starting firing in the direction of Topper.

Foreman entered a code on his iPhone, causing a tree 100 feet from the hole on the left side to explode.

"Shit, I'm hit!" said Topper as he looked down to see blood streaming from his left shoulder. *I hope Foreman was right about the vests*, he thought as he lined up and fired into the chest of one of the guards. The other guards were too low for anything but a head shot. Williams reached into golf bag and took out a rifle loaded with rubber bullets and fired three shots into the right side of each security man. It was enough to incapacitate them and stop any return fire.

"Get in the back," said Foreman as he helped Topper into the car. He sped back to the clubhouse parking lot to pick up Williams. "Bullet exited the back. Get him patched up. I'll call Abby."

Williams dumped some alcohol on the shoulder and wrapped him with bandages and tape that he pulled from his first aid kit. "This is a hell of a lot of blood."

"Abby, we got target P2, but Kyle got hit in the shoulder. Grab your medical bag and meet us back at the hotel. Thanks."

"I had to leave some of my gear on the ridge," said Topper.

"Unfortunately, you left something way more important than your gear," said Williams, "your blood."

Chapter 16

As soon as Aaron Newsome received word of the successful hit on David Backman, he sealed and addressed the twenty padded envelopes containing the flash drives. Sure, it would be much easier to mass email the information, but he wanted to minimize any kind of electronic trail. The best experts in the world were likely trying to track them down, so he wasn't taking any chances.

He drove south with the envelops for three hours to a small town named Prairie du Chien, a town close to the intersection borders of Wisconsin, Iowa, and Minnesota. The envelops would be traced by their postmark, so he wanted to widen the prospective search area for the feds. The town was always a few years behind in technology, so there were fewer traffic and other cameras around the city.

Half the envelops were addressed to the headquarters of a mix of right-leaning, left-leaning, and centrist websites, including Drudge Report, Huffington Post, Wikileaks, and the Media Research Center. The rest were addressed to a fair-minded reporter selected from each of the ten largest newspapers in America, including the *New York Times* and *Washington Post*. It wouldn't be long before at least one of the sources published the entire contents of the flash drives online. As reporters went through the information, facts would start to become widely known by the public, and the narrative on the terrorist attacks would change in a hurry. At least that was the plan.

Newsome dropped the envelops in a side-street blue mailbox and drove to O'Hare Airport in Chicago. It was time to join the rest of his team for the next phase of their operation.

*****

Top Republican Money Man, David Backman, Assassinated on Golf Course. – CNN

White Male Who Drove Golf Drink Cart Added as Third Suspect in FBI's Terror Attacks Investigation. – Washington Post

Terrorists First Communication? Flash Drive's Filled with Documents Mailed to Several Locations. – Yahoo News

Massive Ring of Corruption Discovered in Mainstream Media and Political Organizations. – Drudge Report

Evidence of Bribes Given to Four of Martinez Sexual Accusers. – Breitbart News

Colin Bennett's voice had grown hoarse from the long-string of expletives he'd unleashed as he saw the headlines and learned more about the recent document dump. He had received calls already from five of his media contacts detailing what they received and asking for the plan to handle it. It was critical to set the media narrative on this as soon as possible to minimize damage.

After jotting notes for the past hour, he composed an email to his most trusted assistants and political/media contacts:

Hey everyone. I'm sure most of you have heard the latest news on the flash drive document dumps sent to media sources across the country. First of all, don't panic. We've weathered storms like this before, and we'll do so again. But it's critical that we get on top of this as soon as possible.

Before you do anything else, change all your passwords immediately and implement the security measures in the attached document to avoid further hacks of our private communications.

Start drafting press releases and preparing media interviewees for all cable news shows. Our response strategy is as follows:

1. *Deny, deny, deny! Emphasize these flash drives are fabrications that come from unknown sources. Use the term "fake news" as often as possible in the discussions. Even if you can't convince audiences that the information is false, at least plant enough doubt and confusion that people don't know what to believe.*

2. *Start researching every shred of information on the flash drives that can be disproved with alternative evidence. If we can find 5-10 good examples, we likely can convince most of the population the whole thing is garbage. Regardless of what is found, confidently assert that the documents have been studied and discredited by investigators.*

3. *Point out that the documents are likely from the terrorists who are looking to justify MURDER of so many innocent people. Bring up the families of the murdered journalists and how discussing discredited reports tramples on the graves of the deceased. For whatever media source you're dealing with in the discussion, mention names of people killed or injured from that source. For example, if you're doing a CNN interview, find a way to say the names "Candy Lewis", "Jerome Jones", etc. Whenever a tough question is raised, change the subject to the kids and spouses of those journalists. Tug at the heart strings!*

4. *Emphasize that even if some small pieces of information turn out to be true, there is absolutely nothing that justifies murder. Build as much hatred for the terrorists and sympathy for the deceased as you possibly can.*

5. *Contact whatever editors you have in your network. Try to convince them that even discussing the false documents is an insult to the victims, and they should not reward the terrorists by giving them even one second of coverage. Tell them giving airtime to the flash drive documents is equivalent to Al Jazeera showing suicide bomber videos.*

   6. *As for Martinez and so-called bribes, again deny, deny, deny, but point out the four are only a small minority of the accusers. Were all of them paid off?*

We will be running polls and focus groups at every stage of the game. We will discuss more in person at a later time, but let's control the narrative from the start.

--Colin

    Bennett was a little calmer after re-reading his strategy. Similar tactics had been used with Hillary email and charity scandals. They had been used with the Obama scandals, Fast & Furious and IRS targeting of conservatives. People believed what they wanted to believe. Most Americans liked Obama but didn't like Hillary, which is why the strategies largely failed for one but not the other. Consequently, it was important to control the people likability aspect of things.

    Several journalists and commentators would cover the story exactly as Bennett wished. His buddies at Facebook, Google, Twitter, Bing, etc. would make sure those favorable stories filtered to the top of searches and news apps. Sure, he couldn't control Drudge Report, Breitbart, Rush Limbaugh, Hannity, and other sources, but 60 percent of the country was never exposed to any of that media. Many wouldn't believe anything from them anyway because of the credibility attacks Media World had unleashed against them for years. You only needed 50.1 percent to win an election. And thanks to the third-party element and the large portion of the population that didn't vote, far less than

50 percent was sufficient. Still, if the Martinez accusers retracted their stories, things could get far worse.

Bennett dialed a number from a new satellite phone, "Dutch, this is Colin. We have a little problem."

*****

Patrick Adams limped to the mailbox to retrieve his paper and yesterday's mail. The *New York Times* was starting to resemble its normal thickness after shutting down several sections for a few days. Minimal staff was at headquarters under heavy security. Most articles were being done remotely by reporters healthy enough to do so.

Adams was given the week off to recover, but he had worked almost around the clock for three days doing his own research on the attacks and its victims. He had finally crashed for ten hours of uninterrupted sleep. He glanced through the headlines as he opened his mail. His eyes went wide as he pulled out a flash drive from a padded envelop and read through the contents outline. The *Times* had a small blurb on the front page about some flash drives being mailed out to random media sources, but it didn't describe the contents.

He flipped on his laptop and started pecking through websites. Apparently at least 15 other flash drives with the same contents had showed up in the mail at various locations so far. Why was he receiving a copy? It all seemed to feed into the research he had already been doing. Was someone aware of his investigation? The flash drive contained a mix of both public information and communications that clearly were obtained illegally. Adams spent the rest of the day integrating his own research with that on the flash drive. He had yet to come across a single inaccurate piece of information on the drive. As he listened to interviews on cable news stations, it was becoming clear the information on these drives had scared the hell out of a lot of people.

A chill went down his spine as it set in that it had to be the terrorists who sent him the flash drive. But why? Did they really expect him to help them after watching co-workers get killed and almost dying himself? After making two copies of the information, he picked up his cell and dialed the number of the FBI.

*****

"Thanks for buying a round, Thompson," said the bartender to the second husband of Marie Martinez.

"No problem, I made $3000 in an all-cash contracting gig. My leech ex-wife can't touch the money if I keep it off the books. I still wonder if those two snotbag kids of hers are really mine."

"Have a good night."

As Thompson walked out of the bar, he was approached by a hulking Italian man. "Are you Thompson, ex-husband of Marie Martinez?"

"Yeah, what's it to you?"

Dutch Marcello shot a right-cross into Thompson's nose, shattering cartilage in two spots. Two other men stepped from the sides of Thompson, swinging aluminum bats as they advanced. Thompson had a broken right arm and left leg before he could process what was happening. As Thompson fell to the ground, the three of them kicked him in the ribs until several of them cracked. Thompson howled in excruciating pain.

Marcello tightly clamped onto Thompson's scrotum and said, "By the end of tomorrow, you will give $20,000 to your ex-wife to cover the back child support you've been hiding in your girlfriend's name, and from this day forward, you won't be a single day late in paying the legally required child support amounts, including from your cash jobs. And if you lay another hand on her or her kids ever again, I will cut off every single body parts of yours one at a time— slowly! Do we understand each other?"

"Yes. Yes! Please, no more. I will do whatever you want."

"That's a good boy. Tell your ex-wife her new best friend says hi."

Marcello walked away as patrons from the bar rushed to help Thompson. Marcello dialed a number on his cell, "I'll pay Marie Martinez a quick visit, but I'm fairly confident we won't have to worry about her retracting her story. I have people talking to the other ten. They will keep quiet—trust me. Two attention-seeker women that went public have retracted their story. We didn't pay them and haven't had any interaction with them, but we can certainly change that. I think it'd be better if we just made an example out of someone. Which woman is most shaky on sticking to her story?"

Chapter 17

Backman Shooter Hit, No DNA Matches from Blood in Criminal Databases. – CBS News

Flash Drive Document Dump Pure Terrorist Propaganda, Says FBI Director. – CNN

Martinez Accuser Commits Suicide, Sister Blames Stress and Sexual Trauma. – MSNBC

FBI Terror Investigation Stalls. Still No Arrests. – New York Times

Martinez Pops Back Up in Polls: Miller 41, Locklear 40, Martinez 18. – ABC

Publishing Flash Drive Contents May Make You Criminally Liable as Accessory to Terrorism, Says Attorney General. – Washington Post

Martinez: Government Stomping on Civil Rights in Terror Investigation. – Yahoo News

Shock Poll: 28 Percent of Americans Say Media Terror Attacks Were Justified. – Drudge Report

"Tim, tell me something good," said Bennett, referring to his National Security Agency contact, Tim Gordon. "Have you seen these headlines. Our damage control has been mediocre at best, and I'm not sure how many people are buying the bullshit from the AG and FBI Director."

"As you know, blood was found at the scene of the Backman shooting," said Gordon. "It's not exactly true that no DNA match was found. Special forces DNA and fingerprint samples are normally kept in a database for casualty identification. The FBI is trying to get full access to that database, but the DoD is stonewalling. I hear there's a match to a former Navy SEAL that did several classified missions in Afghanistan and Iraq. He hasn't lived in the U.S. for several years now, so they haven't been able to track him down. That's all I know right now."

"What are they going to do if they catch him?"

"I'm guessing they may want to send him to Guantanamo Bay or rendition him, but if the FBI tracks him down, that's not going to happen."

"Tim, there are some very powerful people that don't want these terrorists captured. They want a more *permanent* solution. If they're arrested, they become public spectacles, which will only bring more attention to our political/media networks."

"I'll see what I can find out, but it will cost you."

"I don't think money will be an issue. Keller's son is out for revenge. Get me the name of the Backman shooter and everyone he served with in special forces."

*****

Abby Benton had finished her third shift of the week in the Slice Café at Google. She sat alone having a smoothie and was getting tired of shooting down programmers trying to hit on her. She had heard more than enough cheesy pick-up lines and boasts about stock options from spoiled, young geniuses. She was waiting for one specific guy who liked to work late and who ate there several times per week.

"Googley Blueberry. My favorite," she heard someone say to her. She was about to queue up another rejection when she noticed the voice came from the guy she was waiting for, Craig Whitman.

"It *is* good. I've made so many of them the past few days that I thought I should try one."

"Oh, you work in this café?"

"Yes, just started a few days ago."

"Hi, I'm Craig."

Abby hesitated before replying, "I'm Doreen." She'd used so many aliases the past couple weeks that it was getting tough to keep track. "What do you do here?"

"I supervise a team that tweaks programming algorithms for the search and news app rankings," said Whitman. "Basically, we constantly put in improvements for the links that come up first when you do a Google search, or in the case of the Google News app, the stories that appear in the standard sections...Headlines, World, U.S., Business, etc."

"Sounds like an important job. Basically, you determine what the world sees and doesn't see, since very few people have the patience to scan through links beyond the first page?"

"Precisely. Our focus lately has been weeding out fake news and hate speech."

"Oh, so you're tasked with trying to prevent another Trump-type presidency?"

Whitman laughed and said, "Yeah, I still can't believe that idiot got elected. It just goes to show you how stupid the average American is, and it's sort of our job to shield them from their own stupidity."

"Sounds noble. How do you determine if something is fake or considered hate speech?"

"It's complicated, but we have teams that write programs to assign credibility to various sources. Fox News, Townhall, Hannity, Breitbart, Limbaugh, and other hate merchants naturally are lowered in value, so they're less likely to appear high in rankings. CNN, *New York Times*, *Washington Post*, MSNBC, and other true journalism sources are programmed to appear higher. At the very least, we try to add some fact-check links besides search results for all conservative and libertarian site links. It's not really official company policy to design the algorithms this way or anything like that, but we have our own unwritten rules."

"Aren't you worried that you're opening up Google to censorship and bias? Correct me if I'm wrong, but isn't about 95 percent of Silicon Valley leftist in its thinking? How are you going to get alternative viewpoints?"

"Trust me, we have some of the smartest people in the world. Google's motto is 'don't be evil.' We know people better than they know themselves, and it's important we keep them away from toxic ideas that conservatives and libertarians spew."

"I'm sorry, I like to play devil's advocate sometime. This stuff is fascinating to me. I did a little programming in college and like to follow current events. I don't have near the brainpower to do what you guys do though. My life is health and fitness nowadays."

"Yes, I see that you keep yourself in pretty good shape," said Whitman.

"Thank you," said Abby. "You look very fit yourself." She pretended not to notice him slip the wedding ring off his left hand under the table.

"Would you like to see some of the code algorithm flowcharts?"

"That would be awesome! But I shouldn't trouble you. It's late, and you probably have a ton of work to do."

"No, no. I would love to show you. It's rare that such an attractive woman shows an interest in my work. I have a corner office on the top floor. Great view at this time of night. Why don't you come up? I'll make us some margaritas."

Abby flashed a smile that made Whitman weak in the knees. "I'd love to."

Craig Whitman's office was the size of a small apartment. It held a liquor cabinet, an L-shaped couch, a big-screen TV, a small refrigerator, and a treadmill. Whitman sat behind a large oak desk covered with a Macbook and four monitors.

"Wow, this office is amazing," said Abby. "I don't know if I'll want to leave. Are all the engineers' offices this ritzy?"

"Well, they're not quite this nice, but I spend an average of about 90 hours per week here, so I spruced it up. Sometimes I just spend the night as this couch pulls into a mattress." Whitman glanced down at Abby's curves. "Here ya go, one margarita for you, one for me."

"Delicious. Come on, let me see the code. Show me your sexy nerd side."

"Well, there's actually millions of lines of code. We have teams tweaking different modules every day," said Whitman.

"Looks like C sharp."

"Wow, you do know your code. I thought that was just a pickup routine," Whitman laughed. "We use a mix of a few different programming languages. The critical component is testing. We feed in daily lists of the most common search terms and phrases, then run them through the search algorithms and tweak them based on the results. For example, if searches are done on Brent Martinez, we want his sex scandals and racist remarks to filter to the top rather than show his speeches and political solution websites. We can't take the pro-Martinez sites out entirely since that would be a little too suspicious, but we do our best to keep the population from being brainwashed by his ideas. It's more of an art than a science. Our stuff is much more sophisticated than something like Twitter. Engineers there use a process called "shadow banning", where a tweet looks like it is successfully posted to all users by the tweeter, but some or all of his followers don't actually see it. Any engineer has the power to ban the hateful tweet. In other words, they have much more flexibility to censor, but it's too easy to get caught by the right-wing nuts."

"It seems like you're crossing some ethical boundaries, but it makes sense to me. Ends justify the means," said Abby as she smiled. "What about the Google News app?"

"It uses a lot of the same concepts, except we start by gearing articles towards the interest of the user, with tweaks by source. We record what users click on and what they ignore. We track both the subject matter they like plus the websites they visit from the app. After that, we adjust the story rankings by the same credibility numerical scores. We entirely weed out the far-right sources like Hannity and Limbaugh. For some sources like Fox News, we use a randomization function that will show one of their links on occasion. In other words, a few times per year, we'll throw a Fox News story in there, so if there's any complaints, we can point to examples where they were listed. It's much more complicated than what I'm describing, but I don't want to bore you."

"No, it's really interesting," said Abby. I'm ready for another one. I'll be the bartender this time. Would you like a strawberry one?"

"Sure," said Whitman. Abby added a small dose of Rohypnol to his drink and handed it to him.

"How did you come to work at Google?" said Abby. "Tell me about yourself. Are you from California?"

Abby talked and drank with him for a little over 30 minutes before leading him over to the couch. As he leaned in to kiss her, she backed away and guided his drowsy head to the pillow. After Whitman dozed off, Abby emptied half a bottle of tequila down the drain and set the bottle and a few shot glasses on the coffee table beside him. She took out her purse and switched off a voice recorder app running on her iPhone. Before leaving, she planted a camera and C-4-packed phone to the bottom of the oak desk.

"How does it look?" texted Abby.

Nate Keeting pulled up a video feed on his laptop and replied, "Good. Ready to take down target P5."

*****

"Who are you and what are you doing in my office?" said Facebook executive, Jack Zimmer.

It was risky for Jim Damon to go to Zimmer's office on only his second day work, but plans were moving quickly. "Hi, I just started yesterday. I know it's a nerdish thing to say, but I'm a big fan. I've seen all your TED Talks and just wanted to meet you."

"Next time knock, or better yet, make an appointment if you want to talk to me," said Zimmer.

"You have a beautiful wife. Isn't she a Democratic Congresswoman?" said Damon as he pointed to the pictures on the wall. As Zimmer turned his head to look, Damon pulled a flash drive out of Zimmer's laptop and put it in his pocket.

"Yes and yes. Now if you don't mind, I have a lot of work to do and so do you. New on the job or not, we expect our employees to hit their deadlines."

"Sorry. Nice to meet you."

Damon took the stairs down to the floor of his assigned cube. As he walked he texted the team, "Zimmer devices planted. I have the code segments and Zimmer contacts copied. He has plane ticket to DC on desk leaving Saturday morning, so we have to make this happen soon. I will finish planting rest of building charges tomorrow. Friday afternoon is probably our best bet here."

"Progress on rest of targets?" texted Aaron Newsome.

"Twitter and Apple ones ready," replied Scott Koonce. "Security too tight at LA Times and SF Chronicle. We can't get to them anytime soon."

"I operated on Kyle's shoulder," texted Dr. Abby Benton. "He's going to be out of commission for a while and need some rehab but should fully recover."

"I'll fill in for Kyle," replied Newsome. "My flight arrives tonight. Let's plan on Friday afternoon. Nate, your call on timing. After that, we'll move immediately to scouting for the next phase of our op."

*****

Patrick Adams was happy to finish his first day of work back in the office of the *New York Times*. He wanted to defiantly prove to the terrorists that he wasn't afraid of them, but in the back of his mind he knew if they wanted him dead, he'd likely be dead already. Plus, there was no reason to send him the flash drive of information if they wanted to kill him.

He still couldn't explain why he was one of the ten reporters chosen to receive the information pack, and he was getting tired of the accusatory looks and questions from his co-workers. He shared everything he had with the Department of Homeland Security, FBI, and the *Times*. What more could he do?

Did the terrorists send him the flash drive as a sort of *apology* for the injuries and sickness they caused? They clearly were going out of their way to prevent deaths among all but their specific targets. Even the substances in the breakroom snacks that caused so much illness were obviously meant to send a message rather than kill. Maybe it had something to do with that cleaning girl. He had looked at her surveillance picture a hundred times. There was something familiar about her that day he saw her at the office, but he still couldn't place her.

As he drove out of the parking lot, he noticed two men in a Ford Explorer were following him. He thought he was imagining things when he saw the same Explorer weave in and out of traffic behind him on his way to work. This seemed to confirm they were following him. He shivered at the thought it may be the terrorists, but the suits the men had on were similar to the ones his FBI interviewers wore. Were they protecting him? Was he a suspect? His best guess was that they were desperate for a lead in the terror investigation.

It would become clear how motivated they were to follow him when he left tomorrow on a drive to Virginia. Interviewing Marie Martinez wasn't the most pressing matter right now, but it was the last thing his editor, Marilyn

Kahn, had asked him to do before she was killed in the 7/31 attacks. This was the least he could do to honor her memory.

Chapter 18

11:30 am

"Zimmer is going to be in meeting until 2:30," texted Jim Damon to the rest of the RAPCA team. "It is one of the Facebook VP's 40th birthday, so most of the staff in the building are headed to happy hour celebration at 5pm."

"That's good for us," replied Aaron Newsome. "Maybe we can get most of the building cleared before the first blow. Try to find out when Zimmer is heading out."

"Copy that," said Damon.

"How's it look at Google?" said Newsome.

"Whitman will likely be working very late," responded Abby Benton. "He came down to apologize early for passing out on our 'date'. Apparently, he slept through a couple of client meetings the next day, so he's trying to make it up to Zuckerberg."

"Twitter?" texted Newsome.

"Their data center is even more sparsely populated than it usually is. Charges are secured," replied Cole Foreman.

"Things are looking good at Apple also," texted Nate Keeting.

"Ok, let's plan for 4:30-5ish. Keeting, give us a sitrep around 4:15," said Newsome, referring to a Situation Report.

4:40 pm

"Still not seeing Whitman," texted Keeting.

"Abby, we only have 20 minutes until Facebook happy hour. Any clue where he is?" said Newsome.

"He came down for a smoothie 15 minutes ago. He asked me to dinner tonight. I said I had to work until 7. He said he'd wait."

"Most of Facebook staff already left. I think Zimmer plans to join, so our window is closing," said Damon.

"He just came back to his office. Both offices clear of bystanders," said Keeting.

"Do it," said Newsome.

Nate Keeting entered codes P4 and P5 into his laptop, which dialed the numbers of the devices in the offices of Zimmer and Whitman. They ignited the C-4 planted under their desks. Metal and wood exploded out from the desk, quickly snuffing out the lives of the targeted Google and Facebook executives.

4:50 pm

Cole Foreman sent signals to explosive devices that devoured power transformers near buildings next to the ones they planned to hit at Twitter and Apple.

Nate Keeting, Aaron Newsome, Darren Williams, and Scott Koonce each dialed one of four phone numbers simultaneously and played a pre-recorded computerized voice, *"This message is from the RAPCAs, the same organization that carried out the 7/31 attacks. We've just blown up the offices of Jack Zimmer at Facebook and Craig Whitman at Google. They're both dead. We've also blown up power transformers near sites at Twitter and Apple. You have 20 minutes to clear the building you're in and get as far away from the area as possible. We've planted dynamite at strategic locations, and your building will soon be turned to rubble. You now have 19 minutes, 50 seconds and counting. You better hurry."*

Security personnel started scrambling at Facebook, Google, Twitter, and Apple. Emergency messages were played on whatever intercoms were available. Emails, texts, and instant messages were frantically sent to company mailing lists. Fire alarms were pulled.

"Calls have gone out. Abby and Jim, clear the buildings and get the hell out; set the detonation at

5:20pm," texted Newsome. Both were given instructions to cover as many floors in their buildings as possible, making sure everyone got the message to exit ASAP. An extra ten minutes was added to the time given on the phone calls as a precaution.

5:00 pm

Cole Foreman set off timers which triggered firecrackers at strategic locations at each of the tech companies they had targeted, mostly in tourist areas and others structures available to the public. The companies were sending out panicked messages to abandon all corporate buildings and data centers, whether threatened or not.

5:15 pm

"Nate, start entering charge codes for Apple and Twitter," said Newsome.
Nate Keeting started pecking away at his laptop. Explosions occurred at the data center owned by Twitter, essentially a building of computers and storage devices designed to handle processing needs of its business. Keeting typed in four more codes and explosions went off in four areas around Apple's spaceship-shaped campus in Cupertino, CA.

5:20 pm

Dynamite-packed devices planted by Abby Benton and Jim Damon detonated at headquarter building of Facebook and Google. While other bombs set off so far that day were only surface hits, these bombs were planted around support structures within the buildings, mostly on lower floors. As support structures collapsed, the weight of the upper floors brought down each lower floor one by one like a controlled demolition. Within ten minutes, both buildings were a complete pile of rubble.

6 pm

All RAPCA team members were packed up, checked out of their hotels, and driving to Las Vegas, NV.

*****

TERRORISTS STRIKE AGAIN: 3 KILLED IN SILICON VALLEY EXPLOSIONS. – Washington Post

First Claim of Responsibility: Terrorists Calling Themselves RAPCAs Strike Big Tech. – Los Angeles Times

Strategic Buildings Hit at Google, Facebook, Apple, and Twitter. – New York Times

RAPCAs: Terrorists Open Second Front in Their War Without Motive. – CNN

Connection to 7/31 Attacks? Two of Victims at Google and Facebook Supervised in News Divisions. – Reuters

FBI: Bomb Threats Called in Before Big Tech Attacks, Victims Likely Chosen for a Reason. – New York Post

"What'd we miss? Who was the third person killed?" said Aaron Newsome. He was addressing all the RAPCA members assembled together in an Excalibur hotel suite in Las Vegas.

"Not sure," said Damon. "Maybe some programmer that had his headphones on that worked on one of the floors I couldn't get to. I can't believe anyone could miss all those communications. Maybe it was someone who wanted to die."

"No, we're not going to ease our consciences by trying to dig up reasons to justify this screw-up," said Newsome. "We've now had a total of three innocents get killed by our attacks. It can't happen again. We've taken out 17 of our 20 primary targets. Our P3 target, Colin Bennett, looked impenetrable before we launched our operations, and he'll have even more security now, so we'll have to wait on him. Our P11 and P19 targets likely still don't know they're on our list. They may have a little more security than usual, though. We'll plan on hitting them next week at the Screen Actors Guild event. After that, we'll go public. Take some R&R this weekend. We'll get to work Monday."

Chapter 19

Patrick Adams sat shaking in his Virginia Beach hotel room after watching on CNN images of the Silicon Valley buildings collapsing. It brought back fresh memories of the explosion that had caused his own injuries. However, the bombs on 7/31 were small and focused. The ones used yesterday functioned similarly to controlled demolitions by construction companies.

The four tech companies hit were widely dispersed with many data centers and offsite backups, so the attacks would likely mean only short-term disruptions, and the RAPCAs targeted only a few people, so why go through all that much trouble? In his head, Adams had called the terrorists every murderous name in the book, but it was clear they weren't killing indiscriminately. With their sophistication, they easily could have killed thousands by now. Instead, they were targeting very specific people and going out of their way to avoid killing others. Who were these people? Nothing about them seem to fit the stereotypes of a terrorist that came to mind.

Adams researched the three people killed on Friday. One was a sales guy who didn't seem to have even a remote connection to the 7/31 attacks. A mistake maybe? The other two looked like they were obviously intended targets. Both not only managed major projects in news divisions but were instrumental in developing programming algorithms on story rankings. Several people killed on 7/31 were editors. Were the terrorists upset at what stories were covered or not covered?

RAPCAs? Probably an acronym, but what? Google search results weren't much help. *Regional Air Pollution Control Agency* made no sense. It had to be something the terrorists made up. Removal of American People that Control the Agenda? Maybe, but that probably wasn't it since no politicians had yet been targeted. *Revolution*

Against something maybe? Clearly the terrorists were launching some kind of war or revolution in their minds. Adams spent the next hour going through possible combinations of words to form acronyms. He circled one as a possibility—*Revolution Against Propaganda and Character Assassination*.

*****

Despite all the attention to the recent terror attacks, there was still a presidential election coming soon, so it was important to continue his other work. Adams hadn't found much in his research of Marie Martinez, ex-wife of the presidential candidate. Their marriage seemed to end amicably, and she never had been in the public eye until the day she did the MSNBC interview making all the accusations against her ex-husband. She was a high school graduate with two kids and jobs at Holiday Inn and McDonald's in Virginia Beach, VA. At least she *used to* have two jobs—a supervisor at McDonald's informed him she gave her two-week notice the day after her TV interview.

She had hung up on him when he tried to call her early, so Adams was hanging around the Holiday Inn lobby, waiting for her to finish her shift. He chatted with the hotel manager for over an hour. He was excited to talk with a *New York Times* reporter who was on the front lines of the 7/31 attacks. He learned that Marie had been in a state of near constant depression since the MSNBC interview. She had requested a decrease in hours to the minimum required to maintain health insurance. At the end of the year, she planned to move back home with her mother in Michigan and enroll in college.

Adams recognized her walking through the lobby as she folded her housekeeping uniform. "Hello, Ms. Martinez."

Marie was startled and let out a muffled breath. Was she scared? Her reaction was like a teenager in a horror movie when the killer came around a corner. "What? I got the message, I'm not going to say anything."

"Ms. Martinez, I'm Patrick Adams, the *Times* reporter that called you last night." He extended his hand for a handshake.

Marie ignored his hand and continued walking. "Oh. I'm not talking to the press anymore. I said what I needed to say."

"Please, Ms. Martinez. We're talking about potentially the next President of the United States. I just need ten minutes of your time."

"I stick by everything I said in my earlier interview."

"Ok, but I found some inconsistencies in your answers that I was hoping you could clear up."

"There are no inconsistencies. Everything in the interview was true," she said as she opened the door of a Toyota Camry Hybrid XLE.

Adams recognized the new-car smell. It started to connect in his mind--new car, quitting a job, tuition for school. "Did someone pay you to do that interview?"

Marie looked him in the eye, then turned her head down as she climbed into her car, "That's absurd."

"You wouldn't be the first. It appears likely several other women may have been paid to make accusations against your ex-husband."

"I'm telling the truth." She started shaking as a tear started to fall from her eye.

"Please tell me the real truth. We can stay off the record if you like. Is someone threatening you?"

"Mr. Adams, I have two kids. I'm a nobody. There's already been one accuser who 'committed suicide', and my ex may never work again due to the beatdown he received. Please just leave it alone." She started her car and sped off.

Adams was good at reading people, and this was an easy call. There was no doubt in his mind she had been both paid off and threatened. He had been a bit dismissive of the money trails in the flash drive documents tied to

Martinez accusers, but it was time to look further into the stories.

*****

Adams drove to Richmond, VA to visit two other Martinez accusers. He tried calling all the rest of the ones that had gone on record who he couldn't visit in person. The conversations were virtually the same. No one wanted to talk very long with him and said little other than terse confirmations of what they had already spoken in TV interviews. All the women seemed to show a hint of fear in their voices and actions.

His investigative reporter spidey senses told him he had stumbled upon a huge story with monster implications on the presidential election. He couldn't help wondering, why did it seem he was the only reporter investigating this? Certainly, the terrorist attacks consumed a lot of attention, but this was the biggest story before the 7/31 attacks. Was it because the terrorist flash drive documents had pointed a finger at the accusers? There seemed to be an organized effort in the media to say over and over the documents should be ignored because of their source. In his experience, when everyone was screaming not to look at source material, there was obviously something they didn't want you to see.

Adams looked down at his acronym decipher attempt, *Revolution Against Propaganda and Character Assassination*. Character Assassination—that is exactly what had happened to Brent Martinez the past month. It was almost as if the entire news media had spent the last month in a coordinated attempt to destroy his reputation and credibility. The sexual accusers were part of that effort.

He pulled up his laptop and started reviewing the notes on each victim, both his own and the ones on the flash drive. It was all starting to make sense. The journalists killed were either corrupt or terrible at their jobs. They were guilty of spreading loads of false and misleading *propaganda*. Many of them were focused only on discrediting or destroying the reputation of anyone who disagreed with them politically. Reverend Louis Holder was one of the worse *character assassination* specialists on the planet. The comedian that was killed, Steve Myers, destroyed reputations using distorted quotes and hate-filled ridicule. Google, Facebook, Twitter, Apple—they all had control over the flow of information through news apps and social media posts.

Fox News displayed the pictures of the three victims in the Silicon Valley attacks. He immediately recognized the face of Facebook's Jack Zimmer. He frantically skimmed through his images to find one in particular. There he was in a picture in a golf foursome with three other men, two of which were also killed by the terrorists—Democrat billionaire, Henry Keller; Political Action Committee coordinator, Bill Reines; and Media World head, Colin Bennett. "Holy shit," he said as he raised both hands to his head.

Adams didn't know much about Colin Bennett, but what he did know fit right into the theories he was building. Bennett had the reputation of being one of the dirtiest players in the political world. He was the man you called if you wanted to run a negative campaign against a political opponent. Could he be so low as to pay off all the women who had accused Martinez of sexual deviancy? He golfed with Henry Keller, so there was no question he could get financial backing to do it.

So far, his theories were a little thin. Other reporters may be tempted to run with what he had, but he wasn't most reporters. He needed to collect more facts. At the very least, he should warn other potential victims.

Who else was guilty of spreading false information on a large scale? One target immediately came to mind—Hollywood. No one would question that it had become a bastion of leftist politics. It came across clearly in movies and TV shows as well as virtually every celebrity awards show and interview. Many took very creative liberties to spread propaganda in their artistic work, which reached billions of people. Would some people from Hollywood be the next target of the RAPCAs? It was all still his own pure speculation.

Colin Bennett, on the other hand, had to be one of RAPCAs top remaining targets. He had a house just south of Arlington, VA, which was on the way home to New York. Adams decided to pay him a visit. He had to warn him.

*****

Patrick Adams pulled into a long driveway in front of a 6000-foot mansion. A 20-foot brick wall surrounded about ten acres of property that held the three-story house. Adams pulled up to an intercom to announce who he was to security personnel. Uninvited guests were normally turned away, but Colin Bennett made an exception for a prominent *New York Times* reporter. He needed new minions for his media network. To have one who was injured and almost killed by anti-media terrorists provided a golden opportunity. The iron fence parted, and Adams pulled his car into the guest parking lot.

As he stepped out of his car, two 6'3" blocks of muscle approached him wearing bullet-proof vests, with firearms clearly visible on their sides. One frisked him and ran a metal-detecting wand over his body. "Please open the trunk," said one of them. Adams did as he was asked. Two German shepherds lingered in the driveway, waiting for commands. One guard stood like a statue watching Adams while the other called one of the dogs. The shepherd sniffed inside and around the car before returning to his trainer. "Ok, you can go inside." He held the door open for Adams and followed him inside. "You can wait on the couch in his office there." The security guard waived him in but stayed right outside the office.

Almost 30 minutes passed before Colin Bennett walked into the room, "Hello, sorry for the wait. Mr. Adams, is it?" he said, extending his hand.

"Yes, thank you for meeting with me. I apologize for showing up here unannounced."

"No problem. I'm sure you wouldn't be here unless it was something important. Let me extend my deepest condolences to the friends and co-workers you lost on 7/31."

"Thanks. The same to you, since I hear you had some friends killed also," said Adams.

"Yes," said Bennett, "relationships with media people are critical in my business. Such a tragedy. So, what can I do for you today?"

"I've come because I believe your life is in danger."

"My life is always in danger, Mr. Adams. I'm one of the best political researchers in the game, and politicians don't like having their dirty secrets dug up, so I make a lot of enemies. It's the nature of the business."

"No, I'm talking about the RAPCA terrorists. I believe you may be their top enemy now that Backman and Keller are out of the picture."

"Based on what, those flash drives?"

"Not just that. I've done my own research, and it seems to confirm a lot of what was there."

"Come on, I've read your articles, Mr. Adams, you seem way too intelligent of a writer to fall for the conspiracy theories of a hierarchy of big-money donors, Media World, yada yada controlling all the media narratives. Sure, we do opposition research and pass it on sometimes, but journalists are free to publish what they like."

"I'm sure there are plenty in the media that remain neutral and fair," said Adams, "but it's clear a large portion of it has become corrupted, even at my own place of employment."

"There's absolutely no evidence to prove that. Those psychopaths that sent the flash drives interspersed a few irrelevant facts here and there with a boatload of bullshit. Again, you're too smart for this. If you dig deeper, you'll likely find many secondary sources are generated from fake news websites."

Adams tried to hold his tongue. He wasn't basing his research on fucking Wikipedia stories. Most of his important research came from primary sources, interviews, public records, and thoroughly authenticated secondary sources. Was Bennett spinning and dodging because Media World and Bennett, himself, were neck deep in the document hierarchy? "I found this picture of you, Keller, Reines, and Zimmer. Doesn't it worry you three of the people you golfed with are dead?"

"I haven't seen that picture before. Photoshop, I'm guessing."

"I found it in a *Times* article discussing a nonpartisan fact-check organization your group was helping to establish." Adams left out his opinion that it was highly unethical to call his organization *nonpartisan* when all the founding members were registered with one political party.

"Sorry, it doesn't ring a bell."

Obviously, Bennett planned to stonewall and deny any questions Adams asked. "Look, Mr. Bennett, you may be right, but in regard to the threat on your life, it doesn't matter what you or I believe. It only matters what the terrorists believe, and my research all points to you as the top remaining target on their list."

"Ok, why don't you give me all the information you've compiled, and I'll take a look."

"I have a copy with me now," said Adams.

"Great, I'll copy it to my Mac. And please stop calling me Mr. Bennett, it's Colin. How about a glass of wine? I believe I have the biggest private wine cellar on the Eastern seaboard."

Adams politely let Bennett give him a tour of not only his wine cellar but his entire mansion. Security was not only tight outside, it was tight throughout the inside. Every room in the house seem to have a locked door that required a keycard, thumb print, or retinal scan to open. Adjacent to the wine cellar was a large steel-encased room with a safe. It was possible the extensive security was to protect his considerable wealth, but more likely, Bennett was well aware that some very skilled killers were after him now.

*****

Bennett spent a few hours reviewing the material before connecting a conference call with Henry Keller, Jr. and a few of his top people at Media World. "It's worse than we thought. We're going to have to start a major scrubbing operation for paper trails and email communication. We also may need to prepare for a credibility attack operation on *New York Times* reporter, Patrick Adams."

Chapter 20

Cole Foreman and Aaron Newsome secured tickets to attend a special Screen Actors Guild event in Las Vegas. It was organized to give a lifetime achievement award to one of the next targets on the RAPCA hit list—a film producer named Gifford Moss. Moss was an avowed communist who regularly discussed in public why the United States was the most evil country on Earth. His films attacked every aspect of capitalism, and he'd developed several unauthorized biographic films of conservatives and Republicans. Since it was fiction, Moss cared little about portraying facts accurately, although he did splash in some verifiably-true information to confuse users into thinking all of the film was true. Libel laws protected him though since he was going after public figures.

A second RAPCA target, Odell Carter, also planned to be in attendance at the SAG event. Carter was a filmmaker who made movies in two primary areas. One was conspiracy theories, including a recent one that described how George W. Bush and the CIA engineered the 9/11 attacks. The second type was historical films about Communist governments, including ones with Fidel Castro, Joseph Stalin, Hugo Chavez, and Che Guevara. All were portrayed as misunderstood heroes.

"We have to be in and out of the hall inside of three minutes tops," said Newsome. "Everyone understand their assignments?"

All the team members nodded. "We've practiced this a hundred times. You are ready. After we've completed the mission, get to your hotel rooms and don't set foot outside them for two days at least. When you're ready, make your way to your designated airports. We'll meet back at headquarters in a week."

*****

Aaron Newsome prepared 20 USB flash drives, the same as he had done in the first mass mailing. Half the drives were reserved for media websites, with the remainder reserved for selected reporters they perceived to be fair-minded. The reporters were all different ones than those chosen in the first mailing. All the media websites that had published the full unaltered contents the first time were again included on Newsome's second list. Three websites refused to publish anything due to its source, and one—the Huffington Post—scrubbed the contents of all but right-leaning reporters and money men before publishing. These latter four organizations were replaced with new media websites.

Newsome updated the media & political diagrams to include connections with each of the Silicon Valley tech companies targeted in the last round of attacks. He created subfolders of files for Facebook, Google, Twitter, and Apple. Each folder contained document sets that detailed communications and relationships with political operatives. Times and dates were released of over 500 visits between top tech executives and high-ranking officials of the Barack Obama, Hillary Clinton, and Elizabeth Locklear administrations.

Two subfolders entitled *Google_Code* and *Facebook_Code* were loaded with programming code copied by Jim Damon, Nate Keeting, and Abby Benton which showed how algorithms altered search results to help leftist sources while hurting conservative and libertarian sources.

Newsome copied another subfolder on the flash drive titled *Brent_Martinez_Search_History*. It included the original unaltered Google search history, the altered one released to the public last month, and the differences.

Lastly, Newsome created subfolders for each of their primary targets killed in the last round of attacks, Jack Zimmer and Craig Whitman. Each one contained images, documents, emails, voice recordings, and videos showing their relationships with the media/political networks as well as their efforts to censor right-leaning sources. A notable inclusion was Abby Benton's voice recordings of Craig Whitman all but admitting to Google's unethical practices in regard to political information.

After completing the duplication of the 20 flash drives, Newsome stuffed them into padded envelops and added a printed description of the contents to each. He slipped the 20 envelops in a mailbox near Caesar's Palace on a walk between casinos. Tomorrow, after they completed the next phase of their operation, he would drop his most important document in the mail.

*****

"And it gives me great pleasure to introduce the man of the evening, a six-time Academy Award winning filmmaker, a man who has taught us so much, a man who has changed the world, Gifford Moss." The mostly-celebrity crowd of 1000 applauded to the introduction and rose to their feet.

As Moss took the stage, Aaron Newsome and Cole Foreman got up from their back-row seats and walked towards the corners of the hall. "T-15 seconds," said Newsome, speaking to the wire microphone strapped to his chest. Security guards were stationed at all four corners of the hall. Newsome and Foreman approached the ones in back by the hall entrances.

Scott Koonce, Jim Damon, Nate Keeting, and Darren Williams entered the hall through an unsecured employee entrance in the front by the stage. The guard by the front held his hand up to stop the four, but before he could say a word, Koonce stuck a needle into his neck that rendered him quickly unconscious. As the count reached 15 seconds, Williams set his Glock sights on Odell Carter, who was sitting in the second row. Williams pulled the trigger of the silenced pistol twice, hitting Carter once in the neck and once below the ear. The first hint of screams echoed from a few audience members who noticed what was going on.

Foreman approached his assigned guard in the corner and casually unloaded a vicious uppercut, following by an elbow strike to the back of the head. Newsome did the same to his guard. They both bolted the doors and start approaching the stage.

Scott Koonce fired canisters of tear gas into the middle of two empty aisles as Jim Damon hurled a flashbang grenade into the corner of the other guard. The blinding light and loud pop disoriented the 4th guard in the hall long enough for Nate Keeting to fire a rubber bullet into his chest.

Most of the audience was still on their feet applauding, oblivious to what was happening until the flashbang noise shocked their awareness. The award winner, Moss, dove behind one of the award presenters, obstructing the next shot Williams was planning to take. Williams sprinted for the stage. Moss hurled the female award presenter towards Williams and ran in the other direction. After stumbling over the woman, Williams fired a shot into the back of Moss. He took a few steps, then fired one more bullet into his head.

Screams rang out through the hall as people started gasping for air and running for exits. "We're at the 3-minute mark, get the hell out now," said Newsome. "Abby, if we're not in the van by the 5-minute mark, drive out of here. We'll blend into the crowd to escape if we have to."

Damon and Keeting each fired a rubber bullet into audience members that tried to rush at Williams. The six RAPCA members met back at the employee stage entrance and made their way to the exit. Kyle Topper entered codes into the RAPCA iPhone app, setting off explosions in trash dumpsters in areas on opposite sides of the building. As they left the building, they hopped into a van driven by Abby Benton.

"Look out, back left!" Most of the extra security rushing to the scene weren't sure which direction to run due to the dispersed explosions, but one spotted them and fired at the group. Jim Damon was knocked off his feet by a shot to his left side, landing hard on the cement. Williams returned fire, hitting the guard twice in the leg.

"Goddamnit, that hurts. He got the vest. Rib is broken, I think," said Damon.

Newsome lifted him into the van. "Abby, get us out of here."

Abby drove the van to an empty area between two buildings. All the RAPCAs jumped out of the van, removed their bullet-proof vests, face disguises, and a layer of clothing. They tossed the discarded clothing into the van, opened up several gallons of gasoline-filled milk containers, and ignited the van. As it burned, they all made their way into the nearest casino entrance. They blended into the crowd. Each took separate directions through the maze of casino walkways. The third round of attacks was complete.

*****

Terrorists Hit Vegas: 2 Killed, 10 Injured in Screen Actors Guild Attack. – Washington Post

Moviemakers Odell Carter and Gifford Moss Gunned Down in SAG Attack. – CNN

Editorial: RAPCAs No Different Than Al Qaeda, Hamas, ISIS Terrorists. – New York Times

FBI Releases Pictures of Six RAPCA Terror Suspects. – ABC

RAPCAs Send More Flash Drives Focused on Silicon Valley. – Washington Times

RAPCAs Claim Martinez Google Search History Altered. – Politico

Senators Push Bill to Make Publishing of Terrorist Material a Felony. – Huffington Post

Politically-Motivated Tampering of Search and News Rankings Seen as Motive in Big Tech Attacks. – New York Post.

No Motives Found in Cold-Blooded Killing of Movie Moguls. – MSNBC

Google and Facebook Programming Code on Flash Drives Appears Authentic. – Gizmodo

Dow, S&P Down Over 25 Percent Since 7/31 Attacks as Uncertainty of More Attacks Shake Market. – Wall Street Journal

"Shorting the market was a brilliant idea, Abby," said Jim Damon. "We've made almost 100 million bucks so far from the market tanking. That should keep us funded for quite a while."

"I hope you know what you're doing moving the money around. I guarantee you the FBI and Homeland will be looking for short-sellers and unusual financial activity. Al Qaeda made a fortune after the 9/11 terror attacks," said Abby.

"I'm not too worried. We used numbered accounts and several small purchases spread across many buyer identifications. Nothing ties back to our real names and all the accounts will soon be closed. Thanks for the pain killers, but maybe I should avoid them to keep my wits sharp," said Damon.

"No, take them. The pain from the broken rib may prevent you from breathing deeply, which can cause you to develop pneumonia. Keep taking the anti-inflammatories and icing it. We shouldn't be stuck in the hotels much longer. Captain Newsome just texted us that police have given up trying to snare anyone in a road block. We're suppose to skip going to any of the airports and drive back to Wisconsin."

"Great, I'm going to sleep for a week when we get home," said Damon.

"We can't get too comfortable. The heat is really going to be turned up in the next day or two. Captain Newsome just mailed the RAPCA Manifesto."

*****

"Are you out of your fucking mind?!" said the interim editor of the *New York Times.*

"I have a mountain of research to back up everything in this series of articles," replied Patrick Adams.

"I don't care if you have enough research to fill the Library of Congress, there's no way I'm going to justify, even glorify, the actions of the terrorists. How could you even think of doing something like that after all the death and destruction they've caused?"

"These will do no such thing. I've gone to independent sources to verify there is a far-reaching conspiracy to bring down Brent Martinez. These articles could stand on their own even without a shred of information from the terrorist flash drives."

"You're crazy."

"As a professional journalist, doesn't it bother you the massive layers of corruption and bias that have been exposed in the past few weeks?" said Adams. "I don't plan to even mention RAPCA in my articles or make any connections with the bastards. This is about our job as reporters to act as an unbiased check and balance on powerful people, and to expose truth, whether we like it or not."

"Are you still suffering the effects of your concussion, Patrick?" said the editor. "I can't believe someone as intelligent as you could fall for this bullshit. There is no conspiracy. And even if there was, it's preventing a racist, scumbag child molester from being elected president. Get the hell out of my office, and if I hear you spending one minute longer on this crap, you're out of job."

Adams shook his head as he walked out the door. He recognized the look on someone's face when there was nothing you could do to change their minds. Once certain people became set in their views, no amount of facts, logics, evidence, or persuasion would convince them otherwise.

As Adams walked out of the office, the editor dialed the number of Colin Bennett. "Yeah, I don't think he's going to let it drop."

Chapter 21

Fifty mailrooms at media organizations around the country opened a business-sized envelope with one printed document on the morning of August 26th.

THE RAPCA MANIFESTO

Freedom and democracy in America have never been more threatened than they are today. The founding fathers of the United States knew true democracy could not exist without the free flow of information and ideas. It was so important to them that they made the 1st Amendment to the Constitution include freedom of the press and freedom of speech. In a democracy, when information is allowed to flow unimpeded, good ideas eventually win out over bad ones. However, what happens to that democracy when the institutions most responsible for information dissemination become corrupted? Let's start with a history lesson.

The Soviet Union was once the greatest enemy of the United States. The two superpowers fought a Cold War for about a half a century. They fought proxy wars through other countries, spied on each other through the KGB and CIA, threatened each other with nuclear annihilation, and opposed each other in every facet of world events. It was a battle of ideology—capitalism/democracy vs. communism/central government control. The Soviet Union proved over time to be no match for the United States in military and economic might, as it dissolved in 1991 back into its original countries. This included its controlling country—Russia. Russia remained a major rival, if not enemy, of the United States ever since the dissolution of the Soviet Union.

While the United States was regarded to have largely won the Cold War, Russia inflicted tremendous damage on the U.S. in one regard—ideology & influence. Leaders of Russia such as Vladimir Lenin,

Joseph Stalin, and most recently Vladimir Putin wisely tried to attack the U.S. from within, using its democracy and freedom against itself. Much of these attacks started with a Soviet program called "Active Measures." This was a program where Russian security services used covert operations to influence the course of world events. In the United States, this consisted of burrowing into the centers of education, influence, and information dissemination. To be more specific— the U.S. press corps, universities & the public education system, and Hollywood. In later years, it expanded to labor unions, protest groups, socialist/communist political parties, and Silicon Valley. Every tool was used in the process—writings, speeches, intimidation, bribes, protests, and more. In many cases, Soviet agents made their way directly into positions of power at these centers of influence.

This was largely a successful effort. Hollywood, the U.S. press corps, and the education system were all very patriotic around the time of World War II. However, over the next half century, they all largely evolved into anti-American institutions that supported the tenets of strong central government control, socialism, and communism while opposing free enterprise. Over recent decades, the Internet and technology have made it easier for anti-American elements to expand their operations.

Joseph McCarthy recognized the turn to communism in the 1950s and tried to root out Soviet agents in Hollywood and the U.S. State Department, and he was partially successful, despite his vilification in the history books. Ronald Reagan, who was a Democrat for 40 years and once President of the Screen Actors Guild in Hollywood, also recognized the threat. He spoke out against communist elements throughout his presidency and wrote extensively in his autobiography about the expanding communist dominance in Hollywood. One example—great tragedies in history are often portrayed in Hollywood-produced movies. The Nazi regime was one of the worst in history, and hundreds of well-known movies have shown the world how terrible they were. However, Soviet Joseph Stalin and Chinese Mao Zedong also led horrific regimes that killed more of their own citizens than Hitler. Yet, it's difficult to think of a single Hollywood movie portraying their brutal dictatorships? Why?! The answer—Stalin and Mao were both communists. In modern times, Hollywood has become unapologetically dominated by leftist, anti-American, anti-capitalism politics. Movies that portray sins in U.S. history such as racism and slavery are released nearly every month. Corporations are portrayed as evil and heartless.

Schools which once emphasized patriotism and American ideals of freedom have turned into tools of anti-American, pro-socialism indoctrination. Textbooks downplay or even ignore positive contributions of America over the past two centuries while emphasizing every wrong. Economics textbooks push the advantages of socialist economies over capitalism but fail to note how virtually every socialist/communist nation has fell into dismal poverty while free capitalism nations live in relative prosperity.

Perhaps worst of all is what has happened to the U.S. press corps. Media news sources have had a liberal bias throughout history—the desire to change the world is what often drives students to the journalism profession in the first place. However, most American journalists historically tried to be fair and accurate while trying to bury their biases by covering both sides of the issues. In recent decades, that is no longer the case. People in American news media organizations have thrown out all basics of journalistic ethics to become outright advocates for their favored political party and their big-government, socialist, anti-American ideologies.

That brings us to the modern era. Super rich donors have developed ways to use these tools of influence to corrupt the flow of information and bring about the political power outcomes they desire. The

Internet and other modern technology enhances these tools.

Money from billionaire & corporate donors, the Democratic party, and the Republican party feed into a complex web of political organizations with innocuous sounding names like Center for American Progress, Media World, Media Matters, and Correct the Record. Often, they're supposedly set up to perform some noble charitable cause. But in reality, they're formed for no other reason than to elect their favored candidates by any means necessary. The number of organizations that feed into this big-money political network is endless—think tanks, lobbying firms, media bias watchdogs, research organizations, fact checkers, public relations firms, civil rights advocacy groups, and on and on. What is their main weapon of choice? CHARACTER ASSASSINATION!

It is no longer sufficient to try to persuade voters to your point of view, which is often a futile effort when a large majority of the American public firmly disagrees with your positions. No, the focus now is DESTROYING your political enemies. It starts with researching everything about an opponent—their writings, speeches, social media posts, interviews, emails, phone calls, recordings, texts, tax returns, donor lists, instant messages, Google searches, and on and on. Computer programs and paid staffers comb through every shred of your history to find any perceived political mistakes. With all the modern techniques of spying, is there really anything we do that remains private? Who among us would survive an orchestrated smear campaign if powerful interests could sift through every inch of our entire lives, especially when even innocent statements can be taken out of context to seem unsavory? What makes matters worse is that smears don't even have to be true. As Nazi propaganda minister, Joseph Goebbels, accurately stated, "A lie told once remains a lie, but a lie told a thousand times becomes the truth." And unfortunately, in the era of modern technology and 24-

hour cable news stations, a lie can be amplified and repeated millions of times in minutes.

Armed with lies and distorted facts, media organizations can destroy any person's character. They can turn them into anything that fits their objective—racist, sexist, heartless, dishonest, sociopathic, whatever they want. The hierarchy of well-funded media/political organizations aid in this effort. They feed well-crafted hit stories to bribed journalists or ones simply friendly to the cause. They feed jokes to comedy shows to add ridicule and further engrain a characterization of a person in the mind of the public. They bombard social media with the character attacks, making it almost impossible for a voter to avoid the negative information. The character assassinations not only destroy potentially good political leaders, they discourage potentially great ones from even running for office in the first place.

Much of the public has become aware of the corruption in the mainstream media sources, instead turning to newer media news sources on the web and in smart device apps—Google News, Facebook Trending, MSN News, Apple News, Google & Bing searches, Yahoo News, Twitter Trending, etc. Unfortunately, Big Tech is dominated by liberal leftists, which inevitably leads to some information sources being emphasized while alternatives are demoted in ranking or censored altogether. Seemingly noble goals of eliminating "hate speech" and "fake news" are being turned into weapons of censorship. Both these terms are subject to human interpretation. Instead of their original meaning, the terms are now applied to "anyone who disagrees with me politically."

So, if we have the education system, Hollywood, the mainstream media, comedy shows, and technology news sources all brainwashing Americans to one political ideology and censoring all others, how can a true democracy survive? The answer is that it can't, which is why RAPCA was founded.

We know many of you reading this won't agree with our methods, and we regret the innocent injuries and loss of life we've caused, but our actions were necessary to shake the propaganda foundations and reset the United States back on a course towards freedom and democracy. We've started our revolution by striking some of the most dishonest and corrupt individuals in the political/media landscape. Anyone who does a thorough, honest examination of the evidence we've presented will see quite clearly these people richly deserved the punishment we've inflicted. Warning: the media and people in power will do everything they can to prevent you from seeing this evidence!

We have several more individuals on our target list, with many more that are close to making our hit list in the future, but we have no desire for anymore destruction or loss of life. We know not everyone will change, but if you want to remain safe from us, you'll meet the following demands:

News Journalists

Cover both sides of controversial stories. *There are pros and cons to every controversial issue, otherwise it wouldn't be controversial! If you don't have time or expertise to fairly present both sides, at least provide a website or some other source where your audience can get more information.*

Stop the use of "anonymous sources" unless confirmed with sources that will go on record. *It is too easy to make up any lie or rumor if another party cannot verify it's true.*

Double-check every fact before reporting it in a story. *Once a story makes its way to the Internet, any lies or inaccuracies can be repeating endlessly until they become "facts" in the mind of the public. It doesn't matter if you retract or apologize for a mistake later since you can't take back all the amplifications.*

Stop engaging in "transactional journalism". In other words, stop trading a story favorable to a certain politician in return for some kind of benefit; for example, exclusivity, access, promises of future political positions, etc.

Cease using anecdotal evidence unless included with scientific evidence. When you use a personal story to advocate for an issue, you effectively are using a sample size of one, which equates to a statistic margin of error of close to 100 percent! In other words, your personal story may not reflect anything close to what is really happening in the larger population.

Describe any biases of organizations that provide research for a story. If a tobacco company releases a study on smoking or an oil company prepares research on environmental energy effects, there is obviously a conflict of interest. The same goes for research organizations or think tanks that are founded by members of one political party. It doesn't matter if they use "non-partisan" in their charter, if it was founded and is run by all liberal Democrats or all conservative Republicans, the research should NOT be presented as an unbiased, non-partisan study.

Provide full context to quotes, voice clips, and videos. Although speech must often be clipped for media time factors, if it portrays a completely different meaning than it would if played in full context, it should not be used.

Stop repeating lies and inaccuracies even if they come from a supposedly reputable source. Even the most honest and thorough sources of information make mistakes, and many once-reputable sources like CNN, the New York Times, and Washington Post have clearly become corrupted. If you use secondary sources for your stories, at least qualify them. For example, instead of saying, "it's a fact that..." or "it's been proven...", say "according to a story in the New York Times..."

Stop using political correctness as a weapon to suppress free speech. True racists, sexists, homophobes, etc. will be exposed by their actions. Nowadays, the media is too often using out-of-context misspeaks to blunt free expression and destroy the character of whomever they dislike.

Stop cherry-picking research and using it to definitively state a fact where alternative research proves otherwise. You can do a Google search to find research to prove or disprove virtually anything you want. Your stories should not say that "facts prove", "this is settled science", "all economists agree", etc. when plenty of alternative evidence proves otherwise. If you use research, qualify it, state its source, provide the information, and let the viewer or reader decide for themselves if it proves anything.

Cover scandals and corruption of politicians of all parties, not just the ones you oppose. In other words, there should be no double standards in coverage. Far too many scandals of the Barrack Obama, Hillary Clinton, and other administrations have been almost entirely ignored simply because the vast majority of the mainstream media supported them politically.

Cease personal attacks and character assassinations. The time has come to start focusing on a person's qualifications for political office and their positions on issues. Beyond that, the personal life of a candidate and his or her family should be off limits.

Big Tech Companies

Don't alter search or news ranks based on any political philosophy. The reputation and credibility of a source is for the reader to determine.

Stop censoring or demoting context based on supposed "hate" speech. Hate speech will always be subject to interpretation and has expanded in definition to "anyone who disagrees with me."

Stop censoring or demoting supposedly "fake news" content. Fact-checking organizations are often founded by one political party or have deep biases themselves, so once again, this has turned into a tool of censorship of "anyone who disagrees with me." Eventually, the public will learn likely sources of completely made-up news, and they will lose prominence on their own.

Protect our privacy and resist efforts to use our information for political purposes. Search histories, personal communication, and social media interactions should never be made available to external parties.

Hollywood

If you write movies about history or topics billed as a "true story", get the facts right. Realize that many Americans don't know their history, and when you change facts in a movie, it only perpetuates lies and myths.

Don't blacklist talented individuals because of their political views. Currently, it's completely understood in Hollywood that if you express any right-leaning views, you'll never work again in movies. We're against all censorship. Using threats to a person's livelihood to suppress their freedom of expression is something we will actively fight.

Comedy Shows

We don't have any specific demands for comedians other than to say they should follow the same standards we've set for journalists. Realize that a whole generation is getting their news and current events from comedy shows. So, if you make jokes about lies and personal attacks, you're only perpetuating the hatred and false information. Comedians are being used as another tool in the *orchestrated campaigns to destroy people's character.*

We realize that all our demands cannot be followed to perfection, but those that consistently chose to ignore these guidelines will eventually make our target list.

Some may wonder why we haven't targeted any politicians. We haven't added them yet because voters have the power of elections to remove them anytime, and we consider the lousy politicians we have in office a symptom of the problem, rather than the cause. If balanced, uncorrupted free speech and press rein in America, we have faith citizens will make better choices and pick people that deserve to be in power. Warning: in the future, any politicians who try to pass laws that suppress free expression in any way will be added to our target list!

For ordinary Americans reading this, we have some requests. Please realize how much our media has become corrupted. Question everything you hear or read. Realize that trending news stories are almost always initiated by orchestrated campaigns. Explore many sources of news and current events across the political spectrum, or you may never get every side of the story or even see certain stories.

As for journalists, movie-makers, politicians, big tech companies, comedians, and others responsible for controlling the flow of information, realize we are out there, waiting and watching. We can get to anyone, anytime, anywhere. You have no idea how many of us are out there. As we've proven by the documents we've released, we can see what is going on behind the scenes. We will institute a short cease fire to give you a chance to change your ways. If not, our Revolution Against Propaganda and Character Assassination will continue.

Chapter 22

Major News and TV Media Unite in Refusal to Publish RAPCA Terrorist "Manifesto." — New York Times

House and Senate Pass Bipartisan Terrorist Ideology Bill; Compels Prison and Heavy Fines for Publishing Terrorist Material; President Expected to Sign. — Washington Post

RAPCA Manifesto Reminiscent of Unabomber and Osama Bin Laden Ramblings. — MSNBC

Trust in News Media Falls to Record Lows. — Fox News

Comeback Kid: Brent Martinez Surges to 28 Percent, Locklear and Miller Tied at 35 Percent. —Rasmussen.

FBI Terror Investigation Stretched, Surpasses 25,000 Tips. — CNN

Shock Poll: 38 Percent Support Actions of RAPCA Terrorists. — DrudgeReport.com

"Will the Terrorist Ideology Bill hold up in court?" said Henry Keller, Jr., son of the deceased billionaire.

"Not a chance," said Colin Bennett. "It's a temporary band-aid. It will help stop the bleeding, long enough for the FBI or Homeland to catch the son-of-a-bitches. At least that is the thinking."

"You know we can't let that happen. Any progress on finding them?"

"I'm meeting with my NSA contact tonight. The blood found on the scene of David Backman's murder belongs to a former Navy SEAL, but until now he's been unable to get me a name. Luckily, the Department of Defense has been stalling the release of his classified information to the FBI, but I don't think they can hold off much longer, especially after this damn manifesto."

"Make sure you get everyone who this guy served with," said Keller, Jr. "We're dealing with a tight-knit unit of professionals, so I'm assuming guys he fought with are involved. Most of our friends in Congress want these RAPCAs taken out as much as we do, so we'll have a lot of resources at our disposal."

"I will get Dutch Marcello to help with the investigation. He's a little more *persuasive* in shaking people for information. He has connections with the Russian mob who can rent us some ex-Spetsnaz mercenaries if we need them," said Bennett, referring to the Russian special forces unit. "They're costly, but they're ruthless and effective."

"Money won't be an issue. We have to turn things around quickly. I'm going to organize some 'spontaneous protests' of any speakers or news organizations that give even a shred of coverage to the manifesto or other RAPCA documents. Get a hold of every one of your editorial contacts and browbeat them into following our fake news, terrorist-propaganda narrative. If any of them give you the slightest flak, let me know, and I will speak to them directly. I can make a lot of people's lives miserable, and they know it."

*****

"The shooter's name is Kyle Topper," said NSA Agent, Tim Gordon. "He's an ex-Navy SEAL, and one of the best snipers in the world. I've compiled a list of all the men he's served with, including a section showing fellow SEALs. There are three SEALs with whom he served that they haven't been able to track down. The one most noteworthy is Cole Foreman. He's supposedly a super-brainy scientist who can build virtually any kind of bomb. Topper was living in Dominican Republic, while Foreman was living in Panama.

Both of them disappeared around the same time, roughly six months ago."

"Motives?" said Bennett.

"Nothing specific that we've found, other than the fact almost all special forces guys hate the media and politicians."

"What else do you got?"

"I've copied the FBI and Homeland investigation documents for you, but it's an endless pit," said Gordon. "There are over 100,000 pages so far. They have more leads and tips than they know what to do with. Half the population has some physical characteristics in common with at least one of the suspects. And we know they keep altering their appearance. These terrorists are clearly professionals. They're very schooled in law enforcement and counter-intelligence techniques. They've planted all kinds of false leads which has sent the FBI on a ton of wild goose chases. We have no idea just how many of them there are, but they clearly have diverse backgrounds. Their tech guys are world class hackers. Homeland was convinced at first that Russian hackers were involved, but it now appears that was another false trail. By the way, the DoD isn't going to be able to keep the identity of Topper classified much longer. Some senators are pushing past remaining bureaucratic barriers. The FBI will know about him in a matter of days."

"Ok thanks, Tim. Your money will be transferred by midnight tonight. Let me know ASAP if they develop any firm suspects or move in for an arrest. And one more thing, as you know, Martinez is rising in the polls again. Get me something on him. I don't care what privacy laws you have to break. I need something sleazy to pin on him, preferably something on video that will take him out of the race once and for all."

*****

Patrick Adams knew he could possibly be committing career suicide. Even if by some miracle he kept his job at the *New York Times*, it was likely most of his co-workers would never speak to him again. He tried everything he could to get the *Times* editors and higher-ups to at least *look* at his evidence, but it was like talking to a brick wall. While documents from the RAPCA terrorists had at times pointed him in the right direction, he confirmed every fact he planned to present with public documents and separate incontrovertible sources.

Since his employer wouldn't publish his story, he shopped it around independently to virtually every prominent news and political source he could think of— CNN, MSNBC, ABC, CBS, NBC, *Politico*, *Time*, *Newsweek*, Associated Press, *Washington Post*, *Washington Times*, Huffington Post, *Newsmax*. The vast majority of mainstream media sources had justifiable hatred for RAPCA, and with such raw emotion, it was tough to separate his story on Brent Martinez from the terrorist documents. This was on top of the fact that many of these same media organizations were complicit in the conspiracy he wanted to expose. He got only one response to his query letters that came from someone with significant public exposure, and it was probably the last person he wanted to go to, Sean Hannity. The Fox News host was known as a far-right conservative, and he was quite possibly the most hated man in media by employees of CNN, the *New York Times*, *Washington Post*, and other liberal news outlets. And that was even *before* the 7/31 attacks.

Hannity, deservedly or not, had a reputation for exaggeration and running with stories before enough facts come out. Adams disagreed with Hannity on quite a few issues politically, but he knew that Hannity's credibility issues were largely engineered by a lot of the same perpetrators of the Martinez conspiracy. He felt had no choice if he wanted to do what was right. As he sat in the Fox News studios, he wondered how he would pay his rent, student loan, and car payments after this interview was over.

"Welcome everyone," said Hannity to the Fox News TV camera. "Today we have a special hour-long edition of Hannity where I'll be talking with *New York Times* columnist, Patrick Adams. Patrick witnessed the 7/31 attacks firsthand, and he has some shocking allegations. Welcome, Patrick."

"Thank you for having me," said Adams.

"First, can you tell us about your experience on 7/31."

"Well, it definitely had to be the worst day of my life. I had some hard deadlines on a couple stories, so I was one of the first to arrive at my office in the morning. I usually arrive first and make coffee most mornings, so it was a bit of a surprise to see a break room full of fresh donuts and snacks. I indulged a little and went to work. Shortly after that, I started getting nauseous. I developed a severe headache. I was dizzy, and I felt a huge knot in my gut. I thought I had some kind of bug, but then I saw some co-workers who seemed to have a sudden onset of the same symptoms. Anyway, from what I hear, the sickness got a lot worse, but I wasn't conscious to witness it."

"Sounds awful," said Hannity.

"One of my co-workers interrupted to inform me of a bunch of explosions that had gone off at the *Washington Post* headquarters. He read off some of the victims' names; they sounded very familiar to me. I knew at least a couple of them were close to my boss, Marilyn Kahn, may she rest in peace. On pure instinct I ran to her office to warn her, but it was too late, the IED went off killing her and knocking me into a wall. I ended up in the hospital for a few days with a severe concussion and a deep gash into my leg from the shrapnel. I don't remember anything for the next couple days after that. I woke up in a hospital bed and had to read about the rest of the carnage of that day."

"I'm very sorry. What a terrible thing to go through," said Hannity. "So, it's safe to say you don't have much love for the RAPCA terrorists."

"No, I hope they burn in hell," said Adams.

"So, what happened after you got out of the hospital?"

"Well, I was determined to track down the terrorists myself. At the very least, I wanted to track down the motives for picking the people to kill that they chose. I started my own investigation into the background of every victim—their work, their associates, their possible enemies, that sort of thing. I started to make a lot of connections. And then, I received one of the 20 flash drives that were sent out in the first RAPCA mailing set. I have no idea why they chose me. I contacted the FBI immediately and gave them the flash drive as well as all my own research that I compiled."

"Did you review all this flash drive information from the terrorists?" said Hannity.

"Yes, there was a lot of it, and I still have quite a bit more to review."

"What did you find?"

"Most of it seemed to fit right in with my own investigation. I proceeded with the assumption that everything from the terrorists was likely propaganda bullshit and not to be believed. It pains me to say this, but virtually everything I've reviewed from them checks out. Some of the information was clearly obtained by illegal methods, but almost everything can be verified with other credible sources."

"Wow, that's hard to believe," said Hannity.

"Yes. Look, I'm not here to discuss the RAPCAs. I don't want it to seem like I approve of what they did, or that their actions are justified *ever*. I'm not relying on any information they provided. They may have pointed me in the right direction, but I rely only on my own research."

"So, what are you trying to say?"

"I'm here to talk about what was the biggest story before the terrorist attacks, the upcoming presidential election," said Adams. "I have zero doubt in my mind that there is a high-profile criminal conspiracy to take down the candidacy of Brent Martinez. It includes some of the highest-ranking members of both the Republican and Democratic parties, billionaire donors, tech company executives, and various media/political organizations and personnel."

"Does it include members that were killed in the RAPCA attacks?" said Hannity.

"Yes, absolutely. It's unfortunate, and I, like most people, don't want to trample on their graves, but it's clear that some of the RAPCA targets were prominent members of this conspiracy."

"Are you saying the RAPCAs launched their attacks to help Brent Martinez?"

"No, definitely not," said Adams. "Few people even knew the name 'Brent Martinez' until a couple months ago. He wasn't even a blip in presidential polls. The attacks likely took months, probably years, of preparation. It's purely coincidental that these same people have been trying to bring down Martinez the past month or so."

"So, this was a conspiracy to do what exactly?" said Hannity.

"To destroy the character and candidacy of Brent Martinez," said Adams.

"You're saying these negative story lines on Martinez are engineered by this conspiracy?"

"Yes, a personal war has been launched against Martinez, and a well-funded one at that, and I wouldn't be doing my job as a journalist if I didn't say that almost all of the mainstream media has been complicit in the criminal conspiracy. Many media members have even been paid in cash to do hit pieces on Martinez. Some of the evidence is so obvious. It is completely shocking to me that arrests haven't been made, that more exposure hasn't been given to some blatantly guilty people."

"Does this conspiracy include people at the *New York Times*?"

"I know I'll probably lose my job for this and invoke a lot of hatred, but yes, it does."

"What about all the women that made various sexual accusations? Are they all part of the conspiracy? Did all of them make up their stories?" asked Hannity.

"I think I can prove that at least half of the original ten women who came forward were paid off. I'm not sure the proof would hold up in court, but there's no doubt in my mind, they were given large amounts of cash. I suspect the other five were also bribed, but I can't prove it. And now that they're getting heavily scrutinized, I believe they're being intimidated into maintaining their stories. Am I the only one that thinks it's suspicious that one of the shakiest Martinez accusers suddenly 'commits suicide' *immediately after* financial evidence comes out against these women?"

"Wow, you realize how crazy all this sounds?"

"I know, and I'm so frustrated that it seems no one in the media wants to investigate this. I have hundreds of documents and files to back all the allegations I'm making, and I want to stress that these did *not* come from the RAPCA terrorists? I just want authorities and people watching this to *look* at my information," said Adams.

"Incredible, shocking story if true. Do you think this is as bad as how the Establishment powers came after Donald Trump?"

"Oh, it's worse. Trump made enemies of powerful people in both the Democratic and Republican parties, but eventually most of the Republican bigwigs realized they were stuck with Trump and switched to helping him. With Martinez, you have the full weight of both major political parties lined up against him, and they'll never relent."

"Amazing. We'll be back with more on this Martinez conspiracy," said Hannity.

Through the rest of the hour-long show, Adams walked through the proof he had against the donors, tech companies, media organizations, Martinez sexual accusers, and the rest of who he thought were part of the conspiracy.

It became the highest rated cable news show of the year. Clips from the show would be replayed on YouTube, Facebook, and Twitter over 30 million times.

*****

Colin Bennett took a flash poll the day after the Hannity interview with Adams aired, and it gave him the bad news he expected. Over 80 percent of people that viewed it found Adams credible, and Martinez had moved into a statistical dead heat with Locklear and Miller in the presidential poll. Time was of the essence if he was to avert disaster. The key was to make sure as few people as possible saw the interview. He fired off a memo to his top assistants and media contacts:

Greetings, everyone. By now I'm sure you've all watched the Hannity interview with Patrick Adams and read the so-called RAPCA Manifesto. Last time I emailed you I told you not to panic. This time I'm telling you it IS time to panic. We have to get ahead of these stories immediately.

Get on the talk shows, write articles, make speeches, post on social media, email your friends. We have to dominate the media narrative so the terrorists don't garner sympathy and the conspiracy theories die a quick death. According to our internal polling, Brent Martinez is now in a statistic tie with Locklear and Miller. Taking him down is still our primary objective. If he stays relevant in the election up to November, the conspiracy storyline may never disappear.

With all this in mind, here is our attack strategy:

1. Compare the Martinez conspiracy theory to other outrageous theories from history—Apollo fake moon landing, Area 51 aliens, George W. Bush rigging the World Trade Center to explode, whatever. Use your imagination.

2.	Attack the credibility of Patrick Adams. Find any inaccuracies you can in past writings and portray him as a conspiracy nutball.

3.	Use the term "fake news" in EVERY single interview or article. Plant it indelibly in people's minds that Adams is relying on planted fake information, including info from the RAPCA terrorists.

4.	Ramp up credibility attacks on Fox News, especially on Sean Hannity. Use any mistakes you can find, even if you have to retread old stories.

5.	Rekindle the Martinez sexual pervert stories. Remind people what he is and dig up new stories to make people believe the women again.

6.	Tie Martinez to the terrorists as much as possible. Imply that they are working to help him, and strongly suggest he may even be leading the RAPCAs.

7.	Deny, deny, deny! Don't admit to a single conspiracy accusation. If necessary, keep changing the subject. Remind people of the terrorist murders and all the innocent people injured. Point out the precarious position this nation is in, and how we can't risk our safety on a racist, cruel child molester like Martinez.

We've dealt with crises like this in the past. We've got through them then, and we will do so again.

--Colin

*****

"This is a fucking disaster, Bennett!" said Henry Keller, Jr. into his phone. "Martinez is surging in the polls, and the conspiracy storyline is gaining fast on social media. You better up your game damn quick!"

"I know, sir, and we have a plan to get everything back on track," said Bennett.

"The other donors want to scrap Media World and most of the other top organizations and reconfigure our hierarchy. At the very least, we will likely need to rename them. The Media World brand name is screwed."

"Whoa, let's not overreact here."

"Overreact?! Martinez is leading in the polls, our media network is crumbling, and we have who knows how many psycho terrorists blowing the hell out of everything! Martinez represents everything my father and I have fought our whole life to oppose. He could blow up Establishment power across Washington. He's a damn libertarian who believes the ignoramuses of the American public are smart enough to make their own decisions. The country and the world depend on having a well-educated elite to save the 90 percent of people too stupid to manage their own lives. We've seen through history the chaos that is caused when there isn't a strong central government to hold things together."

"Yes, I agree, but—."

"Our agreement stands. One million dollars if you get Martinez below 15 percent before the debates and $500,000 per terrorist you help me track down. But if you fail and Martinez goes on to become president, I'm pulling every cent of my funding."

Chapter 23

NYT Reporter Patrick Adams Joins Ranks of Most Idiotic Conspiracy Theorists. — Washington Post

Wisconsin Professor: Patrick Adams Plagiarized Part of College Term Paper in 2001. – Huffington Post

Is Brent Martinez a Member or Simply a Benefactor of RAPCA Terrorist Murders? – MSNBC

Twitter, Facebook Groups Mobilize to Boycott Hannity Advertisers. – Yahoo News

Adams, Hannity Giving Aid and Comfort to the Enemy. – CBS

Patrick Adams Has History of Inaccuracies in Articles. – Politico

Mainstream Media Reporters Resigning in Droves. – Time

Seventeen-Year-Old Campaign Volunteer Accuses Martinez of Inappropriate Flirting. – ABC

Two Senators Confirm Martinez Said in Meeting, "Accusers Should Thank Me for Teaching These Inexperienced Girls About Sex". – CNN

Former Martinez Campaign Manager: "Martinez Wanted to Recruit More High School Girls for Volunteer Staff." – Salon

Injunction Sought to Force Shutdown of DrudgeReport.com Website in First Challenge to Terrorist Ideology Bill. – Fox News

Patrick Adams shook his head as he scanned headlines during his breakfast. He expected some pushback, but did *anything* he said in his TV interview get through? He didn't even take a class from the professor that accused him of so-called plagiarism. And the supposed "inaccuracies in articles" from the Politico story cited very few examples, and the ones they did were more about opinions than facts. Clearly, they just wanted a good headline to hit him with. Adams wasn't surprised in the least by the rekindling of the anti-Martinez media campaign. Some powerful people were definitely rattled.

Adams looked through his iPhone voice mailbox, which was now full. Almost all the calls were either threats or expressions of hatred for "supporting the terrorists." *Thank you, CNN, for publishing my cell number on national TV*, thought Adams. His physical mailbox wasn't much better. One envelope that stood out was from the IRS, a notice of audit of his last five years of income. He had $30 in his bank account, didn't have a business, didn't own any real estate, and had claimed the standard deduction the past five years. What in the hell could they possibly be looking to audit? Another intimidation tactic, perhaps?

Adams left his apartment out the back window. Judging by his mail, a lot of nuts knew his home address. He walked to his car and started his drive to work. As he drove, he flipped through his satellite radio news stations.

"How can a third of the country possibly be supporting a subhuman like Brent Martinez?" said the MSNBC commentator. *"The attention given to the terror attacks has made too many people forget just what a racist, greedy, dishonest pervert he is."*

"Martinez treats young girls as his sexual play things," said the CNN commentator. *"Too many Americans are falling for the fake news stories of women being paid off. There is overwhelming*

evidence to prove he's the worst sexual predator we've ever had run for office."

"I'm very disappointed that my colleague, Sean Hannity, would give a platform to fake news conspiracies coming from terrorists and a junior reporter with a history of plagiarism and inaccurate stories," said the Fox News news anchor.

"It's way too convenient, this relationship between the RAPCAs, Patrick Adams, and Brent Martinez," said the CNN Headline News commentator. "I sincerely believe Adams and Martinez are the public face of a terrorist organization in which they themselves are members."

"If you go through Brent Martinez speeches the last couple years, they're often word-for-word the same kind of things you find in the RACPA Manifesto," said the Bloomberg Radio host.

The expression on the face of Adams went back and forth between eye rolls, incredulity, and the curling of anger. Had he risked his whole career for nothing? Did he make matters worse?

As he drove onto the parking ramp for work, he noticed a crowd of hundreds of demonstrators. As he walked towards the building entrance, he noticed some of the signs. *Fire Patrick Adams! Stop Enabling Sexual Predators! Patrick Adams is Fake News! Patrick Adams is Accessory to Terrorism!*

He started to walk faster towards the door when a protestor yelled, "There he is!"

Protestors started yelling and screaming from all directions. Some pushed him. Some spit on him. He recognized the sister of his former boss, Marilyn Kahn. "How could you dishonor my sister's memory? You're an awful human being," she said as tears fell from her eyes.

Security stopped the demonstrators from entering the building. As he walked through the security checkpoints and up to his floor, he noticed a coldness in his fellow employees he'd never experienced before. There was none of the "hi" or "how are you" greetings. In fact, few people would even look at him. Those who did had a look of disgust. Even an administrative assistant who had flirted with him almost daily since he started there turned her head and walked on without saying a word.

When he arrived at his desk, he noticed all his stuff was boxed up, and two security guards were ready to escort him from the building. It wasn't all that surprising, but a small part of him held out hope that his bosses and co-workers would at least have enough journalistic ethics and curiosity to *look* at the evidence he'd put together.

Security thankfully was courteous enough to escort him back to his car. If not, he doubted he would have made it back in one piece. Even with security walling him off from protestors, he still managed to get spit on, doused with beer, and hit with a few tomatoes and pebbles.

As he drove away, he looked at the *New York Times* sign with a deep sense of loss. It was once his dream job. He had developed what he thought were close personal relationships with some of his co-workers. He thought of a famous quote that never seemed more appropriate to him than now, *"It takes a great deal of bravery to stand up to your enemies, but a great deal more to stand up to your friends."*

*****

Adams tried browsing his Sirius news stations again on the drive home, but he couldn't stand to listen to them for very long. Every station had the same two general themes—Brent Martinez is evil, and Patrick Adams is a nut. Didn't anyone think for themselves in American journalism anymore? Couldn't the media look past their abject hatred for Martinez long enough to see something obviously wasn't right? Most of the evidence Adams put together on the Martinez conspiracy was relatively easy to re-construct for anyone with the slightest bit of journalistic motivation. Why did he seem to be the only one willing to dig into the story? And despite how much he hated the source, the RAPCA-provided information was rock-solid accurate so far in his investigation.

How could people possibly believe he was working with the RAPCAs? That's what bothered Adams the most. While he reluctantly admitted they made some good points in their manifesto, he absolutely couldn't endorse their methods. Their violence made them no better than the corrupt people they were attacking.

Adams suddenly heard sirens and noticed flashing lights in his rear-view mirror. He pulled to the side. Two fire trucks and an ambulance sped by him in a fairly big hurry. He saw large billows of black smoke in the direction they were heading. The realization hit him. No. It couldn't possibly be. As he drove closer, he soon confirmed his own apartment building was engulfed in flames. His badly-burnt neighbor was being put on a gurney and loaded onto the ambulance as his ash-covered golden retriever limped to try to stay with his owner.

"What in the hell happened?" he asked a police officer.

"They're not sure, maybe a bad gas line or something," said the officer. "Whatever it was, it spread quickly. At least half the building appears to be on fire."

Gas line my ass, thought Adams. "Is everyone safe?"

"All the tenants are accounted for except for the #4 tenant, Patrick Adams."

"That's me. Let me guess, my apartment was one of the ones totaled?"

"I'm sorry, but yes. Do you have information on how this started?"

"No, but I can tell you there's very little chance this was an accident."

Adams spent the next hour reviewing his suspicions with the police. When he finished, fire fighters confirmed what he already knew, the fire started in his apartment. In a way, it was a relief. He wouldn't have to pay the rest of his lease, and after what he'd been through at work plus the threats he received by mail and phone, he didn't feel safe there. Other than his clothes, laptop, and team-autographed Packers Superbowl helmet, there wasn't much in there that he cared to preserve. He'd made redundant cloud backups of his research in Dropbox, OneDrive and Google Drive, so that could easily be reconstructed. He would likely push his credit cards to the max to get back on his feet, but he'd probably be ok.

Adams was feeling sorry for himself the entire drive home, and he certainly had more reason to do so now, but he felt something different now. It was anger. It was determination. If he couldn't get his fellow journalists to listen to him, he'd have to go directly to the people. He picked up a cheap laptop, a change of clothes, and some food at Target on his way to a Holiday Inn. He immediately got to work on his own website and blog. It would take him a few days to get all his research organized and made available to the public. Then, he would just need to find a way to somehow spread the word.

*****

Adams used a canned, pre-made website developer tool he found on Google to quickly get something up on his new site PatrickAdams.org. It wasn't fancy, but it was organized and easy to navigate. It was difficult to draw traffic to a new site, so he was hoping to go on Hannity one more time to provide a follow-up to his interview and mention the website. Sean Hannity was clearly interested after he heard of the fire at Adams's apartment and his termination from the *New York Times*. However, Hannity was receiving a lot of blowback from the interview. Fox News was getting bombarded with hate mail and protests.

Also, many high-profile companies had pulled their advertisements from Hannity's show with several more threatening to do the same. The higher-ups at Fox News put the kibosh on any more stories with Adams.

Adams was at least heartened to hear all the positive praise coming from people he knew outside the political & journalism communities. Friends and relatives from back home were emailing and texting their support. Fellow gym goers at his health club frequently came up to complement his work. Maybe it was possible to get his site off the ground using social media and good old-fashioned word of mouth. Several dozen people had unfriended him on Facebook, but he was getting several new friend requests daily, mostly from people he didn't know. He had barely used his Twitter account before the interview, but he had gained over 10,000 followers since the Hannity interview.

Google Analytics showed he was getting a few thousand hits on his website daily. It was a start but wasn't going to make any real impact. Maybe he was kidding himself. The media's labeling him repeatedly as a "conspiracy theorist" had killed much of his credibility. It would take something big to get the country's attention.

*****

"This is *not* the reaction I expected to get from our manifesto," said Aaron Newsome. The entire RAPCA team sat in the large TV and laptop-packed living room of their training headquarters in northern Wisconsin.

"It's not as bad as you think," said Nate Keeting. "The opinion polls we've analyzed show the country overwhelmingly support our message, if not our methods."

"Maybe, but the headlines and cable news coverage are mostly still the same shit," said Newsome. "They're using the same methods of distortion and character attacks. Now, they're going after the credibility of good reporters who give honest, balanced coverage to anything related to us, Martinez, and the people we've exposed."

"I told you that we didn't go big enough. You know there's more we can do," said Abby Benton.

"C'mon, don't start again, Abby. We have to be smart with the risks we take," said Newsome.

"Abby is right about one thing," said Cole Foreman. "The corruption and bias run way too deep in the big traditional media centers to think we can create real change by taking out a few of the worst offenders here and there. In fact, we may have made matters worse, as a lot of the fair-minded journalists that were already the minority at these places are resigning, or more likely being fired for not playing along with the distorted one-sided coverage."

"It's hard to change any of these places because the problems go way beyond bias and corruption," said Keeting. "It's the culture. One of the most powerful techniques of brainwashing is peer pressure. If all the people around you think one way, it's very difficult for someone who thinks differently to speak up. Everyone wants to be liked by their friends and co-workers, so they subconsciously keep unpopular views to themselves. In many cases, when everyone else thinks differently than you, you start to question your own beliefs. If everyone else believes so-and-so, then maybe I'm wrong? In big-city news centers like in New York and Washington, almost all the journalists are liberal and socialist-leaning. They all visit the same leftist websites and watch the same liberal news programs. On social media, they share with each other the same one-sided jokes, memes, and political stories. Their co-workers and friends all reinforce their existing opinions. To put it another way, they live in a bubble. They can't see the world that exists outside of it. It was the same way when I worked at Facebook. Most workers in Silicon Valley are disciples of Steve Jobs, who was very leftist and counterculture in his views and lifestyle. What makes matters so much worse is the way they've successfully attacked alternative-thinking conservatives and libertarians, who are portrayed as stupid, cruel, racist, etc. Fox News, Drudge Report, Rush Limbaugh, etc. are all portrayed as fake-news crazies. It's why most big-city journalists, and really almost half the country, continue to live inside a bubble."

"So, what do we do about it?" said Newsome.

"I think we're on the right track," said Foreman. "At the very least reporters will be a hesitant to make up stuff and take bribes to provide one-sided stories. Many of them will likely retreat to the olden days when they were simply *biased* reporters, not one-sided unapologetic advocates of a political party."

"We have to do more to get the attention of the people," said Abby. "The manifesto and evidence we provided are great, but if most of the population doesn't see them, then they're useless. We need to do something they can't ignore. Something that can't be buried by the press."

"What do you suggest?" said Newsome.

"A TV interview—let's speak directly to the people." said Abby.

"I like the idea, but that might be a little difficult to arrange," said Newsome. "We can't just book a spot on *60 Minutes*. I doubt we can find any prominent outlet that wouldn't go directly to the FBI to set up a sting."

"Plus, the piece-of-shit producers at most TV news stations regularly clip and edit the interviews to the point they have a completely different meaning on air," said Foreman.

"I agree, I don't trust them," said Keeting. "What if we just publish some kind of video statement?"

"I doubt that will accomplish much," said Newsome. "They'll only portray that as more 'terrorist propaganda' and find a way to bury it. Plus, it won't draw the same public interest as an interview. If it's a contentious interview with someone the public recognizes, it would get national attention."

"So, we just need a fair and honest journalist, who will run the whole unedited interview, who won't set us up, and who has been in the public eye," said Foreman. "Sure, no problem. Maybe we can fly one in on a unicorn."

"I think I know someone," said Abby.

Chapter 24

Colin Bennett was getting frustrated with his attempts to track down the RAPCAs. Former Navy SEALs Cole Foreman and Kyle Topper were clearly part of the terrorist team, but he couldn't find any direct motive or ties to the targets they hit. He investigated the men they served with Iraq and Afghanistan, but they were dead ends. There had to be another connection. There was a woman involved. There were tech experts involved. But most of all, there was a leadership element, someone with motive to organize the terrorist group.

"How are you, Colin?" said Dutch Marcello as he shook the hand of Bennett.

"I've been better, Dutch. Thank you so much for your work with the women. I may need you to approach one more, just to keep the story on Martinez in the public psyche."

"Not a problem. We completed our investigation of Topper and Foreman. Kyle Topper was a loner growing up. He had few friends, no siblings. He didn't compete in any sports despite his superior athletic ability. He has never been married. He joined the military right out of high school and has been on the front lines most of his life. As you know, he is one of the best snipers in the world and has been on several classified missions. We could dig deeper, but I don't get the sense they're going to lead to anything relevant to you. He retired from military service five years ago and has been living in the Dominican Republic ever since, at least until six months ago. I'll email you everything we found on him."

"How hard would it be to dig into the classified missions?"

"Very. We don't have the CIA connections that we used to. But for the right price, anything can be had," said Marcello.

"We'll table that for now. What do you have on Foreman?" said Bennett.

"Foreman is the more interesting case. He had a 4.0 GPA in high school and was first-team all-state linebacker on his football team. He earned a degree in electrical engineering at University of Wisconsin in Madison before joining the Navy. He went on to become a SEAL and fought in Afghanistan almost immediately after 9/11. While serving in the military the next 15 years, he earned a master's degree in physics and became known as one of best demolitions experts in the world. Later in Iraq, Foreman and Topper were part of a SEAL team that was ambushed during a mission in Mosul. Apparently, some politician couldn't keep his mouth shut around some *New York Times* reporter, and that reporter published just enough information to blow their cover. Six SEALs were killed in the mission. Foreman was furious. He later saw the reporter at an event honoring the troops and went after him. If he hadn't been restrained, the reporter likely would have ended up in the hospital or worse."

"Interesting," said Bennett. "It seems to at least give him motivation for joining RAPCA, but it doesn't seem enough for him to organize a whole apparatus to go after the big-money donors and such."

"Right, but here's where it gets interesting. We talked with a lot of Foreman's relatives and high school friends. The quarterback on Foreman's football team was a guy named Aaron Newsome. Apparently, Newsome and Foreman were best friends all through childhood and high school. Newsome later joined the Marines and had quite a distinguished military career himself. Newsome was married to a TV anchor who ran for the U.S. Senate."

"Dana Newsome?" said Bennett.

"Yes, exactly. If you remember, you and all your buddies in the media did a total hit job on her until she pulled out of the race. Then, of course, she blew her own brains out. Aaron Newsome is your guy. If I was in his position, I'd want some major payback, I can tell you that," said Marcello.

"You're definitely on to something, Dutch. I'm guessing they're way off the grid, so we won't be able to track them down by their real names, but let's try anyway. Can you also have one of your investigators get me a list of anyone close to Newsome. Relatives, friends, co-workers, anything. I'll cross reference those names with all the terrorist targets in our media database. Something tells me members of the RACPAs have some close personal ties to each other, and they all have some motive for joining."

"You don't have a lot of time if you want to get to these people before the FBI. It didn't take much for us to make the connection to Newsome once we had the names of Topper and Foreman, so as soon as that blood evidence on Topper makes it past the bureaucratic hurdles, the FBI will be hot on their trail, maybe within hours," said Marcello.

"We'll track them down. These RAPCA terrorists are well-trained and particularly dangerous. Are you sure these ex-Spetsnaz special forces guys from the Russian mob are good enough to handle the take-down?"

"With the element of surprise, I have no doubt. These guys are battle-heartened. Some of them went hand-to-hand with ISIS in Syria. They're equivalent in training to American Navy SEALs or Deltas, but for what you need them to do, these guys are better for one simple reason. The Americans have morals, these Spetsnaz fighters do not. They will ruthlessly get the job done, regardless of who or what gets in the way. No remorse. No conscience. No regrets."

*****

Maybe it was time for Patrick Adams to move back home to Wisconsin. He was single with no real friends in the area. Job prospects were dim. He was now an outcast in the New York journalistic community. He didn't have the funds to stay around the city much longer. He could maintain his new website from anywhere. So, what was keeping him here? He couldn't say exactly. There was more to be solved, more to be investigated—the RAPCAs, the 7/31 attacks, the Martinez conspiracy, the Media World network, the new rich donors that seemed to step in to fill the funding gaps left by the assassinations of Henry Keller and David Backman, so many more questions. He could easily write a book with the research he'd accumulated, but who would care to read it?

The thoughts swirled through his head as he walked into his hotel room after completing a 5-mile run. He wiped the sweat off his face and chugged a bottle of Gatorade. Something seemed out of place in his hotel room. He started to turn his head when a hand appeared in front of his face and clasped him over the mouth. He felt the injection sting of needle being inserted into his neck before he completely blacked out.

*****

Adams woke up two hours later in what appeared to be some kind of empty storage shed. His hands and feet were duct-taped to a chair.

"Hello," he heard a man say through a voice-altering device. The man wore a baseball cap and sunglasses, with his face covered in camouflage paint. He opened a folder and started reading. "Mr. Patrick Adams. Originally from La Crosse, Wisconsin. Graduated from UW-Whitewater with a double major, computer science and journalism, minor in library science. Worked 12 years as a reporter for the *Wisconsin State Journal* before breaking the biggest corruption scandals in Wisconsin history, taking down eight Republican state senators and two Democratic ones in the process. Worked less than a year for the *New York Times* before being injured in the 7/31 terror attacks. Investigated a conspiracy to bring down the candidacy of Brent Martinez before pitching the theory on Fox News, after which you were summarily fired from the *Times*. Your apartment was burned down, and now you're living at an Extended Stay hotel, trying to start up a blog website since none of the big-media organizations will give you the time of day."

"Great, you know my history," said Adams. "I'm guessing you're here to intimidate me to burying my story on Martinez. Forget it, you might as well kill me now. I don't have much to live for as it is. In fact, my death would probably bring more attention to the conspiracy, so go ahead."

"Mr. Adams, can I call you Patrick?" said Aaron Newsome in an altered voice. "I'm not here to intimidate you or hurt you. We've already hurt you once, unintentionally so, but we don't intend to do it again."

"What does that mean? Are you supposed to be one of the RAPCA terrorists?"

"Did you ever wonder why you were one of the reporters we chose to mail a flash drive?" said Newsome.

"Holy shit," said Adams. "Is this for real?"

"We screened over 2000 writers, editors, reporters, news anchors, bloggers, and other media personnel. Mostly, it was to find the worst offenders to add to our target list. We wanted to put together the most dishonest, corrupt, and immoral journalists in the country. However, during our research, we came across a small subset of people that still practiced real journalism. Who investigated all perspectives of various issues; who double-checked facts and only used impeccable sources; who had the courage to investigate scandals even in politicians they supported. Who would speak truth, even when it was unpopular with the people closest to him. You're part of a dying breed in America, Patrick."

"Flattery isn't going to change my opinion of you. Your methods disgust me. You almost killed me, and you did kill and injure many people I called friends," said Adams.

"It doesn't sound like they remained your friends very long. We hear it got pretty ugly after the Hannity interview.

Supposedly objective journalists abandon you the minute you say something they don't like? Doesn't sound to me like they were real friends," said Newsome.

"That's beside the point. The *Times* abandoned all objective journalism years before I started. I didn't realize how badly until I worked for them. While I agree with you about the state of the media nowadays, you're never going to get me to support murder as the answer. Why do you have me here anyway?"

"We want you to do a TV interview with us."

"What? You're fucking crazy. I'm not going to evoke sympathy for you or spread your message of hate," said Adams.

"The bias and corruption run too deep at the big news outlets. Deep down you know our message isn't about hate, but about restoring the free flow of ideas in this country, and that message isn't getting through the censorship barriers. As you yourself have discovered, it's easy for powerful interests to censor and bury certain evidence. I'm guessing over two-thirds of the country hasn't seen a word of the documented evidence we released, and probably over a half haven't seen our manifesto. An interview, on the other hand, will be tough to ignore. It will be difficult to bury."

"Forget it. Find someone else. Or just read whatever you want in a statement," said Adams.

"A simple verbal statement will play in the court of public opinion like an Al Qaeda tape release. It won't have the same impact as a back and forth interview. You can ask whatever you want in this interview. It can be as contentious as you like. The only thing I won't answer are questions that compromise our identity or future plans. Look, we want someone honest and objective. We have no desire to continue the violence. We're trying to correct societal wrongs. If we can do that without hurting another person, we'll do it," said Newsome.

"I can ask anything I want?" said Adams.

"Yes. One non-negotiable condition to this interview. It must be played in its entirety with zero editing and released on the web in its original format. Violation of this condition will immediately put you on our target list," said Newsome.

Adams felt his first chill of fear since he awoke in the chair. "And if I say no?"

"If you say no, we'll return you to your hotel unharmed and never bother you again," said Newsome. "This interview is going to happen. If not with you, then some other reporter with courage."

A part of Adams wanted to scream an expletive-filled refusal, but the unattached investigative reporter inside him said this was the story of a lifetime. At the very least, he may be able to bring real attention to the research he'd accumulated on the Martinez conspiracy. "Give me an hour to prepare questions."

*****

"Hello, I'm Patrick Adams, former *New York Times* columnist," Adams said to the camera. "I'm here today to have a conversation with the leader of the terrorist group known as RAPCA. As a member of the media, I can't say it's a pleasure to talk to you."

"That's understandable," said Aaron Newsome. His face was still painted in camouflage. He sat in a chair situated in a darkened part of the storage shed. He spoke through a voice-altering device.

"First, of all, who is RAPCA, and why did you form?" said Adams.

"RAPCA in an organization that was formed to correct a lot of societal wrongs. We have a bitterly divided country governed by a useless group of politicians obsessed only with gaining and holding power. The U.S. government grows bigger every year, eroding our personal freedom and running up a national debt that will soon get so high we'll have to spend more on interest than defense, health care, and social security. But we feel these are only *symptoms* of the problem. The reasons we're in this predicament are a corrupt, biased media and socialist-dominated centers of influence that brainwash too much of the country to one way of thinking. Everything is geared towards programming politically-correct robots who believe big-government is the only solution to every problem. Those with alternative ideas are attacked or censored relentlessly."

"Do you consider yourself terrorists?" said Adams.

"Yes and no. One man's terrorist is another man's freedom fighter, right? No, that's too easy. We've killed, and in many ways, we're no better than any other terrorists or common criminals. We hate the tactics we've had to resort to. Believe me, if we could get our message across and save the country in any other way, we would do so," said Newsome.

"Why use violence? Why not try to run for office, publish a website, or do something else to bring attention to your cause?" said Adams.

"People with a much higher profile have been trying to sound the alarm for years, but they're voices are drowned out by the entrenched powers. How are you supposed to get out your message when the people you're speaking out against control the distribution of that information? Think about it. The educational system is dominated by politically-correct socialists with an anti-American and anti-capitalism bias. Do you think a politically-incorrect, conservative or libertarian could get a university position nowadays? Centers of entertainment, Hollywood and New York, are solidly in the leftist camp, and your acting and comedy careers are effectively over if you take *any* right-leaning position in public. Over 95% of TV and news media is liberally-slanted, and credibility-destruction efforts have been aimed at all alternative voices. Over half the country won't even look at Fox News, Drudge Report, or other right-leaning sources, so they see nothing outside their pre-programmed world."

"Why can't you use social media, the web?" said Adams.

"At first that seemed like the solution to getting around the mainstream media and educational system distortion, but even that is being taken away from the people. It doesn't matter how great of a website you put together, nor how great the content, or how informative & thorough the research. If no one ever finds the website, it's useless. Google and other large tech companies have been shown to suppress conservative and libertarian links while promoting their politically favorable ones. In social media, Twitter and Facebook are suspending right-leaning accounts and removing posts for no other reason than their political philosophy. It's noble to want to remove 'fake news' or 'hate speech,' but who decides what this really means? I personally believe race-baiters like Al Sharpton speak messages of hate. They train minorities to hate whites for no other reason than their race. Are their messages ever censored? CNN and MSNBC have botched numerous stories and promoted thousands of stories over the years that turned out to be false. Are they labeled 'fake news?' Donald Trump would label them fake news, but Google and Facebook would not. Tech companies probably would label Rush Limbaugh broadcasts as 'hate speech,' but Trump would not. You see what I mean? It's all a matter of interpretation. In a true democracy, good ideas will eventually win out over bad ideas. But as soon as you put a small group of people in charge of deciding what speech should be allowed, you in effect have entered a totalitarian state where free thought is stomped out."

"A lot of people may agree with your thoughts, but most people are going to tune out that message once you start killing people," said Adams. "Really, how are you any different than Al Qaeda, Hamas, or any other terror group?"

"That's a great question, Patrick, and I wish I had a good answer," said Newsome. "You're correct, our tactics are awful. I wish there were other ways to achieve our objectives without violence. The problem is accountability. If you get elected to office and do a poor job, people can vote you out of power in the next election. However, when you talk about the mainstream media and all the big-money donors and political/media organizations behind the scenes, there is no accountability. They can spread false propaganda and destroy lives year after year without ever being held accountable. If you go through the research we provided to the public, you will find the people we targeted richly deserved their fates."

"But you've killed and injured many innocent people that had nothing to do with your little war," said Adams. "I count at least three people killed have who no connection to news or media, who aren't described in any of your documentation drops."

"Yes, you're correct, and we have no excuse. We did our best to avoid hurting innocents, and we will provide compensation to the families of the three men killed. It won't make up for their loss, but it's the best we can do. We've done everything in our power to avoid collateral damage. As you probably know, we could have easily killed tens of thousands if we chose to. It's the same as how our military overseas tries its best to target specific people and avoid civilians, but it doesn't always go according to plan," said Newsome.

"Do you have any guilt for the people you *intended* to kill?" said Adams.

"Some. I feel sorry that they gave up their morals and sold their souls. The world will be a better place without them though," said Newsome.

"What do you say to the families of those killed?" said Adams.

"All I can say is that I'm sorry. We had to balance their sorrow with the needs of the country. And remember, these people we killed created far, far more innocent victims through their spreading of false information and character attacks," said Newsome.

"Why did you focus so much of your 7/31 attacks on CNN, *New York Times*, and *Washington Post*?" asked Adams.

"Those three organizations used to be the standard in news. Sure, most who worked there had their biases, but they at least tried to be fair, objective, thorough, and ethical journalists. Those days are long gone. Almost all the people there now who work in news and politics have abandoned all principals of journalism. They exist solely now to spread communist/socialist propaganda and destroy anyone they find politically undesirable. They no longer provide any real watchdog checks on the Democratic party because it would only hurt their agenda. More or less, all they do now is distribute attack stories given to them by political groups run by big-money donors. They have no interest in the truth unless it furthers their narrative and destroys anyone who gets in their way. And remember, bias is not only how you cover a story, but *what stories you choose to pursue*. Patrick, you yourself should know exactly when we mean. You've put together incontrovertible evidence of an obvious criminal conspiracy to bring down the candidacy of Brent Martinez. Not only is your paper refusing to cover the story, but they fired you for even trying to do so. What makes it so bad is that these three organizations often set the national story line, with media throughout the country echoing what they start."

"Are you saying you support Brent Martinez?" said Adams.

"We don't support any specific political candidates," said Newsome. "We have members of RAPCA across the political spectrum. Our opinions on issues are as diverse as the nation itself."

"Some have suggested you're working directly to help Brent Martinez get elected," said Adams.

"With all due respect, that's ridiculous. We began planning for our operations over four years ago. Do you think we'd be able to pull off what we did without extensive planning and training? Hardly anyone, including us, had even heard his name until a couple months ago," said Newsome.

"But it is indisputable that the truths you've exposed in your documents are helping him, correct?" said Adams.

"I suppose, but Martinez is simply one case. There are thousands more cases where political forces have lined up with allies in the media to destroy people," said Newsome.

"Why did you poison the break room snacks of Washington Post and New York Times? You say you want to avoid hurting innocents, but didn't this method almost guarantee innocents would be affected?" said Adams.

"As you know, the substances we used weren't high enough in concentration to cause death. The vast majority of people who consumed the substances in the break rooms were guilty of the actions we're fighting, or at least complicit in allowing it to continue. Only certain people rose to the level of guilt to make our hit list, but most of the rest of reporters there were anything but innocent. It's one of those punishment-to-fit-the-crime things," said Newsome.

"Why haven't you gone after any politicians? Aren't they the ones with the real power?" said Adams.

"Again, we think politicians are a *symptom* of the problem. If Americans have good, accurate, balanced information, we believe they will make the right decisions and vote corrupt, ineffective politicians out of office," said Newsome. "Did you ever wonder why we have such terribly bad politicians leading the United States right now? We have 325 million people in this country. Is this the best we can do? In 2016, we had two candidates with any chance to be elected president, Donald Trump and Hillary Clinton. Were those honestly the *best* two candidates we could find out of 325 million people?"

Adams nodded his head. Without realizing it, he was nodding in agreement with much of what Newsome was saying in the interview.

"There are hundreds of good candidates in every election," said Newsome, "but it's always whittled down to two by the way the media covers some favorably and destroys others. More importantly though, we never get great candidates for office because so many people are discouraged from running in the first place. We all say and do stupid things in life. We all make mistakes. But political groups dig up everything negative about you and use the media as a tool to destroy your character. If that doesn't work, they will make up stuff, or as in the case of Martinez, pay off others to make up the stories. RAPCA stands for a Revolution Against Propaganda and Character Assassination. We're not only fighting for the free, accurate flow of information. We're also fighting against the way people's character are attacked relentlessly. Politics and news are never about solutions nowadays. It's all about making people hate your enemies using any means necessary."

"What if the media attacks are simply *exposing* an inherently bad character rather than creating one? In other words, what if it's just a corrupt politician who deserves to be criticized and attacked?" said Adams.

"If it's fairly done with accurate, provable facts, and if you go after both sides of the political spectrum with the same effort, then there isn't a problem. It's all about balance. If you don't have that, you don't have credibility. Let's take the case of Donald Trump. He was disliked by many people on both the left and right, but regardless of whether you liked him or his positions, almost all of the mainstream media hated him. They spent his entire candidacy and then presidency relentlessly attacking him while ignoring any positive accomplishments. No matter what the story, everything was spun in a way to destroy his reputation and make people dislike him. Add to that an endless amount of false or exaggerated stories. Because the coverage was relentlessly negative, the media lost credibility and most of the nation simply tuned them out.

That in effect gave him a get-out-of-jail-free card. Therefore, when he *did* do or say something worthy of criticism, it simply was buried in the barrage of negative coverage," said Newsome. "The same thing could happen with Brent Martinez if he is elected."

"Explain why you went after billionaires David Backman and Henry Keller," said Adams.

"The engine behind everything we're fighting is the funding provided by superrich donors. Money equals power and control. To protect their interests, rich people in effect buy politicians and buy the media. Who owns the Washington Post? Jeff Bezos, a left-leaning tech guru who happens to be the richest man in the world. What in the hell could the *Post* possibly have to do with his Amazon business? As for Backman and Keller, those two were the worst of the worst. We traced hundreds of millions in political slush funds from them to Media World and other political networks. Everything bad in our national media can be traced to some corrupt money trail. Take a guess—can you tell me where the five richest counties in America are located? You might say Wall Street or Silicon Valley? No, the five richest counties are all in the area surrounding Washington, D.C."

"How long do you plan to continue this little jihad of yours?" said Adams.

"Jihad is a poor choice of words. There is nothing holy or religious about this war. But, to answer your question, we'll continue it as long as it takes. My preference is to *never* have to hurt anyone ever again. I would like the public to rise up and stop the national course we're on through non-violent opposition. That might just be a dream world, though. The establishment power, the corruption, the bias—they're all too firmly entrenched for things to change quickly. Hopefully, we can start the process."

"So, if we, as a society, fixed the issues you're fighting, would you turn yourselves in?" asked Adams.

"We would all gladly trade our lives to accomplish our mission. However, again, we don't live in a dream world, so even if things get better, I think it's best that RAPCAs disappear for a while, but stay out there, watching and waiting to spring to action if the corruption takes hold again," said Newsome.

Newsome and Adams continued the videotaped conversation until 50 minutes of time were filled, enough for an hour-long cable news show with ten minutes of commercials. They spent the end of the interview going over the documents and computer files RAPCAs submitted to public, along with instructions on how to independently obtain confirming evidence.

Newsome and Adams talked off the record a little while after the interview. Adams was given a strong sedative for his trip back to his hotel. As Newsome walked him to the car, he said, "Remember, it must be played in its entirety and made available for download unedited. I think you know we're not the type of people you want to disappoint."

Chapter 25

Fox News, which had been reluctant to give any more coverage to Patrick Adams and his "crazy theories," couldn't resist the ratings bonanza of having a full-length interview of him with the RAPCA terrorist leader. They were the only network to play the interview in its entirety. Most networks played small clips, but CNN and MSNBC steadfastly refused to play even one second of the interview.

Within two days, Adams had 400,000 followers on Twitter. Over 500,000 had liked his Facebook page. The interview he uploaded to YouTube was viewed over two million times. His personal website had over five million hits in the two days following the interview. The documentation he provided for download was retrieved in its entirety 75,000 times. Word was spreading fast.

But everything came crashing down on the third day after the interview was played on Fox. Twitter and Facebook suspended his accounts with a standard "social media policy guideline violation" message they each had used thousands of times for other users. He received no response when he tried to contact the companies. The YouTube link to his video showed a "Video Removed" message. The internet service provider that hosted his website informed him that he must remove his site immediately. He was able to find another service provider on the web to host overseas, but not without a 24-hour delay of service. The small internet service provider was clearly having trouble handling the traffic, so Patrick's website often slowed to a crawl. On top of that, his website was receiving regular denial-of-service attacks, where programs were bombarding his site with activity to slow it down even more and prevent other users from trying to get through.

Adams didn't believe the big tech companies would be so obvious in their efforts to censor him, but here he was, fighting tooth and nail to stay relevant. His eyes were bloodshot from working around the clock trying to make his website navigation faster when he received a knock on his hotel door.

"Mr. Patrick Adams? I'm with the FBI," said the agent as he flashed a badge. "You're under arrest for accessory to terrorism and murder, plus a violation of the Terrorist Ideology Bill. You have the right to remain silent..."

*****

Journalist Patrick Adams Arrested for Conspiracy to Murder and Terrorism. – CNN

RAPCAs Defend Trump, Martinez in Interview. – Chicago Tribune

Presidential Poll: Miller 35, Locklear 35, Martinez 27. – ABC

NYT Editor: Patrick Adams Has History of Pitching Wild Conspiracy Theories and Shoddy Research. – New York Daily News

Opinion: All Information from Patrick Adams and RAPCAs Must Be Considered Fake News. – Washington Post

Did Fired NYT Reporter Patrick Adams Stage the RAPCA Terrorist Interview for Attention? – LA Times.

Former Martinez Campaign Manager Morries: Martinez Spent Time in Psych Ward as Teen. – MSNBC

Shock Poll: RAPCAs Have Higher Favorability Rating Than Congress and Media Combined. – DrudgeReport.com

Death Toll from RAPCA Attacks Reaches 50. – New York Times

*****

"This is horseshit!" yelled Patrick Adams. After spending the night in a cell, he was transferred to an overly warm room with only a table and two chairs. He'd been waiting for three hours in the room before an agent finally came in.

"Calm down, Mr. Adams," said the FBI interrogator.

"I asked for a lawyer ten hours ago."

"Don't worry, you have a bunch of bleeding heart civil-rights lawyers lining up to defend you," said the agent, "but let's not worry about that for now."

"You know damn well I had nothing to do with the RAPCA attacks. They kidnapped me. After the interview, I turned over the original recording and gave the FBI all the information I knew. Why are you suddenly after me now?" said Adams.

"It just seems a little suspicious that you're the only reporter in the entire country to receive a flash drive *and* be invited to give an interview. Why are they so close to you, Mr. Adams?"

"I've been asking myself that from the beginning. They told me it was because I was one of few honest and thorough reporters, but who knows their real motivation."

"So, you're telling me you don't know *any* of these suspects?" said the agent as he laid out six pictures on the table.

"I told the other FBI guys after the interview, the girl seems a little familiar, but that's it. I saw her the day she interviewed for a cleaning position at the *Times*, but there was something about her that made me think I'd met her at some point in my past," said Adams.

"Think, damnit. Maybe you can cut a deal to take the death penalty off the table."

"I've racked my brain ever since I saw her that day. Obviously, she altered her hair or other aspects of her appearance. Maybe someone I met in college. I don't know."

"Why didn't you report your suspicions about her the day of the attacks?" said the agent.

"Because I was unconscious in the hospital. Haven't you read my file? Don't you know I was one second away from getting hit by the same bomb that took out my boss? Do you want me to show you the 12-inch gash in my leg and the other scars from where I was stitched up? You should also have my tox screen at the hospital showing whatever concoction they put in the break room snacks."

"Maybe you've become sympathetic to their cause since then," said the agent. "It certainly seems so by your website and recent stories."

"C'mon, give me a break. I'm solely interested in exposing the criminal conspiracy in the media trying to destroy Brent Martinez. You won't find one piece of information on my website that mentions the terrorists," said Adams.

"Or maybe you even were the inside man that helped carry out the attacks at the *Times*? They seemed way too sophisticated to carry out without inside help."

"Do you even have a shred of evidence against me?" asked Adams. "I'm sure I can provide alibis to prove I was still on the East Coast during the terrorist attacks in California and Vegas. I'm guessing my injuries on 7/31 provide a good enough alibi for those attacks. What is this really about? Are you just trying to intimidate me? Or maybe just get a headline 'Patrick Adams arrested for accessory to terrorism' to kill my credibility?"

The FBI interrogator exited the room without saying another word. Adams talked to a couple of attorneys before settling on a high-profile civil rights lawyer who took his case pro bono. Bail was set at $500,000. Adams was able to secure his release using a bail bondsman and a second mortgage his parents took on their house. His attorney informed him the murder/terrorism accessory charge would almost definitely be dismissed the first time he went in front of a judge. The Terrorist Ideology violation was another matter, but that too likely wouldn't hold up, as the law was already being challenged in court in multiple cases. The damage of the arrest was done, though. Two full days of 24-news coverage were dominated by the "first arrest made in the RAPCA terror attacks."

*****

"Homeland Security will get access to the DoD database tomorrow," said National Security Agency agent, Tim Gordon.

"So, I'm guessing they'll know the identity of RAPCA sniper, Kyle Topper, almost immediately?" asked Colin Bennett.

"Yeah, but you can count on a couple days of delays in communicating with the FBI. They're supposed to be sharing everything, but it's the usual government interagency clusterfuck."

"Ok, thanks. Anything else? It sounded like you had something big when we talked on the phone," said Bennett.

A big smile came across the face of Tim Gordon as he took out an iPad and handed it to Bennett. "Hit 'Play'," said Gordon. A video started playing on the screen.

"Whoa! Is that Alyssa Martinez in a school girl outfit?"

"Yeah, she's pretty damn hot, eh?" said Gordon.

"Very firm. Perky. Where did you get this?" asked Bennett.

"We have hidden recording devices in a few of the ritzy hotels where presidential candidates sometimes stay on the campaign trail. They're there to gauge if any of them are a threat to national security. That's the excuse we use to oversight committees, anyway. This video of Brent and Alyssa was taken in early March this year. Listen..."

"This is your third detention this month, young lady," said Brent. "Obviously, you're not learning your lesson."

"It won't happen again, Mr. Martinez, sir," said Alyssa. "You're the principal, can't you give me another chance?"

"Maybe, but your actions can't go unpunished. New methods of discipline aren't working these days. I'll just have to go old school and take you over my knee." Alyssa lowered her panties and leaned over the knee of Brent. Brent lifted her skirt and gently spanked her five times.

Alyssa popped back on her feet. "I think I've definitely learned my lesson, Principal Martinez."

"You better behave in class or you'll be right back in here. We also have to talk about your poor grades. I'm not sure you're going to graduate."

"Please, Mr. Martinez. All my friends told me there's other things I can do for you to help bring up my grades, but I don't know if I have the skills. You see, I'm sort of a virgin."

"You don't need experience, as long as you put in the effort. Let's see how you do on the oral exam," said Brent as he unzipped his pants.

"This is gold, Tim," said Bennett as they continued to watch for several minutes. "I have no doubt Keller's son will arrange a nice little bonus for this one. It's nice that you have two cameras. Alyssa looks especially hot in the doggy-style position. Man, she has perfect tits. Will the NSA know the source?"

"Probably, if they looked into it," said Gordon. "They won't know who copied it, but they will learn it came from

NSA archives. It doesn't matter though, since there's no way in hell they'd let the truth get out that they make these recordings."

"Awesome. Yes, this will fit perfectly into the story narratives I've been building. Principal Martinez, I think you can kiss what's left of your presidential campaign goodbye."

Chapter 26

Sex Tape of Alyssa and Brent Martinez Leaked on Web. – CBS

Martinez Sex Tape Confirms What We Already Knew About Him. – Washington Post

Brent Martinez Meltdown: Breaks Camera of CNN Cameraman in Angry Rant. – CNN

Alyssa Martinez Walks Off Stage Crying During Veterans Speech. – Fox News

Martinez Plummeting in Polls After Release of Sex Tape. – Bloomberg

Yes, It Was Disgusting Violation of Privacy, But It Saved Us from Racist, Child Molester as President. – Politico

The sex tape release was working even better than Colin Bennett had hoped. The Martinez family tried hard to get the recording pulled from various porn sites, but as soon as they got it off one, it just appeared on ten more. Seven of the top ten links returned from Googling "Martinez sex tape" allowed a viewer to play the unedited recording in its entirety.

Bennett was thrilled to see two full days of cable news coverage dominated by the sex tape release. The news shows even showed a few clips with blue dots covering private areas. Sure, a few whiny guests complained about the violation of the Martinez's privacy and such, but most of the commentary criticized the perverted-ness of the presidential candidate, and how it only reinforced the accusations of the women that had come forward. The news show guests he dispatched were playing their parts of perfection, being sure to remind viewers of Brent Martinez's preference for underage girls.

Newsweek dedicated a 10-page article to Brent Martinez, entitled "Anatomy of a Sexual Predator." CNN ran an hour-long special that played back each and every sexual accusation made against Martinez with follow-up interviews, ending the special with the description of the sex tape. The *New York Times* and *Washington Post* both ran front-page articles that all went over three full newspaper pages long covering the sexual history of Brent Martinez. The stories of *Newsweek*, CNN, the *Times*, and *Post* all had one thing in common—none made even a single mention of the evidence of accusers being bribed, not even to refute it.

Endless Internet memes were created showing Alyssa lying across the knee of her husband as he raised his hand to spank, followed with some kind of joking statement printed across the top. Stephen Colbert, Saturday Night Live, and Samantha Bee built almost entire shows around making fun of the sex tape. David Letterman decided to do a throwback Top 10 list on YouTube entitled, "Top 10 Punishments Alyssa Martinez Has Received on the Campaign Trail," which was shared on Twitter and Facebook over two million times. Jimmy Fallon, Conan O'Brien, and Jimmy Kimmel had monologue jokes about the sex tape in three consecutive days of shows. Most of the jokes, memes, and skit scripts were created by Bennett's organizations.

Bennett had no doubt the campaign of Brent Martinez was finished. He would forever be just a punch line. It wasn't a matter of *if*, but *when*.

*****

"Those fucking, son-of-a-bitches!" said Aaron Newsome. "I thought what they did to Dana was bad, but this campaign against Martinez goes beyond my worst expectations for them. This sex tape has Media World and Colin Bennett written all over it."

"No doubt about it," said Nate Keeting. "Most of the stories on the sex tape are being pushed directly or indirectly by journalists and comedians connected to Media World and other Keller-funded organizations. It looks like his son has picked up right where Keller, Sr. left off and then some."

"Did we accomplish *anything* with our attacks?" said Newsome.

"Of course, we did," said Jim Damon. "There are scattered voices through the media that have returned to being real journalists, and we've awakened the public as to what is going on. Unfortunately, we didn't get enough of the editors and content decision makers. I believe the barrage of journalist resignations aren't caused by fear. They're caused by their bosses continuing to push bullshit political hit pieces which the real reporters are finally objecting to. The corruption runs too deep at the top."

"You also have to remember that the slime bags leading CNN, the *Times*, the *Post*, MSNBC, etc. are in charge of the hiring," said Keeting. "Anyone who isn't far-left in their personal political philosophy simply doesn't get hired at these organizations. And if they do somehow make it through, it isn't long before they get pushed out. Remember, Lou Dobbs and Glenn Beck both are former employees of CNN."

"Plus, we didn't hit Big Tech hard enough," said Damon. "They have thousands of programmers working for them, almost all of whom are hard-core, far-left socialists. Even if company-wide changes were instituted, you can't control everything that goes on behind the scenes."

"We can go a lot bigger with our attacks than we have," said Abby Benton, "but for now, I think we need to send a message by taking out the number one slime merchant out there, Colin Bennett."

"Abby is right," said Newsome. "I want that piece of shit taken down no matter what the cost. Our mistake was not going after him in the beginning. If we can't change things significantly in the media, at least we can go after the sources of the muck."

"I feel bad for Patrick Adams," said Abby. "Something we should have talked about more in our manifesto is how any good journalists who don't stick to their pre-chosen scripts get attacked in the same way as the people they cover. I think I've seen almost as many stories going after his credibility as there have been about the sex tape."

"Absolutely, and I have no doubt Bennett is behind much of that also," said Newsome. "Let's start preparations. I want Bennett taken out before the first presidential debate."

*****

It was getting difficult for Patrick Adams to pay the bills. His credit cards were about maxed out, and now he had the added cost of the second mortgage his parents took on to pay his bail bondsman. His website wasn't generating any income, and he wasn't going to slow it down further or compromise his already-shaky credibility by adding advertising. He'd made a few thousand dollars doing some freelance writing for some fringe publications the past couple weeks, but for the most part he was too much of an outcast in the journalistic community to get any real work. Nearly every day he read a new article attacking his credibility or discussing his accessory-to-terrorism arrest. Almost none of the stories even considered his guilt or innocence; they simply debated whether or not a terrorist should be granted bail at all.

It was expensive to move hotel to hotel, but he had no choice. There were too many crazies after him. The only thing that kept him from moving back home to Wisconsin were the opinion polls of Americans that had seen his TV appearances and visited his website. He had overwhelming support of those that had been exposed to his material unfiltered through the mainstream media distortions and credibility attacks. Maybe he could parlay his support into a book deal. At least it would be difficult to censor printed and digital books.

He decided to shop for book deals and stay on the East Coast until the presidential election was complete. He owed that to the man this conspiracy was trying to destroy, Brent Martinez. Adams hoped he never had to deal with the RAPCAs again. As he left his hotel for a visit to Washington, he noticed another car was following him. Who was it this time? The RAPCAs, the FBI, Homeland Security, or another member of the nut brigade who wanted revenge against the "terrorist conspirator?"

*****

"So, how does it look?" asked Newsome.

"I think we can forget about getting him at his mansion," said Cole Foreman. "There are no elevated sniper positions, and the fencing blocks visibility. He has bullet-proof glass on all the windows, and it would take a good amount of C-4 to get any of the steel doors open. He has three full-time, live-in security people, all ex-military. Plus, he's added some extra security help since the 7/31 attacks. There are always at least three on duty, with the rest usually on the premises. He has highly-trained dogs patrolling around the house. He has alarm systems hooked into his fencing. Security takes the dogs on a sweep of a two-mile radius of the surrounding area every day."

"Does he ever hang out in his yard or walk his dogs?" asked Newsome

"If he does, I've yet to see it. He rarely leaves. He works from home and has all his necessities delivered. The only way we're going to take him out in his home without casualties is to nuke the whole area with some heavy explosives," said Foreman.

"What does he have for other staff?" asked Abby.

"He has three women that share all the cleaning, cooking, and serving duties," said Foreman. "All of them are young, probably early 20s. I wouldn't be surprised if they were occasionally called upon to service his sexual needs, as they're all very attractive. But even if they do, it's not enough. He usually brings in $1000/night call girls a couple days per week."

"At some point we may have to consider taking some chances on collateral damage if the target is worth it," said Kyle Topper, "and Bennett definitely is."

"No, forget it," said Newsome. "We can't recklessly risk the lives of innocent people with the justification that a target is *worth it*. We can't cross that line. Once you do that, there's nothing you can't twist and justify in your mind. I can't stand to see another innocent victim get caught in the crossfire."

"So, what do we do?" asked Topper.

"We just have to be patient," said Newsome. "Bennett is too wired into the media power structure. At some point he's going to have to schmooze some politicians or rich donors. We just have to be ready when that happens and take advantage of the opportunity."

"His network firewalls are impenetrable," said Nate Keeting, "but Jim and I have been able to hack the email of some of the people he corresponds with. We might be able to get some advanced notice when he plans to go out."

"Alright, let's try to find out his patterns of travel," said Newsome. "Does he have certain monthly or annual events that he attends? Does he go to any debates or other campaign events around the time of a presidential election? Does he ever take his call girls out to the opera? Whatever. Bennett thinks himself immortal, but his cockiness will eventually cause him to slip up. When he does, we'll be ready."

Chapter 27

"So, what did you find out, Dutch?" said Colin Bennett.

"Aaron Newsome, Kyle Topper, and Cole Foreman all vanished around the same time," said Dutch Marcello. "I have no doubt they're the military core of the RAPCAs. After Newsome left the military, he needed a few surgeries and some rehab. His doctor was named Abby Benton. You may remember her, she was the doctor accused of botching that QB's operation because of his flag protests."

"Yeah, I remember now. Some crazy fan attacked her and almost killed her."

"Yep, I'm sure all the bullshit antics of Louis Holder didn't help. It definitely gives her motive for going after him. And get this, Benton was thrown out by her partners after she settled the lawsuit. A friend of hers helped get her a new job in Madison. That friends name was Dana Newsome."

"Wow. Were you able to track her down?" asked Bennett.

"Nope, she's suddenly disappeared also. Sound like a coincidence to you?" said Marcello.

Bennett shook his head. "You have more?" His eyes widened as he tried to suppress his excitement.

"I do. I had some of my best men on this. It won't be cheap. The RAPCAs appear to be a real tight group where everyone has a personal connection. We looked into all the friends and relatives we could find of those four members. Abby Benton's ex-husband was a police officer named Darren Williams. He lost his job for shooting a black teenager. Guess who was first on the scene of that shooting to raise hell?"

"Louis Holder?" said Bennett.

"Correct. Williams has gone missing. Aaron Newsome had a cousin named Nate Keeting, an M.I.T. grad who was fired from Facebook. He's gone missing. Keeting's roommate at M.I.T. was named Jim Damon. He was fired from Google. He's also gone missing. Keeting and Damon both graduated near the top of their classes. There's your tech brain core of RAPCA."

"Awesome work, Dutch. I knew I could count on you. That's seven terrorists. Anyone else you know of?"

"Not so far. We haven't been able to figure out who the black dude is that took down the *Washington Post*. I'm sure he has a relationship to one of the other seven, but we haven't tracked it down yet. There has to be a lot more terrorists involved. There's no way they could pull off such a sophisticated operation with that small of a group," said Marcello.

"No question there has to be more," said Bennett.

"You know what you need—you need to capture one of them. Let my people extract some information from him. We'll find out everything there is to know about these RAPCAs," said Marcello.

"Any idea how we can track them down?"

"They need to have some kind of base of operations. Some place where they did all their training and planning. If I had to guess, I'd say somewhere near a hometown of one of the members. Possibly California or Wisconsin. Newsome, Williams, and Benton all lived in the Wisconsin area. Damon and Keeting lived in California. I would look for some remote area. Something wooded or isolated. You also could be looking at something outside the country since Foreman and Topper both at one time were living in the Caribbean area. The military guys all served in Afghanistan and Iraq, so I guess it's a possibility they had a camp over there."

"Nah, the government keeps close tabs on the terror training groups over there. It would have been too risky. Newsome was the founder of RAPCAs," said Bennett. "I'm guessing it's a place in the U.S. connected to him." An idea flashed through his mind. "Can you get me a list of all aliases they've used in the past? They've used a ton of different identifications. I wonder if they purchased property under the name of one of those aliases."

"It shouldn't be a problem," said Marcello. "Benton, Keeting, and Damon all were doing well financially. One of them may have owned the property where they based operations."

"Henry Keller's son is on the warpath. He wants these guys found, and nothing less than a permanent solution will do."

*****

"We know Bennett has a meeting in Washington sometime around 2 or 3 pm," said Nate Keeting.

"Do we know how much security he'll have with him?" asked Aaron Newsome.

"In the email we hacked there was a reference to getting two extra visitor passes, so I have to believe those are his men. His limo driver is usually packing also," said Keeting.

"Ok, Cole, Abby, and Scott—head out on I-66," texted Newsome. "Jim, Kyle, and Darren—head out on I-395. Nate and I will follow him out of his house. I want to have at least one car ahead of us in case we lose him."

"I think I see some activity near his garage," said Keeting.

"He's headed out now in his limo," texted Newsome.

"Tinted glass—big surprise," said Keeting.

"Yeah, and that glass looks like it's bulletproof," said Newsome. "Don't get too close. It won't be hard to locate him if we fall too far back. Traffic won't pick up for another hour or two."

Newsome followed the limo about a half-mile behind. They temporarily lost the limo after it made a few extra turns not on a usual Google maps route which added to the travel time. "They're watching for tails," texted Newsome. "They just got on I-395, black bulletproof limo, tinted windows. We'll have to wait for a destination. Stay alert."

Newsome dropped back and continued to follow Bennett's limo. "We're about a mile or so back. Crossed Potomac exactly two minutes ago."

"We acquired the target," texted Jim Damon. "He's headed towards Capitol Hill. No way we'll be able to get an opportunity with that level of security."

"Dammit," said Newsome. "Ok, abort."

*****

FBI Identifies Former U.S. Marine and Two Ex-Navy SEALs as Prime Suspects in Terrorists Attacks, Four Other Suspects Not Identified. – New York Times

Patrick Adams stared at the pictures of the men who had kidnapped him. The names given in the newspaper were Aaron Newsome, Kyle Topper, and Cole Foreman. It wasn't totally a surprise that members of his own country's military were involved. Clearly, they were highly trained and effective, yet they valued the lives of innocent people in a way that the country's enemies would not.

Adams scanned through some of his research. Newsome, who was identified as the RAPCA leader, had been in the list of about 500 suspects he'd put together. That was likely the man he'd interviewed. Many things bothered him about the off-camera discussion he'd had with Newsome. In particular, Newsome seemed to know things about him that weren't available in public sources. As he read the research on Newsome, he learned the Marine had lived in Madison, WI around the same time Adams was a reporter for a Madison newspaper. Did Newsome know him? He didn't appear the least bit familiar to Adams.

Adams had used some of his extra time since being fired to program some custom cross-referencing applications on his laptop. Now, it was time to put them to the test. He fed in all people associated with the FBI's three identified suspects. It included all the friends, relatives, and men who'd served in the military with those three. He then fed in his suspect list, the terrorist victim list, and all the people mentioned in the documentation provided on the flash drives sent by the RAPCAs.

Only a few names were kicked back from the program as associates of Topper and Foreman, but 23 names came back for Aaron Newsome. He spent the next two hours researching the names on the lists. He came across the name of Dr. Abby Benton associated not only with Newsome but also Reverend Louis Holder. How could he possibly not catch this earlier?! He knew her! He'd even gone on a date with her. Was it after-effects of the concussion? Too little sleep? It didn't matter now. Shortly after the attacks, he'd spent very little time on the research of Holder since the focus of the attacks seemed to be on the mainstream media.

Adams pulled up all the pictures he could find of Abby Benton on the web and put them side-by-side with the pictures of the cleaning woman suspect at the *New York Times*. The girl in all the pictures was as attractive as he remembered. The body build was the same. Most of the facial features were the same, but there were enough changes that facial-recognition software would likely not match them. It had to be her though! The more he thought about that day he saw her at the *Times*, the more he became convinced. Her voice had been vaguely familiar. Her presence and mannerisms seemed familiar.

This could be the whole key to the investigation. It was the non-military connection to the terrorist group. It could bring everything together. He searched his suitcase for the card of the FBI agent that had arrested him. He started to dial the number. On the second ring, he hung up. He sat and stared for several minutes as thoughts raced through his head. He was still a suspect in the investigation. Finally, he made up his mind and re-dialed the number. "Can I please speak to the special agent in charge?"

*****

Colin Bennett used his special secure phone to dial the number of NSA Agent, Tim Gordon. Bennett hadn't left his house in over a week since his last trip to Washington. "What have you heard about the FBI investigation, Tim?"

"They have a couple of the same names you gave me on their list of suspects besides the three they've went public with," said Gordon, "but they don't yet have enough evidence for a conviction. The Attorney General is pushing them to do everything by the book."

"What did you find on the seven names I gave you?"

"Quite a lot, actually. I'll upload everything I found to the secure website I gave you last time we met. We picked up a lot of chatter when Newsome was in the recruiting stage. After the I.T. guys Damon and Keeting came onboard, their communication became much more sophisticated, so there's not much after that. I might have identified one of their fake-ID sources, so maybe if you send some of your muscle guys there you could figure out some of the aliases they've been using."

"Thanks. Any doubts we have the correct suspects?" asked Bennett.

"None. I picked up a couple calls made by Abby Benton talking to a man about RAPCA that doesn't match the voice prints of any of the others. That may be the mystery black guy who was at the *Post*," said Gordon.

"Anyone else you picked up that could possibly be connected? There's got to be more involved."

"Sorry, nothing else that's useful," said Gordon, "but again, they became smarter with their communications after the tech guys joined up, and they were still in an early recruiting stage. It was about nine months before the 7/31 attacks when the trail went cold. After that, it's almost as if all of them vanished from the Earth."

"Alright, I'll data mine everything you have and cross-check it with everything I got from Marcello. Have you found anything on the other matter I mentioned? Someone was following me when I met with the Democratic senators the last time I went to Washington. I know I'm on the RAPCA hit list. I'm guessing they called off their attack when they saw the barrage of security they faced near Capitol Hill."

"As a matter of fact, I do think I found something.," said Gordon. "They didn't hack you. *No one* could get through the firewalls I help you set up. However, I found a weak link in one of the people you emailed about the meeting in Washington."

"Can you use it to back-trace the location of the RAPCAs?" asked Bennett.

"No, but I can show you how to close the security hole and prevent it from happening again."

"No. Don't," said Bennett. He paused for a minute. "I think I have a better idea."

Chapter 28

"We hacked this email of one of Colin Bennett's top assistants," said Nate Keeting as he displayed it on the projected computer screen:

Rick,

Sounds great. Let's go to a late show on Saturday. I will buy us all seats and text you the time & info. Have a good night.

Colin

Sent from my iPad
=====================================
From: Rick Morries <Rick.Morries@MediaMatters.org>
Sent: Wednesday, October 14
To: Colin Bennett
Subject: Movie

Hey Colin, why don't you come out of hibernation to join my wife and I for a movie Saturday night? We could go see the new Gifford Moss movie Stalin: Misunderstood Revolutionary *that they say is going to sweep all the Oscars this year. Bring one of those gorgeous girls that always seem to flock to you.*

Rick

"Rick Morries? Isn't that Brent Martinez's old campaign manager?" asked Darren Williams. "The one he fired who's been all over the cable news show ripping apart his former boss? He's working for Media World now?"

"Yeah, big surprise, eh?" said Keeting sarcastically.

"This might be our last, best chance to get to Bennett," said Aaron Newsome. "We'll have multiple exits

243

and limited security. We have two main problems. One, we don't know which theater or the exact time of the movie. Two, there's likely to be a lot of innocents around for a Saturday night show."

"Looking through Rick Morries past credit card purchases, he's most often gone to movies at AMC Courthouse Plaza in Arlington," said Jim Damon. "It's most likely going to be where they go since it's also close to Bennett's home address. There are three other theaters in the area that have the movie playing on Saturday night that are also possibilities. We'll try to get more exact information, but on this short of notice, I wouldn't count on it."

"I'm going to split us into groups of two," said Newsome. "Each group will be assigned one of the four theaters. Scout out your location and supplement it with whatever you can find on the web. Memorize the layouts, exits, and best escape routes. Buy a couple seats to every show playing Saturday at your assigned theater and map out a plan for how to take him down. On Saturday, we'll put a tail on both Morries and Bennett. If the two of them go to your assigned theater, you'll be running point on the take-down with the rest of the team running support. Ok, we have a day and a half left to prep this operation, let's get to work."

*****

On Saturday night, Rick Morries drove out of his garage. He carries a revolver with him everywhere but didn't have any hired security. "Morries just left his place with his wife," texted Jim Damon. "It looks like they're headed towards AMC in Arlington."

"Hold positions until we know for sure," replied Newsome. "It may be a diversion."

Fifteen minutes passed as Damon and Williams followed Rick Morries to the theater. "He just pulled into parking lot at AMC," texted Damon. "Looks like 9:30 pm show."

"Bennett limo is pulling out of his gate now," texted Abby Benton.

"Jim, do a quick walk through the theater," texted Newsome. "Let me know if you see anything unusual. Get some diversion bombs set for ignition at the six points we talked about. After that, hang in the parking lot with Kyle and be ready to set them off on my signal. Cole and I will handle the take-down. Nate, handle police chatter. Darren, you wait on stand-by in the right-side theater. Abby and Scott, be ready in the getaway car positions." Newsome received a series of thumbs-up texts from the rest of his crew. "Cole and I will arrive in five minutes. Any intel on who's with him?"

"Bennett has a woman with him on each arm," texted Scott Koonce. "Guessing they're paid help by their attractiveness and the way they're slobbering over him. I see three guards with him. Bennett and his bodyguards all have vests. Bennett also has some kind of metal hat or helmet on him. I'm guessing a headshot from behind is out."

"Roger that," replied Newsome. "He's not stupid," he said to Cole Foreman. "This could be tougher than we thought. I don't think we can get him in his movie seats."

"We'll get a chance at some point," said Foreman. "Maybe when he's getting popcorn, in the restroom, or leaving the theater."

"I don't know if I like hitting him when he's leaving—too many bystanders and his guards will be in firing positions," said Newsome. "Maybe they'll go out for a drink or something afterwards. Normally when you go to a movie with another couple you do something else like a dinner or bar visit."

"I don't want to chance it," said Foreman. "There's his limo. Looks like his driver is hanging in the parking lot—one less gun to worry about."

Bennett sat in the center fourth row of the theater. One of his dates sat in the recliner to his left. The second girl shared a recliner with him and sat to his right, practically on his lap. Both of the 20-year-old girls were hired to stay cuddled close to him throughout the night. One of his security guards sat to the left of the threesome, with Morries & his wife on the right. His other two guards took solo positions in the back rows, flanked on opposite sides of the group. Foreman and Newsome took their seats near the aisles in the middle section about ten rows back.

"What a piece of shit," said Foreman. "I see he brought two human shields. They look like high school girls. Al Qaeda would be proud of him."

"Be ready, everyone," texted Newsome. "We're going to wait for a better time. Movie previews are starting now."

Newsome and Foreman sat patiently through the previews and first half of the movie. The theater was about 80 percent full, which didn't make their task easy. Newsome ran different scenarios through his mind, but each one had too much risk to either his team or innocent bystanders. The movie would end around midnight, and Bennett had never gone to a bar a single time since they'd been following him, so they'd likely have to get him in the theater or not at all.

As the movie came to the Yalta Conference scene, the women to Bennett's left looked back in the theater and waived her hand towards Bennett's bodyguards in the back of the theater. One of them got up and left the theater briefly. The other stood up and walked to the entrance of the theater. He waited there a minute until his partner returned. The bodyguard walked up to the fourth row as Bennett and one of the two girls stood up. The guard escorted the two of them as they walked out of the theater.

"RR", Newsome texted to the group, his shorthand for restroom. This might be their only chance. He stood up and walked to the back of the theater. One of the guards stood in his path as he tried to leave.

"Sir, please wait here," he said, extending his powerful arm into the chest of Newsome.

"What are you talking about? I have to use the bathroom and don't want to miss too much of the movie?" said Newsome. "You don't work for the theater, so get out of my way."

"I can let you go, but I have to search you for weapons."

"Fine, but let's go outside the theater so we don't disturb anyone," said Newsome. As the guard started to pat down Newsome, Darren Williams came up behind him and tasered him into unconsciousness. The two of them dragged the guard to a corner out of sight of other theatergoers. Cole Foreman exited a few seconds later to join Williams and Newsome.

The three of them approached the men's room down the hall. One guard was stationed outside the restroom, with the other guard and Bennett presumably inside. Without giving the guard a chance to think, Williams walked right up to him and extended the taser, then gently guided him to the floor.

"Ok, just like we planned," said Newsome. "I'll take down the guard inside. Darren, you take out Bennett. Cole will cover the outside." Newsome holstered his Beretta pistol and pulled out a tranquilizer gun. Williams pulled out his Glock and removed the safety. The two of them slowly walked into the restroom. Bennett and the other guard were side-by-side at the urinals. Newsome approached in the lead and took aim.

Just as Newsome lined up his sights, the bodyguard yelled "Now!", then tackled Bennett to the ground and covered him like a secret service agent protecting the president. All the bathroom stalls simultaneously opened. Dutch Marcello and five of his men came out firing. Two bullets went into the brain of Darren Williams before he could process what was happening. Smoke filled the room as bullets and broken glass flew in all directions. Newsome dropped the tranquilizer gun and reached for his holstered Beretta. Two pistol shots hit him in his bullet-proof vest before he could bring the gun to firing position. A third shot hit his knee, knocking him off his feet and pounding his head into the floor. Newsome's vision blurred until he slowly closed his eyes.

"Shots fired," Foreman said to his mic, alerting the rest of the team. "At least five tangos. Not police." He ran into the restroom. Foreman shot the man to Marcello's right with a bullet between the eyes. His second shot grazed the side of Marcello's head. Marcello took aim and fired a round into the neck of Foreman. Two shots immediately followed from the others, entering the forehead of Cole Foreman and quickly snuffing the life out of the Navy SEAL.

"What in the hell is going on?" said Nate Keeting. "Talk to me guys. Police are on their way. One minute away."

"Jim, blow the diversion bombs, 30 seconds," said Abby Benton.

Bennett put his fingers on the neck of Newsome, "He's still alive," he said to Marcello. "Sorry about your cousin, Dutch."

Dutch Marcello made the sign of a cross as he looked down at the blood-soaked face of his closest cousin. He pointed at Newsome. "Put him in the van and let's get out of here." As Marcello exited the restroom, a 16-year-old usher looked him in the eye from the side entrance towards which they were headed. The boy stood frozen in fear. Without hesitation, Marcello raised his pistol and fired into the middle of the witness's chest. Marcello and his four remaining men hopped into the van with the unconscious body of Newsome.

"This is taking too long," said Kyle Topper. "I'm going in." Just as Topper walked in, three police cars pulled up. As officers stormed into the theater, Topper noticed what was left of the face of the man he had served with since BUD/S training. "Cole is down," he said in a broken voice.

"Police are swarming the scene. Abby, pick me up in the front. If any of them are alive, we won't be able to help them." The five remaining RAPCA members drove from the scene just before a SWAT team arrived and police sealed off the area. It was the first time they lost a battle in their Revolution, but it may have been one from which they could never recover.

Chapter 29

Four People Killed in Foiled RAPCA Terrorist Hit at Movie Theater in Arlington, VA. – ABC

Bodyguards Thwart RAPCA Attack on Media World Leader Colin Bennett and Ex-Martinez Campaign Manager Rick Morries. – CNN

Sixteen-Year-Old Theater Worker Killed in Terrorist Attack. – USA Today

Was Former Martinez Campaign Manager, Rick Morries, Main Target of Attack? – MSNBC

Attack on Ex-Campaign Manager and Vocal Critic of Brent Martinez is More Evidence He is Associated with RAPCA Terrorists. – New York Times

Brent Martinez Sinks Further in Polls. – Bloomberg

Two RAPCA Members Killed: Ex-Navy SEAL, Cole Foreman, and Fired Police Officer, Darren Williams. – CBS

FBI Finds Blood of RAPCA Leader Aaron Newsome at Theater. – NBC

FBI Identifies Disgraced Physician Abby Benton as New York Times Bombing Suspect. – Washington Post

    Patrick Adams had a swirl of emotions as he scanned the day's headlines. He couldn't say he was happy or sad about the RAPCA deaths. He supported their message, and when he researched the background of each identified terrorist suspect, he understood their passion, especially Aaron Newsome and Abby Benton. However, he just couldn't support their tactics. The boy that was killed in the theater was obviously a mistake. He couldn't say if one of the RAPCAs killed him or if it was one of Bennett's bodyguards, but it didn't really matter. When you use murder and terror to strike at your enemies, these kinds of unfortunate accidents are bound to occur sooner or later.

His mood switched to anger as he reviewed the latest stories on candidate Brent Martinez. At this point, he likely had no chance of winning the presidency, but the media would just not let up in their effort to destroy him. Releasing the sex video may have been the cheapest political stunt he had seen in his lifetime. Adams had zero doubt Bennett was behind the release, which is probably why the RAPCAs went after him. Perhaps emotions overtook good judgement in their preparations. That would explain how they'd failed so miserably at the theater when they'd been so flawlessly professional in every other operation.

Nothing Adams saw in the media surprised him anymore. To suggest the Martinez was associated with the terrorists was beyond ridiculous. There wasn't a single shred of evidence to support that argument. Martinez had spoken almost daily voicing his opposition to the tactics of the RAPCAs. That didn't stop almost every news source from insinuating the connection. To say Rick Morries was the real target defied logic. He had no personal bodyguards and was left unprotected in the theater. He was mentioned more as the main target of the theater attack than Bennett, obviously to provide a motive they could tie to Martinez. The comedians and Internet meme producers continued the daily barrage of jokes aimed at Brent and his school-girl-dressed wife, Alyssa.

Every day Adams watched and collected more information. It was all added to his website to show the coordinated conspiracy to destroy Brent Martinez. The website reliability was still spotty due to the denial-of-service attacks, but the information had caught the eye of a publisher that specialized in libertarian books and magazines. The publisher gave Adams a $50,000 advance to write a book on the subject.

Adams had enough material to write ten books, so the challenge would be chopping it down to the most despicable actions of the media/political cabal. After that, to be a good reporter, he felt he had one last task before he could start writing. That task was to interview the subjects, so they had a chance to respond to any accusations and tell their side of the story. That meant he'd have to talk again to a guy that now made his blood boil every time his name was mentioned—Colin Bennett.

*****

"Clearly, they were ambushed," said Nate Keeting. "I'm assuming Bennett knew we were after him and hired some of Dutch Marcello's thugs to set us up. The email we hacked must have been a plant." The five RAPCAs sat in a Holiday Inn in Pittsburgh contemplating their next move.

"Captain Newsome has to be alive, but where?" said Abby Benton. "If he was ok, he would have contacted us by now. Someone has to have him."

"The Feds?" asked Kyle Topper.

"It's possible, but I doubt it. They'd be anxious to trumpet their capture," said Abby, "but I suppose they might want to stick him in Gitmo or rendition him to some other country to extract information from him on us."

"No, they have too much of the public watching this case closely," said Jim Damon. "Is it possible Marcello has him?"

"We can't rule anything out," said Abby. "Check all the hospitals, and let's see if we can hack the investigation to find out what is going on. We can't go near Arlington or DC right now. The Feds have a dragnet around the whole area. Monitor what communications that you can in the Marcello organization. I know Aaron would want us to forget about him and lay low for a while, but we're not going anywhere until we know more. And if it was Marcello's organization that did this, we'll have some new names to add to our target list."

*****

Aaron Newsome spit out water after being awakened with a bucket to the face. He was propped up into the sitting position on a large metal chair. His wrists were handcuffed behind him, and his chest and legs were heavily duct-taped to the chair. His shirt and jeans had been removed. The injury from the bullet to the knee had been patched up, but judging by the throbbing pain, little or no anesthetic had been given.

"Mr. Newsome," said Dutch Marcello. "Captain, isn't it? You've cost some friends of mind a considerable amount of time and money. I do admit that it's been entertaining to watch, but it's over now. I've been hired to even the score."

"Dutch Marcello. Big surprise," said Newsome.

"So, you know who I am? That's good. Then you should know my reputation. It should save us some time."

"Yes, I know you and your piece of shit thug family has been doing much of the political dirty work for the Keller's and others for the past two decades at least," said Newsome. "Don't worry, the RAPCAs will get to you in due time."

"I love it! Someone in your position with that kind of attitude. This will be more fun than I thought," said Marcello. "You were the unlucky one in your strike team, Captain Newsome. Your buddies, Cole Foreman and Darren Williams, received a quick death with minimal pain. You, on the other hand, well, I'm guessing you'll be begging for a bullet to the head in a matter of hours, if not minutes."

"Give it your best shot. Whatever happens to me, it doesn't matter. My team will figure out you and Bennett were behind this. Your days are numbered. We won't be constrained by any rules when we fight back," said Newsome.

"You have spirit, Mr. Newsome, but I'm feeling little patience or mercy today after you killed my cousin. You had a good run, but it's over now. Tell me how to find the rest of your team, and I promise I'll kill you quick," said Marcello, snapping his fingers.

"I'm sure you know my background by now. You're not going to get a damn thing from me. Let me go, and I'll direct my team to focus on going after the people that *hired* you instead of picking off you and every one of your thugs one-by-one," said Newsome.

Another man walked into the room wearing a leather apron and gloves. He put on a welding helmet and flipped the face shield up as he approached the two of them. "This is my cousin, Bruno," said Marcello. "It was his brother that was killed at the movie theater. He has no interest in extracting information from you, only inflicting pain. Lucky for you, I'm a reasonable man. Last chance—tell me how many are in your organization and where I can find them."

Newsome looked up at Marcello, then cleared his throat and spit directly between his eyes. An evil smile crossed the face of Bruno. "Ok," said Marcello, wiping the spit from his face. "Get started."

Chapter 30

"Dutch Marcello's cousin was the other body found at the theater," said Nate Keeting. "Blood from two others was found at the scene that they haven't been able to identify yet."

"Based on the forensic evidence, the FBI estimates 5-7 additional shooters," said Jim Damon. "They know it was a Marcello-led ambush, and they plan to question some of his family to figure out how they set up the RAPCAs, but the agents on the case are getting pressure from above to bury his role in the attack."

"So, it confirms what we already knew. Marcello specializes in doing the dirty work of Keller, Bennett, and a ton of politicians," said Abby Benton. "I see that reporter, Patrick Adams, has added a whole section to his website on the connections of Marcello to the media networks. He strongly implies that Marcello was the one who paid off all the women who made all the sexual allegations against Martinez. Any word on Captain Newsome?"

"Not specifically," said Damon, "but in an email, Marcello references a 'valuable treasure piece' picked up at the theater. He talks about moving it to keep it out of the hands of the FBI."

"Alright, see if you can find out where he's being held," said Abby. "We'll mount a rescue if we can get some decent intel. Regardless if we can save Captain Newsome though, it's only a matter of time before we burn the whole Marcello organization to the ground."

*****

"This is the third time I've tried calling Mr. Bennett," said Patrick Adams.

"I understand, Mr. Adams," said Colin Bennett's secretary. "I will give him the message, and I'm sure he will get back to you. He's been busy. As you know, he almost lost his life in a terrorist attack last week."

"Yes, sorry. I'm writing a non-fiction book where he is a central figure. I wouldn't be doing my job as a writer if I didn't give him a chance to tell his side of the story and refute the allegations I will be detailing in the book."

"I'll let him know. Please don't call again," said the secretary before cutting the line.

Pure bullshit, thought Adams. Bennett engineered that whole scene at the theater using Marcello as the muscle. Adams had the money from the advance on his book to get an apartment, but he continued to move from hotel to hotel every couple of days. If he wasn't already a target, he was now after publishing all the material on Marcello and his connection to Bennett and Keller. Adams had resigned himself to the fact he'd likely meet an untimely demise sooner or later, but he was going to keep working to expose the corruption every day until then.

*****

Aaron Newsome had barely flinched or made a sound through the first round of torture administered by Bruno Marcello. Bruno was skilled in both the psychological and physical aspects of the activity, so he started with the least painful methods and progressively got worse. Each time he warned Newsome what was coming so the mind could build it up and make it even worse than it was. Newsome had a broken nose, three cracked ribs, and numerous minor cuts spread out over his body.

"Are you ready to talk?" said Dutch Marcello. "It's going to get worse every hour, and we'll be pumping you with stimulants and adrenaline to make sure you never get a break from the pain."

"Fuck off, I enjoy the pain," said Newsome. His team had trained on techniques for withstanding torture. The psych aspects were usually what caused people to break. Newsome redirected each new infliction of pain. He thought of his wife Dana, which brought waves of anger that masked the physical trauma and created new levels of defiance.

Bruno ran a blow torch up and down Newsome's extremities, turning the skin alternate shades of red and black. He then pried off each of his fingernails on precisely two-minute time intervals. A timer was used so Newsome could watch each second tick, knowing what would happen each time the clock hit zero. Newsome let out angry grunts as each nail was removed, but he returned to scowls as he stared directly into the eyes of Bruno and Dutch Marcello.

"You're strong, Newsome," said Dutch. "I'll give you that. Most people break within the first hour or two. What do you have to gain by continuing though? Everyone, and I mean everyone, breaks eventually." Dutch paused. "Nothing? Continue," he said to Bruno.

Bruno Marcello pulled out hedge clippers. He ran them along the surface of Newsome's hands and feet for a full 15 minutes. He smiled, then clipped off the left pinky toe. Newsome flinched but kept his mouth shut. Bruno waited precisely 120 seconds, then clipped off the right pinky toe. Another man dressed in white stepped up and bandaged both toes. He took Newsome's blood pressure and checked his heartbeat, then nodded at Dutch.

"How many do you have on your team?" said Dutch.

"Three hundred million," said Newsome.

Dutch shook his head. "Continue." Bruno clipped off both index fingers. Once again, the medic stepped in to treat the wound and stop the bleeding. Newsome felt pain throughout his body. His vision grew bleary as he faded into unconsciousness. "Wake him up. Keep him alert and feeling the pain. Don't let him close his eyes a single time until we return. Bruno, let's take a break."

*****

Eight hours later, Bruno returned to the room. "Are you ready to talk yet?" Newsome only scowled. Without hesitation, Bruno clipped both of Newsome's big toes and exited the room. The pattern continued for the next 16 hours—Bruno would ask Newsome for information, Newsome refused, and some new kind of pain was inflicted.

After almost 36 hours of torture, Newsome was losing all grasp of reality. He'd been pumped with so much adrenaline and other drugs that his brain was having trouble processing where he was. Fatigue was breaking down his ability to resist. During their torture-resistant training in boot camp, they hatched a plan to release a series of old aliases that team members had used. It had to be convincing though and wouldn't be believed if the information came too early in the questioning. Of course, planning always was easier when you weren't actually experiencing the pain. The truth was, Newsome never envisioned any of the team would be subjected to torture from someone like Marcello. The more likely situation was waterboarding at Gitmo or some other government-sponsored interrogation techniques.

"How many are in your organization?" asked Dutch.

Newsome looked down and said in a low voice, "Twenty."

Dutch eyes widened. Finally, some hint of progress. "Names, give me names." Newsome responded with silence. Dutch nodded to his cousin, who was now holding a power drill. Bruno drilled through the right shoulder blade.

Newsome let loose an unrestrained scream for the first time. "Stop! I'll tell you." Newsome started calling out a memorized list of aliases. He paused several times involuntarily as flares of pain shot from various spots throughout his body. His brain was foggy and fatigued. He started repeating names he'd already said in random order. Without realizing it, he mixed in names of reporters they'd targeted. Everything was blurring together. Newsome felt a surge of awareness whenever he came to a team member's real name. He managed to keep those names hidden through his ramblings, but he made one huge mistake—

mentioning the name "Tracy Niehaus." This was the alias Abby Benton had used to purchase the property of their training headquarters in Wisconsin. Newsome passed out with zero awareness of the fatal mistake he'd just made.

*****

"That's all the names I've gotten so far," said Marcello into his cell phone.

"It's sounds like mostly aliases they've used in the past," said Bennett. "There are at least four or five I haven't heard before, but I'm not optimistic. I'm guessing he was planning to feed you these bullshit names when the time was right."

"Fine. I'm done fucking around. I'll get back to you," said Dutch as he ended the call. "Wake him up."

The medic tried some smelling salt, which did nothing. He then administered another shot of adrenaline. "This is going to kill him if we keep going at this pace. His heart can't take it."

"Just shut the fuck up and get out of my way. Alright Newsome, I'm tired of the bullshit. Give me some real names and a location of your headquarters or I'm going to start hacking off limbs."

"Asafaggi pbtt sees," mumbled Newsome in a barely audible voice.

"Say again?" Marcello stepped closer to Newsome and lowered his ear to the whispering Newsome.

Newsome came alive and chomped down on the ear of Dutch Marcello. Every ounce of strength was used to consume Marcello's full ear and bite until upper and lower teeth met each other. Marcello screamed out louder than Newsome had at any time in the past 36 hours. Bruno and the medic rushed to pull Newsome off, but not before 95 percent of Marcello's ear was detached completely from his head.

"Goddamnit! You fucker!" Marcello pulled out his Smith and Wesson pistol and fired into Newsome's head and chest repeatedly until he pulled the trigger on an empty chamber.

"Dammit Dutch, what the hell?" said Bruno. "We finally got him talking! And you said I could kill him after all this was over."

"Shut up, will you look at the side of my head right now?" The medic picked up pieces of ear from the ground and did his best to patch the blood dripping from Dutch's head.

"What do you want to do now?" said Bruno.

"Just get rid of the body. Leave it somewhere that the cops will find it. Maybe it will get the FBI off our back if they find him. Fuck!"

Bruno and the medic wrapped up the body of Aaron Newsome in plastic and carried him to the trunk of a Cadillac. They drove him to the parking lot of a local apartment building and hurled him into the dumpster. Aaron Newsome, war hero and founder of the RAPCA terrorist group, was reduced to a rotting corpse, falling far short of the goals he had set out to accomplish.

Chapter 31

Mutilated Body of RAPCA Leader Found in Dumpster. – NBC News

Mystery Surrounds the Death of RAPCA Leader Aaron Newsome. – Politico

NYT Editorial Board: We Hope He Suffered. – New York Times

Terrorist Newsome Got What He Deserved. – MSNBC

Aaron Newsome Can Burn in Hell Next to Osama Bin Laden. – CNN

Most Common American Reaction to Newsome's Death? Anger. – Fox News

Shock Poll: 44 Percent of Americans Call Aaron Newsome a 'Hero'. – DrudgeReport.com

Did RAPCA Torture and Kill Their Own Leader? – Washington Post

    Being the only woman in RAPCA, Abby Benton always felt the need to overcompensate on the toughness scale. She had been nothing but a rock since the moment they started forming their group four years ago, but that tough exterior collapsed when she saw the tortured pictures of her best friend's dead body. She burst into tears and left the room. Shortly thereafter, the team could hear a martial arts punching bag in the next room being brutalized by a very angry woman.

    The remaining four RAPCA members sat in stone silence for several minutes, hit below the belt with the new reality they were facing. "I want a piece of Bennett and

Marcello so bad I can taste it," said Kyle Topper. "I don't care if I have to stalk the rooftops of New York and Washington for the next 20 years. Eventually, they will pop their head out somewhere public, and I will be ready with my rifle that will not miss."

"Marcello wouldn't have made such a move without major financing behind him," said Damon. "There are bigger fish to fry, but yes, we have to take them out, preferably something slow and painful."

"Marcello must have been trying to get information out of Captain Newsome on us," said Nate Keeting. "Judging by his condition, he held out quite a while. If I know Aaron, he either tried to escape or provoked his own death so he wouldn't roll on us."

"We're heading back to Wisconsin," said Abby, returning to the room. As the last remaining member of the founding threesome, she was now the unquestioned leader. The murderous, determined look in her eye captured the undivided attention of the team. "We'll regroup and retrain. It's time to start preparations for retaliation."

*****

"Your boy Marcello majorly fucked up," said Henry Keller, Jr. "How could he be so stupid to kill a captive member of the terrorist group? We still don't know how many there are or bases of operation."

"Sorry sir, but we *did* kill the leader and two of their most capable fighters," said Colin Bennett. "Cole Foreman was the brains behind their bomb-making capability. And the interrogation of Newsome wasn't a total loss. We confirmed and added to a long list of aliases they've been using. We'll monitor for their usage in the future. Also, one of the names, Tracy Niehaus, was used to buy a large chunk of property in northern Wisconsin. Newsome and Benton are both from Wisconsin. We scouted out the location. It's fairly isolated and fenced in all around it. My people tell me there are some military-style defenses, and a large house on the property is protected by bullet-proof glass."

"Ok, it sounds promising. Is anyone still there? It may be their base, but who knows where they're set up now," said Keller, Jr. "They could be anywhere around the country planning their next attack."

"Marcello and his men are watching the location 24-7 now. They've spotted at least five people there—four men and one woman. We've seen them doing calisthenics and running together in the morning. There maybe more of them, but we haven't spotted them yet. And as you said, some may be out on assignment. We haven't been able to pick up much communication from inside. I'm guessing they have some thick, sound-proof walls and noising-cancelling devices. Marcello is shipping in some more powerful equipment."

"So, what do you recommend now?" said Keller, Jr.

"We'll watch and wait. As we talked about, Marcello has some connections with the Russian mob. They have 12 ex-Spetsnaz fighters ready to be called into action if you're ok with spending the money. When you add in the cost of manpower, weapons, referral fees, and other equipment, the cost will come to about $18 million for a take-down operation," said Bennett.

"Can they guarantee their results?"

"Marcello said they need half up front and half when the operation is complete. If you want to guarantee the kills, we can just firebomb the whole fucking compound, but I'm guessing you might want at least some of them alive," said Bennett.

"You're correct. Thanks to Marcello's fuck-up we don't have anyone to pry for more information. Tell them I'll pay $15 million, but I will throw in an additional $5 million for each RAPCA member that they can bring to me alive. I will have my own people do the interrogations next time. I personally would love to participate in the questioning," said Keller, Jr.

"I think they'll go for that. I'm told they want a few more days of time to collect intel, then they'll mount an assault," said Bennett.

"Ok, I want it done within a week. To change the subject, how are things going with the Martinez operation?" said Keller, Jr.

"He's still around the low teens by some miracle, but we're still doing the daily barrage of negative stories. It's hard to find a single journalist in any major news organization that supports him, so he'll keep falling. Our internal polls show him with stronger support than the publicly-cited polls, but they're not factored into the 15 percent threshold equation. His only chance at election in the first place was getting into the debates, which didn't happen. Miller and Locklear have done a good job beating each other up the past few weeks, which is probably why his numbers ticked up a little, but as usual, the hatred is too strong on each side for Democratic and Republican voters to waste a vote on a third-party candidate."

"Great work. I've wired your million-dollar bonus to the Cayman account. I'll throw in an additional $5 million if you can get him out of the race entirely. After seeing Donald Trump get elected with all the polls against him, I don't want to take any chances. There are way too many dipshit hick American voters out there, especially in the South and Midwest."

"No argument here," said Bennett. "If Martinez somehow wins a state or two, with the rest of electoral map split the way it usually is, you may have a situation where no candidate reaches 270 votes, meaning the evenly-split House decides the next election. With the recent number of Congressmen switching to Independent status, that result could go either way."

"Tell me something I don't already know," said Keller, Jr.

"We'll keep up the pressure," said Bennett. "Martinez became popular largely because of his cool, friendly, confident demeanor. However, he's been short with several reporters lately. He's starting to lash out, and his wife is turning into a basket case. Ok, if I must, I'll take your additional $5 million, but I have to admit, I'm quite enjoying this."

*****

"The Marcello family has businesses, legal and illegal, all across the U.S. and Europe," said Nate Keeting. "The usual—drugs, gambling, unions, prostitution, weapons trafficking, and so forth, but Dutch Marcello doesn't get involved in much of those enterprises. His sole specialty seems to be doing dirty work for political campaigns. He's helped set up protests and riots. He paid off some individuals to start fights at Trump rallies way back when, and he helped organize almost all the anti-Martinez violence going on now."

"We found out Bennett, Marcello, and the Keller family are all making a large chunk of money on a relatively new phenomenon—gambling on elections," said Jim Damon. "*PredictIt, Paddy Power, Ladbrokes*, you name it. You can buy and sell real money based on the percentage chances of certain political events occurring. For example, Bennett made some large bets immediately before the Martinez sex video came out. We also traced bets from Marcello, Bennett, and Keller right before all the female accusers started coming forward. They're smart about spreading the money around and betting from international accounts."

"Speaking of international accounts, the Marcello family also has a love-hate relationship with the Russian mob," said Keeting. "I intercepted one call spoken in Russian with a Marcello caporegime. I couldn't decipher what they were saying though."

"Any ties to the Russians we heard speaking to Keller at the hotel where we hit him?" said Kyle Topper.

"It's possible," said Damon. "The enterprises of the Marcello family and factions of the Russian mob don't really crossover; however, they do seem to share information and muscle when it's needed."

"So how do we get to them?" said Abby Benton.

"Hitting them personally will be difficult," said Keeting. "Marcello doesn't communicate much electronically, for obvious reasons, so he is tough to track. We could strike back at some of his family's financial interests, but that's about it right now. As for Bennett, he is holed up at his fortress mansion, and he appears to have added even more security."

"Alright we'll wait. Let's start collecting data on every dollar Marcello earns, legitimately or illegitimately," said Abby. "And I want to know every single politician he's ever had a conversation with."

*****

"Their daily schedule and patterns are unpredictable," said Boris Puchkova in a heavy Russian accent. "The security of these terrorists seems top of the line. To move in, we'll need the power cut to the entire area. They probably have backup power, but the more we can disable, the better."

"When can you be ready to move in?" said Dutch Marcello to the ex-Spetsnaz fighter.

"A few more days at least," said Puchkova. "We need to check the area and do more research on their security vulnerabilities. We'll need some heavy explosives to blow those doors, bullet-proof vests & helmets, flash bangs, night-vision goggles, and some extra ammo. We have all the rifles we need. I'd like blueprints and architectural designs of the inside if you can get them."

"Make a list—whatever you need," said Marcello. "How's this going to go down?"

"We'll wait until the middle of the night. Cut the power. I'll have a sniper ready to shoot out any lights used with backup power. We'll set up explosions on the east and north side of the house, blocking the back way opposite the direction we're coming. Five of my men will approach from the west, five from the south entrance. The explosions, flash bangs, and gas will disorient them. I'm guessing all but one will be asleep. They're unlikely to have NVGs, so we'll have the advantage on vision. I'll have another man covering the outside in case any of them try to escape."

"I want to be there when it happens," said Marcello.

"My team doesn't work with outsiders?" said Puchkova. "We don't need any interference. This whole thing will be over in 15 minutes. They won't know what hit them."

"I'll stay out of the way. Henry Keller, the man paying for this operation, wants me to film it live. It's a personal vendetta for him," said Marcello.

"Fine, but if you get in the way of my men, I'll shoot you myself. Saturday night, we move in on them," said Puchkova.

*****

"Hi, Tim," said Colin Bennett on a secure phone line. "Did you find any more good stuff on Richard Miller? Locklear still has a lead, but just over half the votes leaving Martinez are going to the Republican, so we need some more dirt."

"I found a few interesting recordings that I'll upload to the website," said NSA agent, Tim Gordon. "But that's not why I called. Listen, the FBI investigation has had some break-throughs. Among other things, I came across some communications that included that alias you mentioned, 'Tracy Niehaus.'"

"Ah, fuck. How long ago was this communication?" said Bennett.

"It came through last night. If they don't know about that headquarter location in Wisconsin by now, they will by the end of today at the latest. If they connect all the dots, which I suspect they will, then I would expect a raid on that compound within a day or two. So, if you have something planned, you better do it damn soon," said Gordon.

"Thanks, Tim." Bennett hung up the phone and sent a text message to Dutch Marcello, "FBI closing in fast. You have to go in tonight!"

Chapter 32

It was a cold Wednesday night in northern Wisconsin on October 14th. Two inches of snowfall covered the ground. Boris Puchkova noticed fresh footprints in the snow in several spots inside the fenced-in headquarters of the RAPCA terrorist organization. The whole area was pitch black except for one light inside a room of the 4000 square foot cabin that Puchkova was viewing through binoculars.

"I don't like going in without more prep time," said Puchkova. "This is 100 acres of property to scan."

"We don't have any choice," said Dutch Marcello. "The Feds will be coming the next day or two, and there's not a damn thing on this land other than trees and that cabin."

Marcello, Puchkova, and 11 heavily-armed men dressed in black approached the compound outside the fence at a spot where a dirt road ended. An empty UPS truck was backed up to the fence, ready to exit the scene quickly when the mission was completed.

"Sync watches 2:46 am, 00 seconds now," said Puchkova, speaking Russian. "Power transformer, door, and back-side explosions will be set for 3:00 am. Team A take south entrance. Team B take the west side entrance. Vitkor you have the sniper position in the high ground oak tree. Alexei cover the outside and be ready to move. We need them alive if possible but shoot to kill if you must. Everyone understand their assignments?"

"*Da*," came the simultaneous responses.

Puchkova nodded to two of his men, who then proceeded to cut through the wire fence, carving out a hole large enough for the men and equipment to move into the compound. Each Russian carried a Colt M4 carbine rifle, a holstered Sig Sauer 9mm pistol, and a grenade strapped to their backs. Two carried duffle bags of pre-assembled C4-laced explosive devices. One carried a bag with tear gas canisters and flashbang grenades. They were ready for anything. Marcello had two holstered Beretta pistols and carried a video camera and tripod.

Night-vision goggles guided five Russians as each planted a bomb at their specified locations. So far, nothing inside the house indicated their presence was detected. Marcello set up the camera 200 yards from the house, zoomed in, and took shelter behind a set of maple trees. "Are you receiving?" he texted to Henry Keller, Jr.

"Yes. Mostly all black but I see the outline of house, barely," replied Keller, Jr.

"There will be plenty of light and fireworks around 3 am," texted Marcello.

Viktor climbed into a large oak which held a level branch that would have been perfect for a tree house. The oak tree sat on a hill, which in combination with the branch gave Viktor about 20 yards of elevation over the house they were attacking.

"One minute," said Puchkova into his wired mic. Five men hugged the ground 50 yards from the south entrance, and five laid down the same distance from the west entrance. Five explosions went off simultaneously at 3 am. The light inside the house went out. Canisters of tear gas were fired in through the holes blown on the doors. Puchkova's team sprinted to the entrances. Flashbangs were tossed in immediately before each team entered. "Go," said Puchkova. Return gunfire erupted from an unknown direction inside the house. Puchkova expected this—blind, panicked, disoriented gunfire. The teams met in what appeared to be the living room. The house was still complete darkness other then the light coming from the outside bombs. Puchkova's men proceeded room-to-room in 2x2 formation, checking every corner from every direction. The gunfire appeared to be coming from the basement and an upstairs bedroom.

"Enjoying the show?" texted Marcello.

"Love it." replied Keller, Jr. "Zoom in a little more."

Marcello did as requested, but the live video feed ended, turned into nothing but a solid blinding orange light. The entire house exploded out in a wall of fire, demolishing everything and everyone inside the house. The fire and impact of the bomb stretched out a radius of 225 yards. Viktor and Alexei were both close enough to be vaporized by the blast. Marcello's camera blew into pieces. The maple he was sheltering behind protected him from the impact, but the left side of his body caught fire, which soon spread to the rest of his body. Ten more simultaneous explosions occurred on trees spread out through the property. Marcello rolled around in intense pain as he extinguished the fire on his clothes. Pure adrenaline carried him back to the UPS truck at the dirt road entrance. He hopped in and sped off without giving a second's thought about Pochkova's men.

Neighbors from miles away were observing the astonishing light show now occurring. They'd heard gunfire and what sounded like minor explosions before, but nothing like this. It was a total war zone.

As Marcello exited the scene, three police cars pulled up to the outside of the fencing on the main entrance to the fenced-in property. The officers exited their cars and grabbed shotguns and vests from the trunk but were unsure how to proceed. Luckily, they didn't have to make that decision, as a stream of cars quickly followed carrying FBI agents in their blue and yellow jackets. They took up positions around the fencing, but no one moved in.

An hour later a SWAT team arrived on site. Together with the FBI agents and local police they entered the compound. It didn't have the feel of entering a crime scene but rather the aftermath of some aerial bomb that had nuked the whole area. Fire trucks were set up but were ordered not to move in until the area was secured. It didn't take long though. There was nothing alive inside that fencing. It was just scattered piles of wood, metal, debris, and body parts.

*****

The FBI Director took the podium in front of a room filled with reporters. "I'll make a short statement and then I'll take your questions. As all of you know, three members of the RAPCA terrorist group, including the leader, Aaron Newsome, were killed a week ago. We've had APB's out for four additional suspects—Abby Benton, Nate Keeting, Jim Damon, and Kyle Topper. We also suspect others but have yet to identify them. However, we've located their headquarters in Wisconsin. Approximately 3 am this morning, a series of explosions occurred on the property. We've found the remains of at least ten bodies on that property and expect to find several more. The 100 acres of property may take weeks to go through, and probably longer to identify the bodies. We'll do a thorough investigation, but as of now, our preliminary theory is that remaining RAPCAs were testing some new powerful explosives that went off unintentionally. Regardless of what happens in the investigation, we will continue the larger hunt for RAPCA members. I'll take your questions now."

"Are you saying the four suspects you named were killed in the blast?" asked a CNN reporter.

"Yes, that is what we expect. Witnesses have identified all four as being in the area within the past week. One witness also identified an African-American man who we suspect carried out the *Washington Post* bombings."

"You said you've found ten bodies so far," asked a Fox News reporter. "Have you been able to make any positive ID's on the bodies?"

"Yes, we've identified two bodies. Two Russians were identified in the group. One was named Boris Puchkova, the other was named Viktor Safin. We're still collecting information on these two, but we've determined they're both former soldiers in Russian special forces. We've contacted the Russian government for more information. They've confirmed their identities and informed us none of them were still active in the military. The personnel folders they sent seem to credibly back their claims. We haven't found a connection to the other RAPCA members at this time. It's clear they needed a lot of extra manpower and expertise to carry out the simultaneous attacks they did, so it's not surprising they had more help."

"Are you saying the Russian government may be behind these attacks?!" said an MSNBC reporter.

"We have no evidence of that. All the American suspects we identified had motives for targeting the media. It's likely the Russians were just hired mercenaries," said the FBI Director.

"But it's at least possible, the Russian government is involved?" said the same MSNBC reporter.

"Sure, I guess anything is possible. It's highly unlikely though given the information we've obtained so far."

"It's been rumored that the presidential candidate, Brent Martinez, is affiliated with these terrorist groups," said a *New York Times* reporter. "Have you investigated him in connection with any of the attacks?"

"We've investigated and have found no evidence that he's involved."

"What about the reporter, Patrick Adams? Does he have any connection to this? He is from Wisconsin originally, if I remember correctly," said a CBS reporter.

"We've dropped the charges against Patrick Adams. In fact, information given by Mr. Adams was instrumental in us tracking down the headquarter location and identifying some of the suspects."

"Could you elaborate? If he gave you this information, doesn't it make it more likely he's a suspect?" said the CBS reporter.

"Mr. Adams had airtight alibis for all the attacks and was in fact severely injured in one of them. I can't get into all the details, but he gave us a mountain of research and tips that helped us connect the dots."

"Back to the Russians that were killed," said a *Washington Post* reporter, "Given the fact that Russia interfered in the 2016 election and the fact that Brent Martinez directly benefited from the RAPCA attacks, shouldn't the focus of your investigation be on the Russian government?"

"Again, we have zero evidence that the Russian government was involved in any way," said the FBI director.

"Will you be interviewing Vladimir Putin or any other Russian officials?" said a CNN reporter.

"You're not listening to me. We have *nothing* to indicate RAPCA is anything but a domestic terror group."

"But shouldn't at least explore that angle?" said the CNN reporter.

"Just because a suspect is from another country doesn't automatically mean that the entire country is guilty."

"But you said they're former special forces, the kind of men Russian intelligence may hire?"

"Yes, maybe," said the increasingly impatient FBI Director, "but given all the other positively-identified suspects, the motives, the evidence, the manifesto, and all the connections, it's completely ridiculous to think the Russian government was behind the RAPCA attacks!"

*****

End of the RAPCAs? Explosion Kills At least Ten at Headquarters in WI. – ABC

Two Russian Special Forces among Dead at RAPCA Site. – USA Today

Was it the Russians All Along? – New York Times

Russia Likely Trying to Steal Another Election with RAPCA Affiliation. – CNN

Act of War? How Many Elections will Russia Try to Sway Before They're Held Accountable. -- MSNBC

Russia, RAPCA, and Fake News: What They All have in Common. – Newsweek

The RAPCA Russian Connection and the Martinez 'Conspiracy': The Fake News Stories All Makes Sense Now. – Washington Post

Chapter 33

Brent Martinez took the stage in front of a room filled with about a hundred of his campaign staff and 20 reporters.

First of all, I want to start by thanking all my campaign staff and volunteers. I can't praise you enough for your hard work, loyalty, and dedication through this very stressful campaign. I wish we could have accomplished more, but it saddens me to say that it hasn't.

I started this campaign wanting nothing more than to help my country and the American people. I've sought to bring people together and break down the artificial barriers of political parties. I've sought to change Washington, removing corruption and waste, while restoring freedom and returning power back to the people. All I wanted to do was find real solutions to our ongoing problems together in a respectful way. I care nothing about the presidency itself, but only being a position to do good for the greatest amount of people.

Unfortunately, whatever it is about me or my candidacy, I've stirred up a hornet's nest in Washington. I've undergone one of the greatest engineered campaigns to destroy a candidate ever—politically, professionally, and personally. Anyone who knows me can see that the image, the caricature, of me that exists now in the public has been put together by some very powerful and corrupt people. When I look into the mirror, I see many faults. However, I can't begin to see anything resembling the evil monster that's been constructed by a very corrupt and biased media.

I'd like to go on fighting, and if it was just me, I would do so. I would continue to endure every criticism, every attack, every humiliation, every lie and distortion. Politics is a blood sport. I knew that when I got into it. What I didn't expect is just how big of a burden it would be on my family.

And I didn't fully appreciate just how much the American media and celebrities today have abandoned all sense of morality and empathy.

My wife Alyssa has never been interested in politics. She's never been anything but a loving, loyal, and caring partner who's supported me through all the vicious attacks and lies. She doesn't give political speeches. She doesn't attack opponents. She's never given any reason whatsoever to justify the attacks hurled at her. I'd love to keep the following fact private, since it's none of the business of anyone outside the family, but I know it will eventually become public knowledge, and I know there is nothing to stop so-called journalists and comedians from adding to her humiliation. Alyssa has checked herself into a psychiatric hospital for depression. I beg of you to leave her be. Focus all your attacks on me. I'm sorry to say though, that at this point, I have little faith you'll do so.

If you haven't guessed by now, I'll be withdrawing my candidacy for president. I must do what is best for my family. It angers me that I'm in effect rewarding the perpetrators of this disgusting attack campaign, but my will to fight is gone.

I would hope, with me out of the race, that whatever true journalists are still left in the cesspool of the America media, will finally start examining the facts. I would hope that you finally investigate in an unbiased way to seek the truth rather finding any way possible to further slander me and destroy my character.

Maybe some of you listening to this speech will never believe me, that I'm not anywhere close to the person the media has constructed. But I know in my heart the person I really am. And it terrifies me that if the media can turn a person like me into the evil person some of you have in your minds, then there may not be any hope for the future of this country.

There are millions of people out there who would make great leaders. Senators, congressmen, cabinet members, mayors, governors, and yes, presidents. But we may never find those great leaders, since they'll either be destroyed by well-funded media campaigns or worse yet, be too afraid to run for office after witnessing what has happened to others.

It's up to you, the American people, to right this wrong. Only you can fix this broken system.

*****

Colin Bennett stared out his living room window. He couldn't stop smiling. It was a hard-fought victory, but he'd done it. The RAPCA's, if there still were any alive, were in shambles. And having Russians die at the scene—what an incredible stroke of luck! Many of his remaining contacts in the media had recently been queasy about running the story narratives he created, but with the RAPCA's out of the picture, they were slowly returning to the gullible minions he knew and loved. They were moving forward full throttle with the "Russia interfered with another election" storyline. Everything was following into place. Americans would soon fall back into their oblivious idiot roles they usually played at election time.

And Brent Martinez was out of the race! Bennett had to admit, there were times he was starting to doubt himself, times he thought he may never be able to get Martinez to drop out, but patience and persistence had paid off. He confirmed another $5 million deposited in his off-shore accounts. That was the tip of the iceberg. He had proven his effectiveness to Henry Keller, Jr., who was now the top political financier in the world. Bennett's expertise would be needed in hundreds of elections every two years.

A voice came through the intercom, "Sir, there's a Patrick Adams here to see you."

Bennett rolled his eyes, "Does this guy every give up?" he said to himself. He pressed the intercom button, "What does he want?"

"He says it something about an interview for a book he's writing."

"Fine, send him to my office. I'll be there in a few minutes." Bennett paused and thought for a moment. "Take his phone and check him for recording devices."

Adams drove up to the guest parking lot. Two security guards patted him down and ran metal detection devices over him, while a third guard guided a German Shepard through a search of his car. "Ok, follow me," said one of the guards. He guided him through the house to Bennett's office. "Wait in here. He said he'll see you in a few minutes."

Forty-five minutes later, Bennett walked into the office, "Mr. Adams, Patrick, good to see you again," he said, extending his hand.

Adams refused the handshake. "I'm sorry to show up here unannounced, but you wouldn't return my calls."

"I apologize for that. The past few weeks have been crazy. I was sad to hear you left the *New York Times*. I really enjoyed your columns. I hear you have a website or something now?"

"C'mon, cut the bullshit, Bennett," said Adams.

"Excuse me?"

"You know damn well what I've been doing the past month, and I know you've been behind many of the credibility attacks on me lately, so let's stop the phony friendliness act."

Bennett's fake smile turned into a genuine smirk. "Fine, you want to be direct, I can do that. You should have known the powers that be would never let you get away with publishing the shit that you did. And going on Hannity? C'mon, that killed your credibility with half the nation without my having to lift a finger."

"I can't say I'm a huge fan of Hannity, but thanks to you, he was the only one who would take my call. But this isn't about me. I really don't care what happens to me personally or my career. What's important is exposing the rampant corruption in the media and political world today," said Adams.

Bennett rolled his eyes and sighed, "You're never going to get it. Americans already know about the corruption and bullshit, but most people, unlike you, have figured out it's never going to change. You're trying to live in a world that doesn't exist. Money and power are the greatest motivators, the greatest aphrodisiacs in existence. One percent of the world population controls more than half the wealth and almost all the power. If you try to take that away from those chosen few, there will always be incredible push back. Sure, people are disgusted with me and the work I do, but if it wasn't me, they'd just find someone else to do the dirty work."

"Maybe if we actually exposed these people and their corruption to the nation, we could actually change things, so the character assassinations and attacks would no longer have any effect?" said Adams.

"You're hopelessly naïve, Patrick. Every person who enters journalism starts out with a wide-eyed optimism about changing the world, but they eventually come to their senses and join the party. The system never changes because Americans don't want it to change. They don't want to have to think. They don't want to wrestle with pros and cons of issues, the advantages and disadvantages of new legislation, blah blah blah. They just want someone to hate, some easy reason to vote for or against a candidate."

"I think you're oversimplifying. Americans are a lot smarter than you give them credit for. If you gave them a chance to make good decisions based on all the accurate information, they may surprise you."

"Are you fucking kidding me?" said Bennett. "You're talking about a population that flocks to idiotic reality shows and superhero movies, who don't have the barest knowledge of economics, history, and science. There's a reason the show 'Are you smarter than a 5th grader' was so popular because most Americans aren't. You have 80 percent of the public out there who have little or no net worth despite the endless amount of educational and investing opportunities. Do you think I want to put the fate of the nation in the hands of those morons?"

"I think it's you people that don't get it, you so-called elites in New York, Washington, Hollywood, and Silicon Valley. You live in a bubble and really have no idea how the world works outside of it. You pass judgement, belittle, and take advantage of good people you know nothing about. Americans are caring, hard-working, loyal, patriotic, and a lot smarter than you give them credit for. Who cares if they remember some useless facts they were taught in grade school? And they would love to be involved in fixing the problems of the nation, but they've become so jaded by the system people like you have created. The entertainment you scoff at is simply a way to escape from that toxic environment created by the powerful elites."

"Wow, I must admit, Patrick, that you're damn good at spinning bullshit. And your investigative research is incredible. I'd love to hire you. The first year you could probably make ten times what you could for that stupid book you're working on. I suppose it's about the damn Martinez 'conspiracy' crap?"

"Brent Martinez is one of the greatest human beings to ever run for office," said Adams. "He has more integrity and character than I've ever seen in a candidate. I've researched everything about him and have never come across a single hint of corruption. He is simply a brilliant, well-educated, hard-working man who had intelligent solutions proposed for virtually every problem he have in society today. You destroyed him. And for what, because he threatened the happy, perfect existence of you pampered elites?"

"I like Martinez personally, but think about what he was proposing—radical cuts in government spending, term limits, cutting regulations, scaling back executive and legislative controls. He basically wanted to remove a ton of power and money from the system. Do you think there wasn't going to be a massive campaign to fight that?" said Bennett.

"It's just not right, what you all did to him. He didn't deserve it. No one deserves what he and his wife had to go through," said Adams.

"Ah, you're breaking my heart. He knew the risks when he got into the race. By the way, I was serious about hiring you. You're one of the sharpest reporters and researchers I've ever met."

"I'll pass," said Adams.

"C'mon, Patrick, join the real world. Look at this house. Look at my cars. Hang around if you want to see some of the women that come visit me every night. I'm thinking about buying a private jet later this month," said Bennett.

"Yeah, I heard you were paid a million bonus for getting Martinez out of the race," said Adams.

"Correction, I made a million for keeping him out of the debates. I made an additional *five* million for getting Martinez to drop out of the race, plus an additional $1.5 million for facilitating the deaths of the first three RAPCAs. I'm waiting to see how many additional $500k bonuses I get as they sort through the rubble at RAPCA headquarters. And keep in mind this money is just *bonuses*. They're on top of the substantial salaries I get from my different organizations."

"That is just sick," said Adams.

"I'll take that as a complement. You could be part of this elite group," said Bennett as he popped the cork on a bottle of wine. "Instead of wine from Costco or Walmart, you could be drinking something like Chateau Mouton Rothschild 1896," he said, holding up the bottle. "Cost me ten grand. Don't get me wrong, my drinks aren't always this expensive, but I have sort of a tradition when I knock a political opponent out of a race, and this was my biggest victory yet."

"Doesn't it bother your conscience even a little? The lives you destroy? The families you tear apart with your politics of hatred and division? The long-term damage you do to the health of the nation?" said Adams.

"Yes, it bothers me terribly, so much that I have to dry my tears with $1000 bills," said Bennett, smiling ear to ear. "You make me laugh. You don't understand how much fun this is, how intoxicating. I can determine who does and doesn't get elected. I'm a true kingmaker. I control the way history books are written, I—." Bennett choked on his words as he started to get dizzy. His vision blurred. "I—." The room was spinning. His heart started racing as he struggled for breath. He staggered to his knees.

"You should have examined your cork a little more closely." Adams held up a small hypodermic needle and a tiny empty plastic bottle. "These were tucked into the Green Bay Packers mini helmet on my keychain, which is how your security team missed it. You'll be dead in about 60 seconds I'd guess, a far better fate than you deserve."

Bennett fell to the ground. Foam started coming from his mouth as he convulsed with his eyes wide open, still aware of what was going on, but unable to stop it.

"Ever since I started as a journalist, I've tried to do everything by the book. I've tried to be ethical and honorable, to provide balance and fairness to every story I wrote. I've always held lofty goals of changing the world, accurately informing the public, and stomping out corruption. I never believed in violence. I figured the American 1st Amendment freedoms were all that were needed to have a fair system. But after I witnessed what you did to Brent Martinez, I finally realized, the system is badly broken. And that system will never be fixed as long as people like you are a part of it."

Chapter 34

Adams grabbed his phone as a guard escorted him out of the residence of Colin Bennett. As Adams started his car, the guard glanced into the office at Bennett, who was propped up in a sitting position at his computer with his back to the door, Beats headphones around his ears. The guard closed the office door and watched Adams speed off in his car. Adams drove a few miles to a parking lot, where he got out and hopped into a rental car packed with suitcases. He headed out on the interstate, starting the long journey he had ahead of him.

*****

Dutch Marcello likely needed a few weeks in the hospital. Extensive skin grafts would be required to repair at least half of the surface of his body, but he'd live. The missing ear and scars covering his body would always be there to remind him of his battle with the RAPCAs. His only solace was that the last of that wretched group was likely incinerated along with the Russian mercenaries he hired. Part of him wanted some of the RAPCAs to still be alive so he could provide some real retribution. He was sure the Russian mob felt the same way, since to them, the soldiers killed weren't mercenaries. They were family.

*****

Elizabeth Locklear Elected President of the United States! – MSNBC

Democrats Narrowly Win Control of Both House and Senate. – Washington Post

Two More Women Retract Accusations Against Brent Martinez. – Fox News.

Locklear Wins Presidency with 274 Electoral Votes, Despite Winning Only 41 Percent of Popular Vote. – DrudgeReport.com

Brent Martinez Wins Home State of Virginia and 20 Percent of Popular Votes Based on Write-ins, Fueled by Social Media Campaign. – USA Today

Media World Leader Colin Bennett Poisoned in Home, Reporter Patrick Adams Suspected of Murder. – ABC

We Have to Face Facts that Despite Their Methods, the RAPCA's Cause was Noble. – Breitbart News.

Unlike 2016, Russians Are Foiled in Attempt to Manipulate U.S. Election. – CNN

    Patrick Adams glanced through the headlines as he exited his plane in Punta Cana, Dominican Republic. His hair was now dark brown and his eyes blue. He wore dark glasses and a stars-and-stripes ballcap. After clearing customs, he saw a driver holding up the name "Robin Molitor", the current alias he was using, an amalgam of the names of his two favorite baseball players growing up.

    The car drove for over an hour beyond the city limits where he was dropped off, seemingly in the middle of nowhere. He got out and walked two miles following a hand-drawn map of a trail into the jungle. He came to a small worn-down house that would likely be described as a dump in the U.S. but was considered a mansion in Punta Cana. He walked around to the back entrance and knocked twice as instructed.

    "Patrick, I was getting worried you wouldn't make it here," said Dr. Abby Benton as she opened the door and hugged him.

"My flight was delayed a couple hours, but there were no major problems. The ID papers you provided me worked like a charm," said Adams.

"Great, but don't get too used to that 'Robin Molitor' name. The Dominicans know their baseball, so you might get some second looks. C'mon, meet the rest of the team. Guys, let's welcome the newest member of RAPCA, Patrick Adams. Patrick, meet Nate Keeting and Jim Damon, our tech gurus. This is our world class sniper, Kyle Topper. And this is our explosives specialist, Scott Koonce." Adams was swarmed with handshakes and pats on the back.

"Someone get this guy a margarita," said Damon.

"Please tell me Bennett suffered an excruciatingly painful death," said Topper.

"Yeah, I want to enjoy a complete play-by-play on his last minutes after a few more pina coladas," said Nate Keeting.

"That call you made to the FBI that led them to our headquarters couldn't have come at a more perfect time," said Abby. "I give them a few weeks before they figure out our bodies aren't there, and then they'll realize they're back to square one."

"I wouldn't be surprised if they try to keep it under wraps," said Damon. "The FBI and Homeland directors have constantly been on camera since the explosion occurred. It'd be too humiliating now to go on TV and admit they're back to being clueless. Plus, the press is loving the Russian angle way too much. CNN broadcasts have been like Saturday Night Live skits with their braindead 24-7 Russia stories. I swear those dipshits would rather start a war if that's what it took to misdirect people from their own corruption."

"I have to ask," said Adams. "It sounds like these Russian guys were pretty bad ass. They must have had constant surveillance before they went in. How did you get out and set them up with such precision timing?"

"We had cameras and sensors all over the property," said Koonce. "We knew they were coming, and we knew they weren't the Feds. Bennett had some sources in the government that fed him inside information, so we figured your call to the FBI would be passed on quickly, and it was. Thank you, Mr. NSA agent, Tim Gordon."

"Cole and I had a tunnel constructed from the basement to a dense part of the woods outside the fence," said Abby. "We figured we'd need it at some point."

"And after we were out," said Keeting, "well, you can simulate and control almost anything remotely with today's smart home technology. We programmed movements, heat patterns, voice recordings, and some automated weapons, among other things. I'll explain in more detail later during your training."

"Training?" asked Adams.

"Yeah, we have a whole intense training and blood initiation thing we put all team members through. It'll be fun," said Abby as she winked.

"I can't wait," said Adams as he was handed a margarita.

Abby held up her drink, "Everyone, let's have a toast. First of all, a toast to the great men we lost in battle, Cole Foreman, Darren Williams, and Aaron Newsome. May they rest in peace knowing their sacrifices were not made in vain." The six of them paused in silence with their heads bowed, then took a sip of their drinks.

"We've accomplished quite a bit so far in our Revolution," said Abby, "We've taken out some of the worst actors in the media/political world. We've awakened the public to what's going on, or at least some of it. And as for Big Tech, Hollywood, mega-rich donors, and remaining journalists, maybe, just maybe, we've given them a little something to fear, something to encourage some new behaviors. But we couldn't save Brent Martinez, and not as much has changed as we hoped, but this is just the beginning. We're going to recruit. We're going to train.

We're going to acquire even better technology and weapons. We're going to strategically plan and prepare." Abby paused for a minute. She looked down as new thoughts raced through her mind. Her face turned serious. "I think it's time we take our Revolution to another level. We're going after the Deep State, and this time politicians won't be exempt from our target list."

"The media's the most powerful entity on Earth. They have the power to make the innocent guilty and make the guilty innocent, and that's power. Because they control the minds of the masses." – Malcolm X

"Every two years the American politics industry fills the airwaves with the most virulent, scurrilous, wall-to-wall character assassination of nearly every political practitioner in the country, and then declares itself puzzled that America has lost trust in its politicians." – Charles Krauthammer

"It's easier to fool people than to convince them that they have been fooled." – Mark Twain

"By the skillful and sustained use of propaganda, one can make a people see even heaven as hell or an extremely wretched life as paradise." – Adolf Hitler

"Until you realize how easily it is for your mind to be manipulated, you remain the puppet of someone else's game." – Evita Ochel

Acknowledgements

A big thank you to my wonderful wife, Doreen Messerli. Without your love and support, I couldn't have undertaken this new venture. Thanks also to my mother, Peggy Messerli, for her proofreading, critiquing, and encouragement. I'd also like to thank former Navy SEAL, Carl Freeland, for his consultation on some of the military details in the book.

About the Author

Joe Messerli is a writer and I.T. professional living in Green Bay, WI. He was the author/creator of the website https://www.balancedpolitics.org/ (which was sold in 2012) and is the author/creator of the website https://politicallyincorrecthumor.com/. For more information on his background, go to https://about.me/joemesserli. He can be contacted by emailing jpmesserli@gmail.com.